CHAINGE

BY
KEN DEAN

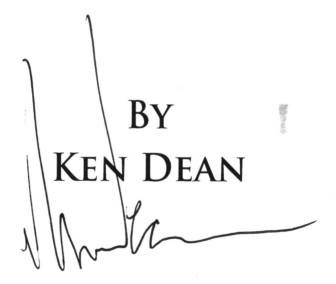

Thank you for your interest in my work.

Please feel free to follow me on Facebook at www.facebook.com/progressive17.

I look forward to hearing from you.

For Jules,

You are my inspiration, you are my bliss.

I love you.

To family and friends that supported me throughout this project, many thanks.

Special thanks to John David Kudrick for his editing prowess.

For assistance with bringing my cover vision to reality, thanks to eBook Launch.

When those who seek power promise change, the chain may be as subtle as a trick of the mind, a poisonous thought, or as obvious as links of iron, but guard against it.

It is sure to follow.

Chapter 1

The clack-clack-clack of the cold steel wheels on the track droned on as the train crawled its way toward the tenement. Soot mixed with steam and crept through the cracks in the rotting, wood-framed windows of the train car. The sweat of this ancient beast condensed and frosted on the dirty panes; its pungent odor tickled the nose. Splintered bench seats creaked in time with the methodical lunging of the iron serpent, forward and forward, on through the cold night.

Not long now, I thought, then gave a quiet sigh. *This is the third time Our State has moved me to a different Medical Rights Facility in a different Progressive. Seems that whenever I begin to grow roots, I am plucked, planted anew, to be reaped and consumed by another faction of the Collective. Alas, it is within the power of Our State to do with me as they wish, as I am a Server and I am theirs.*

"Look alive, Servers. Twenty minutes out!" yelled the Black Cat as he marched through the car.

His shout was authority and raw power made verbal; his stride, giant. He must have stood about six-seven, a hulk, even more intimidating in his black regalia. His black beret immaculately crafted, a perfect fit over his black, full-head mask. His mirrored glasses and black, spit-shined boots reflected the Servers' fear back toward them, intensifying it, reducing most of us to sniveling puppets. His black jacket and pants were crisp, every crease perfect. The insignia of Our State adorned both his beret and his left sleeve, the Greek delta—Δ—its legs interlinked chains; inside the delta, the parallel black and white

1

lines below the setting orb that surrounded the all-seeing eye of the Provider. A baton was the Cat's only weapon, although with the fear his presence instilled in most, there was scant reason he'd need it. As cold as the train had been, the Black Cat's presence had made it even colder; no wonder they were referred to as "change agents."

With my eyes, I followed his mechanical movements as he marched along the aisle toward the rear door of the car. As he reached for the door handle, he stopped and turned in my direction. Instinctively, I averted my eyes—only to catch upon the most angelic face I had ever seen. From the corner of my eye, I could tell the Black Cat had not caught my gaze as he turned again and continued to exit the car; my eyes, however, were still transfixed on the young woman with the striking features, a bright spot in this dark vessel of solemn faces. From fear to reverence in an instant, what a serene feeling washed over me. I was mesmerized. I wondered what her duties were. How could such an exquisite creature be made to serve? She moved her arm to brush a strand of hair from her face... such radiant grace, such freedom caught in the fluid movement as she tucked the free-falling strands behind her ear. Her eyes were the bluest of blue, pools of serenity perched atop high, prominent cheek bones; the soft, curved features of her nose provided a most elegant profile. Her jaw line was strong itself, but somehow weakened ever so slightly with carrying the burden of her teary eyes. Her lips... I had never seen so full a set. How I focused on her lips; they stirred me, conjuring thoughts that had never before entered my mind. My stare must have pierced her as she slowly moved her eyes to look toward me. Fear once again overcame me and I glanced down to avoid the contact. I chuckled to myself, disgusted at my weakness.

Out of nowhere, my head was grabbed and thrust forward, slamming against a scanner. The crack against the cold plastic resounded throughout the train car. I registered the green blink and the beep of the scanner.

"What the hell are you staring at, Server?" yelled the Black Cat as he held the back of my head. "Answer!"

"Nothing, nothing. I was looking out the window, just looking out the window."

"Looking out the window, were you?" he yelled as he dropped the scanner and thrust his baton into my groin, sending an explosion of pain through my useless testicles, up through my spinal cord to my brain, giving it a pulverizing kick.

I let out a scream of anguish like a little boy.

"So you're a Medical Server and you think you're so damn smart. Smarts won't get you far in this world. I better not see you even looking in that direction again or your introduction to your new tenement is gonna be one you'll never forget."

"I won't look that way again. I won't. I won't. You have my word," I said, whimpering like a child.

"Your word—ha. I have all of you... more than just your worthless word. Remember that, Server."

The Black Cat pulled his baton from my groin, the release of pressure sending another rush of pain screaming through my body. I hunched forward, sniveling and rocking, my hands pressed between my legs. Allowing his arm to swing free, with the baton as an extension, the Black Cat stepped down the aisle toward the exquisite, innocent Server. He forced his way between the other Servers in the row and the girl, standing before her like a looming tower. He moved his baton under her chin and pulled her head up to face him. She trembled, her cheeks twitching, sobs escaping her mouth.

I brought this on her.

The Black Cat seemed to caress her cheek, working the tip of the baton down to her neck. Her tattered shirt gave way ever so slightly as he moved the shaft tip down, pulling her collar to a point that exposed the soft, supple-looking cleave between the mounds of her chest. I didn't know what the hell was going on in my head: I was mixed with rage and arousal, neither of which I'd felt before. The baton moved around each mound, concentrating briefly on the most prominent area of each before the Black Cat moved the tip farther down. The woman's arms were extended down at her sides, elbows locked tight, pushing herself off the bench, her chin dipped as she whimpered, gasping at breaths stolen from the chilling scene. The Black Cat chuckled as he moved his baton to her umbilical area, moving it around in small circles, occasionally pushing inward, only to pull out, moaning as he toyed with her. He stopped and turned to me, catching me off guard as I stared in disbelief, my odd feelings confusing me. I dropped my head as quick as I could.

"Won't look this way again, huh?" he said, followed by a sickening laugh.

I couldn't say a word; I had no idea what to say. I couldn't even come to terms with why I should care what happened to her, or the sensations the scene had released in me. I heard the door to train car open and a moment later slam closed. I looked up and the Black Cat was gone. The girl sobbed, holding her hands to her face.

How stupid are you? Contact is expressly forbidden. Desire is forbidden. It is not for Servers to partake of such wantonness.

I traced the outline of the delta insignia tattooed on the back of my right hand with a finger from the other as I continued to rock, willing the pain in my testicles to decrease, listening to the aftermath of what my unlawful interest in another had caused as she continued to sob. The delta pointing away from me reminded me that it was I who served.

How foolish can I be that I filled my head with such nonsense of late? Remember, you are but a drop of water, condensation. Your path is marked by the rights of the Collective. You exist for the sake of and by the grace of Our State and the all-giving Provider.

Moments passed and the pain began to subside. I chose to move my gaze to the world beyond the frosty, condensation-covered window. I felt the coolness on my palm as I wiped an arc across the glass. Cold, soot-infused water pooled on my hand, sending a shiver through me. I watched as a bead of condensation made its way down from my fingertip to my palm—all along its path, the route of least resistance taken, and no choice in the matter, to eventually evaporate into nothingness. Was that all we were, beads on a path of another's choosing, destined to evaporate at the end of our journey? Closing my hand into a fist, I gazed out through the arc I had cleared on the frosty window, out into the darkness. The full moon eyed the countryside as it peered through the breaks in the spotty cloud cover. Brightness blasted the snow, reflecting the light over the skeletal remains of charred trees, and craters peppered the landscape as scars marring a once exquisite face. The thought of a beautiful face pulled my mind back to the angelic Server who had caught my gaze, but I refrained from turning toward her. Through the pane, all I could see was black and white. In utter shock, my head turned, as my eyes became fixated on a body dressed in rags amidst the wintry land. It scrambled over the high snow banks along the sides of the train tracks.

Run, run! I found myself thinking, not quite understanding why such thoughts would enter my mind.

A high-pitched squeal echoed through the car as the steel wheels skidded along the rails. My body flew forward with the sudden decrease in speed, and my head smacked against the wooden back of the bench in front of me. As I rose to my feet, slightly stunned, I looked around at my brethren.

"Is everyone okay?" I asked.

Nothing, not a single response from any of them. All the Servers simply adjusted themselves in their seats and returned their gazes to the floor in front of them.

Lifeless animals.

I turned again to the car window. I could make out the person in rags trudging through the high drifts, moving slow against the blowing snow.

Run, run!

The door to the car creaked open on its hinges as a gust of icy cold wind rushed in—followed by a Black Cat.

"Stay in your seats. Do not attempt to move!" the Black Cat said. He stopped his dash through the car and held his hand up to the side of his head. "We've got a runner," he said into thin air, nodding as if the person he was speaking to was standing in front of him. "Yes, Consular. Right away, sir." He dropped his hand and continued his run to the door on the opposite end of the car.

Placing my hands against the glass, the coolness of the window on my hands and the visage of the runner became invigorating as I stared out. "Run, run!" I whispered, louder than I had intended.

The Black Cat turned as he reached the door. I froze as I realized I could hear my own voice. Out of the corner of my eye, the raising heads of my fellow Servers in response to the scene served as an acknowledgement of my foolish comment. I felt the gaze of the Black Cat on me like a dark shadow as I jumped to my feet.

"Run, run! He's getting away!" I yelled at him.

The Black Cat's head cocked to the side, looking like he was unsure of how to respond. In a moment, he turned and jerked the door open, then rushed out against the incoming gust, the door slamming shut behind him. Letting out a sigh of relief, I turned and scanned the faces of the other Servers. The brief shock shown in their wide eyes melted as their lids relaxed and their gaze returned to the floor in front of them. Falling against the bench, my attention returned to the scene beyond the pane. The runner was making little headway against the wind and deep snow.

Hardly a runner.

Three huge black bodies drew closer and closer to him. The glow of the moon against the backs of the hulking figures cast shadows along the white canvas of snow. Like three talons, the shadows of the Black Cats engulfed the runner as the distance between them closed.

A moment later, the lumbering runner fell. The Black Cats pounced on their prey, and clubs began to slice through the air to land upon their victim, rendering him helpless. One of the Black Cats stood tall; I guessed it was the same Black Cat that had run through our car, his hand reaching to the side of his head, checking in with his master again. As they began to drag their quarry back to the train, I slumped back into the bench, realizing the futility of the runner's poor effort to escape.

Fool… Yes, you're a fool. Why would you root for a runner? We are here to serve. That is our freedom. There's no freedom out there in the cold, barren waste…. Fool.

I pulled my tattered coat around myself and shivered. The cold was creeping through the car, through my spent frame again as the warmth of the adrenaline rush now began to fade.

At some point, this never-ending night would soon give way to sun; it had been weeks since the darkness had enveloped the land. We'd been told that tomorrow we would once again begin to see the sun, although its warmth always seemed so far off. I couldn't decide which was worse: this darkness, occasionally brightened by the moon, or the month-long vigil of the sun where not a day went by with darkness. We had been taught how the holocaust had put our planet off kilter, destroying the regular day and night cycles. Now we only enjoyed such regularity for ten months of the year.

How odd. My training in the sciences as a Medical Server Provider left me without an explanation as to how such an event could have altered the cycles for only a portion of the year. The Progressives—or cities, as they were once called— were not affected by the event. In those places, it was always sunny during the day and darkness at night, just as it should have been.

I gathered that the Black Cats had pulled their prey aboard the train, as it now lurched and then began to move forward. The window next to me had once again frosted over, so yet again, I cleared an arc with my hand. As we rounded a bend in the tracks, I could begin to make out the lights of Progressive 17 where I would soon be afforded, by the immanent grace of Our State, the opportunity to serve the Collective. Progressives were scattered about Our State in areas still capable of sustaining life. We had been taught that much of the land had become inhospitable, as bombs had rained down like tea leaves over a harbor during the revolt.

The train car door opened yet again and was quickly closed. I cringed down in my seat and leaned my head closer to the window, its coolness chilling my forehead. As I waited for the oncoming beating, I scanned the land beyond. The moon had become curtained by a veil of clouds, its glow muted, painting the night all the more dark. The lights from Progressive 17 made it look as if it were a campfire on a pitch-black night; however, those lights offered no sense of safety, protection, or warmth. As the train rounded another bend, I lost sight of Progressive 17, which made my mood, briefly, a little brighter. The Black Cat paused as he reached my bench. I expected a blow from the baton, but he turned away and continued down the aisle to the far end doorway. He turned, his reflective lenses directed toward me. Raising his massive arm, he pointed his baton at me; he held it for a brief second, lowered it, turned, and left the train car. I wondered what had become of the runner.

Curious, why should I care?

A screaming whistle pierced the silence of the car. We had to be quite close to the Progressive, although from my vantage point, I could no longer see it. The train would sound the whistle whenever near a Progressive. I'd always wondered if the Served, the Progs within, ever heard the whistle.

Do they know it's us? Do they even care? I suppose not, as long as they are provided their rights. I believe that's as far as their minds can carry them. But forget a lab test, forget an X-ray, forget anything that is covered in their rights, and then they'll care. Their screams of injustice then become the piercing whistle… and what a shrill sound it can be.

The train veered right, along the winding track, as the car became illuminated by the light emanating from Progressive 17. I pulled my tattered red handkerchief from the torn pocket of my jacket and wiped the window from top to bottom. The Progressive came into view. The twenty-story walls appeared to scrape at the cloud-covered sky as shafts of light rocketed upward to stab at the clouds' underbelly. Through the translucent walls, one could see the buildings sprouting up from the blemished earth, though not a single building approached the height of the walls. A near-invisible dome covered the Progressive. The members of the Collective within were unaware of the dome as they, in their freedom, never left the Progressive. On a day of rain, a day of snow, from a distance one could make out the arc of the dome as the precipitation danced off the structure. I remembered once, during my advanced indoctrination, seeing a picture show of a jellyfish. Peering through the outer layer of the jelly, one could make out the tiny fish it had all but paralyzed with its nematocysts, pulled up into the dome to be devoured, still motioning back and forth, but unable to break the grip, unaware of its ultimate fate. The Progressive before me stood as a larger version of the same dance, its inhabitants held with promises of rights and anesthetized with ignorance—blissful in their ignorance. Freedom in a bottle, kept in a jar, held in a crucible, entangled in the tentacles of Our State.

Farther on, another turn, and the Progressive's lights faded behind us. Up ahead, the dim outline of the tenement was traced upon the grayness of the snow-blanketed fields. The short transport from a Progressive to its tenement was like a leap back, a return to a primitive time, a regression in technology, from a laser to glowing ember. So much change in so short a time—*How unnatural.*

The snake of iron and wood slowed to a stop, groaned a heavy sigh, and belched clouds of steam and soot. The hiss of the beast diminished as it took itself to rest atop the steel tracks alongside the depot platform. Two seats ahead of me, a Server whimpered: "I can't keep this up. Why is this happening? Why?"

I shook my head. *Another fool.*

"This is Progressive 17 tenement," I whispered. "The strictest—the end of the line for Servers. Freedom will be constantly forced upon you."

"This is not freedom. I can't take it," he whined.

"Shut up," I said. "You're going to get us all beaten. Just shut up and keep it together!"

The Server continued to whimper, the moans now barely audible. Peering through the glass, I saw the sentinels fixed upon their posts, their uniforms as black as the surrounding night, their clubs at the ready. Each appeared equidistant along the platform, like chessmen, pawns standing their watch, awaiting the next move. A Black Cat emerged from the reception building, bullhorn in hand. Raising it to his mouth, the Black Cat yelled, "Servers will disembark the trains by car number, starting with number one and ending with number nine. Remain in your seats until your car number is announced!"

I looked up. On the ceiling of the car, a large number *4* was painted.

"Servers in car number one, on your feet and make your way to the train exit. Form two rows on the platform, parallel to the train, and wait for further instructions!"

I wasn't sure whether it was the increasing chill or the uncertainty of a new tenement, but I could feel my body quivering. I slowly looked toward the beautiful creature near the rear of the car; she seemed focused on her fidgeting hands, her lips constantly moving in a rapid fashion. The look of fear, of terror, had stolen the former glow from her face. She was petrified. I cleared my throat in a loud obnoxious fashion hoping to gain her attention, but she continued her silent chattering and fidgeting unabated. Looking around behind me, the other Servers in the car seemed oblivious to my throat clearing. All just sat, hands folded in their laps, staring at the swollen, warped floorboards of the car, like beaten animals lacking an ounce of fight. The sniveling Server had finally quieted. All the while, I could hear the shouting on the platform, the Black Cats growling their orders to the lowly Servers, instilling and re-instilling within them the fear that overpowered the Servers' intelligence and left them cowering. Once again, I cleared my throat, yet louder this time. She looked up, and tears seemed to well within her eyes, their burden becoming heavier; lips trembled. We caught eyes and held for split second, yet a lifetime swam by.

"It'll be okay," I mouthed. "It'll be okay."

I was rewarded with a half smile, as she lowered her head to continue her fidgeting.

I heard the Black Cat with the bullhorn announce the third car. A few more moments and we'd be off into the chill of the winter's night air. I reckoned it to be about 2:00 a.m., four hours until wake-up.

And we are not even to our new bunks yet. "Service makes you free" is what we are told. I must remember that. I am free, free of guilt as I give myself, my sweat, my toil, my days and nights to the Collective. I sacrifice myself for the bliss of the Collective. The cold is but an inconvenience. I shall not allow it, or anything else, to interfere with my abilities to provide the members of the Collective with the service they have the rights to.

"Car four, on your feet. Move toward the exit and fall in line behind car three Servers. Move, move, move!" yelled the Black Cat.

The trembling female Server whimpered and jerked her head up with the most startled look. I motioned to her to get up and fall in line behind me. All Servers were on their feet in moments, lined up single file in the car aisle, moving in step toward the door. The first Server in the car opened the door, and a blast of frigid air rushed in, slapping each Server as it passed, swallowing up any trace of remaining warmth. The angel was out of step, and her left foot kicked my heel while her left arm swung forward as mine went back—and our hands connected briefly. I felt her softness, her sensitivity, her vulnerability, and her fear, and then gone—she changed her step. I swore to myself I would never forget that moment, that contact. I exited the car and stood in line behind the Servers from car three. The angel was a few people ahead of me now, in the next row. I could see her head was hung, and I imagined the terror racing through her. With my concentration so focused on the angel, I hadn't even noticed the bitter wind until my ears began to throb. Numbness crept slowly over my exposed skin as the wind sprinted down the corridor created by the train and the in-processing building. The shredded rags bestowed to us by Our State offered no protection against the elements; my tattered jacket might as well have been a burlap potato sack. We Servers stood shivering like penguins in the Arctic as we waited for the remaining cars to empty their sacrificial beings.

The last car emptied its load as the Black Cat with the bullhorn ordered the columns forward. The Servers marched along the platform, down the slope toward the reception hall. Through the iron gates they led us. *SERVICE MAKES YOU FREE* proclaimed the ethos above the metal trap, welded letter by letter above the entrance. Along either side of the gate, chain-link fence capped with concertina wire stretched out for hundreds of yards in both directions, broken occasionally by a guard tower fixed with large-caliber weapons. Single-bulb lights hung every twenty yards or so, illuminating the area around the fence. Open wires were strung lamp to lamp along the length of the fence. The ground was frozen solid. The footprints of previous Servers left impressions that made the marching painful on my soles through the thin tread on my shoes. The breath of the Servers condensed in the icy air as we marched toward the assembly area adjacent to the reception building. It was as if we marched through a foggy dream state—only this was terribly real.

"Halt!" shouted the Black Cat through the bullhorn.

The two columns of Servers came to an abrupt stop at the command.

"Right turn!" yelled the Black Cat, followed by our instantaneous acknowledgement and action.

Before me stood a row of posts with numbers one through twenty-six from left to right. Before we turned, I noticed the two rows of long, single-story buildings to my left, seemingly the standard layout of the Servers' tenements. However, this was slightly different, as a large steel tub sat between us and the posts.

"First row, take two steps forward."

We opened our ranks as ordered. Several Black Cats gathered in front of the first rank, talking amongst themselves and adjusting the scanners they were carrying.

"Any Server wearing anything on their head, remove it now."

A Black Cat holding a shovel in each hand approached the first row of Servers. He thrust his arms out, smacking the shovels into the chests of two Servers. "Take them."

"Yes, sir. Yes, sir," both Servers mumbled as they took the shovels.

"Get over there and start shoveling snow into that tub!" yelled the Black Cat.

The two Servers took off, over to the tub. The snow was packed so hard from thousands of Server footsteps that the Servers had to smack and smack at the ground to break it up. I could hear water sloshing around in the tub as the Servers tipped their shoveled chunks into it. Once again, a shiver ran through me. The thought of the vat of ice cold water on the blustery, lunar-lit night was too much, too much to keep even a spark of warmth alive.

"That's enough! Drop the shovels and get back in your ranks," the Black Cat said.

The sound of crunching snow and ice arose from my left as a gargantuan Black Cat made his way to the front of our formation. His massive size and weight pushed his tread into the hardened snow, leaving tracks as he stepped. Behind him trailed two smaller, but equally menacing Black Cats dragging a mass of tattered clothing. As the two Black Cats made their way to the front, I could see that the tattered pile of clothing they pulled behind them was actually a man. His body appeared limp and lifeless as his heels bumped up and down over each ridge in the hard-bitten ground. The Black Cats released his shoulders, dropping his upper body to the ground with a thud, a groan emanating as his breath condensed in the frosty air.

The runner...

The gargantuan Black Cat was standing with his back to us, between the runner and the tub, facing the tub of water and snow. He stood up tall, righting his huge frame, his height towering over both the tub and the runner. In an effortless move of precision, he completed an about-face and looked out over our ranks.

"It appears one of your brethren has forgotten his place and has developed a distaste for freedom. Remind him of his freedom!" the Black Cat yelled.

"Service is freedom!" we yelled in response.

The Black Cat scanned our ranks. "Are you free?"

"We are free to serve!" we replied in unison.

"I can't hear you. Are you free?" the Black Cat yelled.

"We are free to serve!"

The towering Black Cat looked down upon the man in tatters. "See, Server? As your brethren have boasted, you are already free. No need to go running away."

His face pushed into the ground by its own weight. Clearly spent and unable to move, the runner responded in a soft voice: "Yes... free... free."

The Black Cat drew back his leg and swung it forward, smashing his colossal boot into the runner's back.

"Arrgggg!" he yelped in response, his back arching against the blow.

Is this freedom? I thought as I watched the scene play out before me. *If we are free, would all of this be necessary, this fear, this torment? No... Stop it!* I told myself. *Stop it! You are free. You are free to serve.*

The Black Cat looked down at the runner, shaking his head. "You need to be cleansed of those ill, self-serving thoughts. They are dirty. They soil your mind, and in doing so, they soil the System." The Black Cat's voice was deep and it resonated with authority that seemed to carry out over our ranks.

"No, no! I don't need a bath! No!" the man screamed, breath rushing from his lungs to meet the frigid air as if he knew what was coming.

"Clothes!" yelled the Black Cat.

The two other Black Cats jumped on the runner and pulled his shoes and clothes off as he thrashed about trying to fend them off.

"No!... No! I don't need a bath.... Please, please don't! I won't run again, I swear. Pleeeease!" he screamed.

"Bathe him," the huge Black Cat ordered.

The runner kicked and flailed as the Black Cats grabbed him and hefted him up off the ground. For a moment, they held him aloft, over their heads, pausing, as if to relish the moment. His body writhed as he tried to break their grip. In a quick heave, the Black Cats threw the runner into the tub but didn't let go of him. Water splashed up and over the rim as his body went under, and his scream became muffled. As quickly as he had been thrown in, the Black Cats released their grip and up popped his head. I watched as he gasped and gasped, the breath clearly stolen from him as the iciness of the water acted as a vise around his chest.

Breathe! Breathe, man.

"N-N-N-No-No, n-n-no more, p-p-p-p-please." His voice was but a whisper as his breath still escaped him, he slapped his arms against the sides of the tub in an attempt to pull himself out. The tub looked like a steam bath as the heat dissipated from his body and condensed to be taken away on the chilly breeze.

"Again," said the giant Black Cat. "Make sure we cleanse those thoughts from his mind."

"Nooo! Ple—" The runner's words were cut off as his head was pushed beneath the surface of the water.

He won't last much longer, this night and the temperature of that water—hypothermia will suck the life out of him within the next several minutes if he's not released.

"Do any of you need a good washing of dirty thoughts that may be hiding in the corners of your minds, or do you realize your freedom?" the Black Cat said to us.

"We are free to serve!" we yelled in unison.

"Again."

"We are free to serve!"

The Black Cat turned to the others and nodded. The two Black Cats released their grip on the runner's head. Shooting up from beneath the surface, his mouth sucked in a hard breath, and his eyes were as wide as any I had ever seen.

Fear—that is the face of fear.

The Black Cats yanked him out of the water and threw him to the ground in front of the tub. He just lay there, shivering uncontrollably, panting, yet with visibly little air exchange. I wanted to break from the ranks and help him, but at the same time, I didn't want to. He'd brought this upon himself, after all.

One of the two smaller Black Cats threw the runner's clothing at him. The massive Black Cat pulled a dirty green woolen blanket from behind the tub and threw it toward the runner in the most nonchalant manner, as if this act was simply a part of the daily play.

"I'd like to welcome you to Progressive 17 tenement, your new home. As you can see, we are fair and merciful; your freedom here is serious business."

We all continued to stand there in the bitter chill as equally nonchalant as the Black Cat. I couldn't catch onto any particular thought, but something just didn't seem to sit well. I couldn't put my finger on what it was. More Black Cats began to appear on either side of our formation.

"Carry on," the lead Black Cat said to the others before turning and marching off toward the administration building.

A pair of Black Cats approached each end of the first row of Servers. One Black Cat carried a scanner and one carried a rectangular object, a type of electronic register. The Black Cat with the scanner grasped the back of the first Server's head and pushed the face of the scanner to the Server's forehead.

"Hold still, Server!"

With the trigger control depressed, the scanner illuminated the skin of the Server and registered the serial number etched on his skull beneath his skin. The Black Cat released tension on the Server's head, touched the base of the scanner to the electronic register held by the other Black Cat, and said, "LS, Lesser Server, post sixteen—move!"

As the Server ran to the post with the number *16*, the two Black Cats moved to the next Server and repeated the process. The Black Cats moved to stand in front of the angel, her head still down, but I could see from my vantage point in the back row that she was still fidgeting.

"Look up, Server!" the Black Cat ordered as he grasped the back of her head.

She let out a whimper as the Black Cat smacked the scanner against her head. Releasing his grip, he shoved the scanner forward pushing her, back a step. He touched the scanner to the register.

"As I thought, another LS. Post twenty-six—move, move!"

The first row had been completed; the Black Cats followed on with the remaining rows. It seemed like days since disembarking the train, as the wind and cold were taking their toll on all of us, and we were all tired, all feeling weak and chilled to the bone. A pair of Black Cats stood in front of me. One grasped the back of my head and pushed the scanner to my forehead, touched the scanner to the register.

"MS, Medical Server, post two—move!"

I shuffled to post two as fast as I could. My muscles were cramping from the cold, fighting against my movements. Standing in the line, I waited with several other Servers already queued up, facing the post, one behind the other, all motionless and silent. I turned my head slightly to the right, looking for the angel; I was unable to see beyond the next few posts. I wondered whether I would ever see her in person again, although I was sure I'd always see her in my mind. Deep inside, I smiled.

The crunching of the Servers' feet against the frozen ground had ceased. I began to wonder how long we would have to stand there when the blare of the bullhorn sounded.

"Post one Servers, turn around."

To my left, out of the corner of my eye, I saw the Servers standing at the first post turn on their heels as ordered.

"Move out, post one!" the Black Cat yelled.

The Servers moved as ordered, off toward their sleeping quarters, the crunching of their feet marking time as their stiff bodies lumbered forward. There looked to be only six new people at post one; at my post, maybe ten—it was hard to tell exactly how many had joined this line after me. The higher post numbers had the higher number of people. I remember an elderly Servant from my previous tenement confiding in me that the lower the post number, the greater the level of ability and, therefore, importance of the Server to the Collective. Even back then, I had been afflicted with moments of wonderment, of pausing to question the ways things were. That terrible faculty of mine, I felt, would one day be my undoing.

It may very well be the reason I have ended up here at Progressive 17 Maybe they suspect that I am beginning to suffer from the insidious affliction of individual thought.

"Importance," the old Server had said.

I also remember how I had laughed when he had told me this. The way they treated us, how could anyone believe we were of any importance at all?

Stop it! Don't start again. Just do as you're told.

"Post two servers, turn around!"

We turned around as ordered.

Only seven of us, I noted. *I must be getting tired—can't even count to seven I'm so worn out. I feel like a Prog!*

"Move out, post two!"

Finally, soon *I'll be able to close my eyes and rest, perhaps dream of the beautiful angel.*

I could see the Servers from post one ahead of us, almost at their bunkhouse. There were two sets of identical bunkhouses, one situated on either side of a common dirt road. The closest bunkhouses were for post one and two Servers. Directly behind these bunkhouses stood bunkhouses three and four, and each of these were longer than one and two. The pattern continued for the remaining bunkhouses. From above, the footprint of the bunkhouses formed the shape of the delta—Δ—a delta situated within a rectangular barbed wire compound, replete with machine gun towers.

We approached our bunkhouse and received the order to halt. A Black Cat with a register board approached the first Server. "ES Paine, Jonathan… bunk number seventeen."

The bunkhouses looked identical to those of both my previous tenements: short, rather narrow bunks on one side, two high, with numbers painted at the foot of each.

The Black Cat approached me. "MS Huxley, Blair… bunk number nine," he said and then continued on with the remaining Servers. "All Servers to your bunks. Lights out in five minutes. Wake up at zero six hundred. Move!"

We scrambled for the bunkhouse door, and the first Server there attempted to slide the iron bolt away from the frame to allow the door to open. Although the large key lock was unlocked, it still hung through the hole in the bolt and the corresponding catch on the frame, probably due to the fact there were Servers already inside.

Security… It's for our own protection. At least, that was what we had been told as the reason for the bolting of the bunkhouses at night—bolted from the outside, of course.

I reached toward the lock and removed it from the bolt hole, then nodded to the other Server for him to attempt to unlatch the bolt again. With some effort, the iron bolt slid back along its track as I hung the lock through the hole on the door frame. The Server pulled at the handle on the door, opening the iron slab to reveal the new home Our State had

21

provided us. We all hurried in to take refuge from the icy night chill.

A pile of green woolen blankets, similar to the one thrown to the runner, sat on a small shelf just inside the door. I grabbed a blanket as I made my way down the aisle. *At least I have an odd numbered bunk.* The nearly all-seeing eyes of Our State had a difficult time seeing the lower-level bunks. I didn't see many open bunk spaces, and I guessed that we had a full complement in this bunkhouse. The more Servers in a bunkhouse, the warmer it was, which was fine with me. I reached bunk number nine; seven and eleven were occupied, with both Servers sleeping. In keeping with my usual luck, the Server in bunk eleven was snoring like a lost goat; his presence here indicated, however, that he lacked the rights of a goat.

How peculiar.

I crawled onto the makeshift, community straw bedding, doing my best not to wake my bunkmates. There were no partitions between the bunk spaces, but fortunately, nine and eleven were considerate enough to stay within their respective slice of the platform. I eased out of my tattered jacket, rolled it into a ball and placed it at the head of my sleeping area. For some reason, I'd never been able to sleep without a pillow, even if it meant choosing a pillow over being cold. Such items were in short supply in recent years. The Provider had told us that in order for more of the masses to experience freedom, all such goods were being directed toward the needs of two new Progressives currently being constructed. As it was within the rights of the Collective in those Progressives to enjoy an existence devoid of inconvenience, it was for us to go without in order to provide such rights.

"Lights out in one minute. Eyes and ears are on. You know the rules: keep still, keep quiet!" The Black Cat slammed the iron door shut.

Beyond the door, I could hear the lock moving through the latch, and then the metallic snap as the lock was closed on itself. We had been secured—caged… but we were free.

Chapter 2

"I know it's frowned upon, my angel," I said. "I know if we're caught, it'll be our lives, but we're worth the risk."

She smiled and nodded in agreement. "I know, Hux. We are."

It was as if we had just met: the happiness, the jittery feeling in my stomach when I saw her. I couldn't help myself. *It has been years, and we've gotten away with it for this long, so why should we be worried now?*

We had only a few areas where we could steal a moment to be with each other, and this was one of them. We stood at the far end of bunkhouse twenty-five, nearest the outer fence. A tall pile of decaying relic vehicles blocked the view from the corner guard tower to this spot. The light bulb perched atop the gable of the bunkhouse had burned out many moons ago and had yet to be replaced. There we stood, in the darkness of the night, enjoying the moment as if it would be our last. I pulled my angel close to me so I could feel the warmth of her breath on my cheek. Our ability to experience each other had been stripped from us as children in an effort to prevent Servers from engaging in such bodily sharing, but we had this. Despite Our State's desire to control the entire being, thought had to remain intact in order for us to serve the Collective. As an extension, emotion occasionally found fertile ground. Within my garden, the angel had taken root. This was all the freedom we had.

I turned my head slightly, my lips touched hers, the sweetest sensation one could ever feel. The coolness of the dark night was melted by the heat of emotion. It was a world of polar opposites. I have served many members of the Collective—the blank, empty, emotionless herd. I had never noted within a single one of them the ability to feel with this intensity. Where was their freedom? In what form was it made manifest? Questions persisted, permeated my mind in increasing episodes. A beautiful woman rested herself in my arms, and I... I was elsewhere, thinking of the out-of-kilter world in which we played our parts. She knew my mind, knew my predisposition for inquisitive avenues; this, I believed, served as her attraction to me.

I pulled back a little to gaze into her eyes.

"Don't move! Don't move, maggots!" came a yell.

I turned to see two Black Cats rushing toward us. Looking back into my angel's eyes, I leaned forward and brushed my lips against hers, then whispered, "Run!"

She took off running toward the other end of the bunkhouse, trying to reach the common road. The Black Cats closed in on me as I began to run toward the back fence of the tenement.

"Over here, over here! Follow me!" I yelled to them.

Glancing over my shoulder as I ran, I saw that despite my yelling, the Black Cats split up, one chasing me while the other went after my angel. A Black Cat closed in on my angel, and in a completely impulsive move, she turned and began to run toward me.

"No! No, the other way!" I yelled.

I had slowed my pace while focusing on my angel, and the Black Cat chasing me took advantage and hurled his baton at me. His aim was perfect, and the baton struck the back of my head, sending me headlong into the ground. My angel screamed, changed her direction, and ran full-on toward the fence. I looked up, feeling oozing warmth flow over the back of my scalp.

"Don't... Don't..." I moaned as I fell in and out of consciousness.

She reached the fence and began to ascend the chain link. The Black Cat in the rear corner tower turned, training his machine gun on her. Charging the weapon, the Black Cat yelled, "Halt!"

My angel maintained her upward movement.

"AARRGGGHHH!" the Black Cat yelled as he pulled the trigger and released a hail of steel and flame from his fiery beast.

"Noooo!" I shouted.

BLEEER—BLEEER—BLEEER!

I shot up from my bunk space at the sound of the blaring alarm, hitting my head on the bunk above me. My heart was racing like a fox, my head covered with sweat. *A dream! It was only a dream.* My breath raced for a few more moments as I gained my composure.

The Servers on either side of me were already awake, sitting up. The Server in bunk seven was rubbing his eyes and yawning, and he paid no mind to my outburst and sudden movement. He seemed preoccupied with his stomach, rubbing it, dry-heaving occasionally. Eleven gave me a puzzled look, furrowing his brow. Holding his blanket up in front of himself, he pointed at me with his index finger, then made the "okay" sign with his index finger and thumb. I raised my blanket in front of me, held my hand behind it, and gave him the thumbs-up. It was a welcome feeling to know I had a rational bunkmate. His blanket up again, eleven gestured toward seven. Bending his head behind the blanket, eleven pointed to his ear, then he sat back up and waved his finger from side to side.

Ahh, seven is deaf. No wonder the lack of surprise at my outburst. But... I'm not sure what all the heaving was about. An illness, maybe...

As an MSP, I'd had the misfortune of noting many a malady and permanent condition afflicting Servers. It wasn't unusual, given the absence of health care for us. Health care was one of the many Provider-bestowed rights for the indolent, the lazy, the inept, the Progs. This tenement housing was not even a right for us; it was merely a matter of convenience. If our self-proclaimed leader, the Provider, had his way, we would have been sleeping in the snow, dying sooner. For us to die later, though, was much more convenient for the Provider.

Servers from the upper bunk space were dropping their naked bodies to the bare, cold wooden floor. My residual fear from my nightmare still had its grip on me, and I was already falling behind in the morning ritual. As I already had my jacket off from a few hours ago, it was just a matter of my shirt, pants, shoes, and underclothes. All Servers had such things down to a routine of a few seconds. Out of my clothes, I shuttled my way to the edge of the bunk space and hopped off. I was now standing between Servers eight and ten, now down from the upper bunk space. The shafts of natural light began to enter the bunkhouse as the Black Cats began to hoist the metallic shutters up from the sealed window spaces. This was the first time we'd enjoyed the sun in weeks, and the added warmth was a welcome feeling. A fierce, high-pitched squeal pierced my eardrums with each heave of the rope as the metallic window covering moved upward along its rusty tracks. With the shutters full open, the Black Cats peered in, taking a visual headcount. Once satisfied, the Black Cat at the first window gave a nod to Server one, at which point we began to move into the hygiene area.

This group of Servers must have been around for some time, because our execution was flawless. We filed into the individual sanitation area. Eight Servers headed to the sinks, eight to the toilets. The remaining eight stood motionless, silently awaiting the rotation. We were allotted four minutes at each area before rotating to the next. As the time elapsed, the rotation began: the Servers from the toilets headed to the showers, those from the sink to the toilets, those who waited, to the sinks. After emptying my bladder in the toilet and rubbing hair-dissolving lotion over my face at the sink, I moved with the others to the showers. Each of us frantically scrubbed our cold, dirty skin. The water was tepid at best, as the wood-fired water heater never kept up with the water demand. Next to me stood a tall Server, his back covered with long scars.

"What happened to your back?" I said, the sound of my voice concealed by the sound of the water from the showers.

He stared at me for several moments, a look of uncertainty on his face. "I think too much. You'll end up the same way if you question too much."

I didn't know how to respond, I was dumbstruck.

After exiting the showers, I grabbed a towel from the pile to the left of the hygiene area entrance. Returning to the bunk area, we dressed and stood, facing the bunkhouse door and awaiting the remaining Servers. From start to finish, all Servers toileted, shaved, washed, and dressed in twenty minutes, like clockwork.

I heard the metal on metal of the key in the bolt lock as the Black Cat unlocked the bunkhouse door, followed by the slap of the bolt being slid out of the jamb. The door swung open to show the Black Cat preparing to welcome us to the new day.

"You know the drill, geniuses. Get out here and get lined up. Move!"

And a good morning to you, too, I thought as we double-timed out to the initial headcount zone.

The Servers from bunkhouse one had just begun their trot from their initial headcount zone to the common yard in front of the reception building, the area I'd stood on just a few hours earlier. The tub had been removed; a glassy patch of ice now marked the previous evening's "bathing" area. A Black Cat passed in front of us, counting each Server as he passed.

"To the common yard! Fall in on Servers from bunkhouse one! Move!" ordered the Black Cat.

We hustled off as ordered and fell in on the other Servers. The forty-eight of us stood at attention, waiting for the remaining Servers to arrive and fall in.

Inching its way above the horizon, the sun's rays raced toward us, bathing us in its wonderful light and warmth. Once again, we welcomed its presence as one of the only lights and sources of warmth in this dark world. External warmth was all we had. The times of warmth from within had long passed, emotion subdued to the point of nonexistence, at least for most. A cold, fist-sized lump of muscle was all that throbbed beneath the ribs of most. Anything other than blood emanating from that organ was a detriment to Our State. To control emotion, one had to control thought, and the easiest way to control thought was to retard it. Hence, the Collective. Hence, the Served—or Progs, as we referred to them.

"Move, Servers. Move, move!" a Black Cat yelled.

The Servers from the remaining bunkhouses continued to file into the common yard as commanded by their respective taskmasters. The groups in the yard grew in size with each passing moment. With all Servers in the yard, there were six groups made up of eight ranks, with an equal number of Servers in each.

"Open your ranks!" yelled a Black Cat in the front of the formation into his bullhorn.

In a procedure identical to our arrival scan, the Black Cats began the Server-by-Server scan. Up and down the rows Black Cats marched, jamming scanners into forehead after forehead, checking serial numbers and yelling out names and titles. Despite the many years of being a recipient of this practice, I still found it difficult to fathom.

We are treated like the domesticated animals I recall from my medical training—creatures used for a lifetime of work, only to be left to perish once their value to Our State declines. We are the intelligent people—creators, builders, doctors, and craftsmen—and yet we are fed upon and weakened, left to wallow in this sty.

The thoughts became choked in my mind. My feeling of indignation had come quickly, as it often did of late. For an individual moment, within the confines of my mind, I wandered free—free to feel the rage of my treatment, of our treatment... free to object... just free to roam. I was no longer a Server, nor was I among the Served. I was not a Black Cat, a Prog, a Medical Server Provider. For a few moments, I was just a man—a man objecting to being treated like a piece of property, a man tired of not being truly free. Then, in the next moment, my mind cleared of the dirty thoughts, as it usually did after these bouts of mental weakness. I saw the perfect order of things, the Collective of which we are all a part. I saw my freedom... the freedom of the Server... the freedom to allow my life and service to be the property of the Collective.

As the Black Cats drew near, I found myself instinctively listening to the names of my fellow Servers, paying close attention to the bunkmates I had already met, numbers seven and eleven.

"Hold your head still," the Black Cat ordered as he grabbed the back of seven's neck. He then jammed the scanner up against seven's forehead, depressed the trigger and the scanner beeped. The Black Cat tapped the base of the scanner on the cradle the second Black Cat carried; another beep indicated the scan had been acknowledged.

"Mead, Peter, GS: General Servant—check."

General Servant, in with the specialty servants? Quite odd, It must be his massive hulk of a body, a workhorse; he must be able to lift a ton.

The process continued, Server eight, then me, and then ten. The Black Cats came to number eleven, the bunkmate to my right.

"Arnold, Colin, HSC: Housing Server, Carpenter—check."

A skilled craftsman... I can just imagine the wonderful furniture he provides for the Served. Tables, chairs, settees... all for their right to comfort.

From my left, a gut-wrenching sound broke my thoughts and the frigid tension of intermittent silence, like a combination of choking and gagging coupled with the splashing of refuse and water from a rusty bucket. I turned to see that Mead had vomited directly in front of himself, leaving a murky puddle of grayish, red-streaked bile all over the snow-packed ground at his feet. One of the Black Cats, who had just passed by, doubled back and grabbed Mead by the back of his neck, bent his already leaning body over, and thrust his face down into the vomit-stained snow. Despite his mammoth size, Mead never resisted, just moaned. He just took it like a broken steed, lacking even an ounce of self-worth or survival instinct.

"We gave you time to empty your stomach half an hour ago, Server!" the Black Cat yelled, smearing Mead's face into the snow as if he were trying to spread a cold piece of butter onto a cold piece of toast.

None of us reacted to the brutality of the scene; we just stood there, same as always. I'd seen the same thing happen repeatedly at my last Progressives, and I doubted this would be the last. When at last the punishment had been doled out, the Black Cat left Mead to pick himself up off the sullied ground, as he continued down the line to scan the remainder of the Servers. While he walked on, I turned to look at Mead. He stood, half doubled over, arms across his abdomen as if guarding it. I could make out something forming around his eyes. I couldn't tell if it was melted snow making its way down the anguished creases on his face, or if it was something else.

At last, roll call was complete. The gargantuan Black Cat strolled out to the front of our formation while the others took up positions around us.

"Open your ranks!" he yelled.

There were few Servers that began their days of freedom at Progressive 17. Many came from elsewhere, so we all knew the drill. We opened our ranks as ordered.

"Your freedom to serve is dependent on your physical ability to do so. For this reason, the Provider, in all of his graciousness, has granted you time for physical conditioning. And so we shall begin," he proclaimed, holding his arms out wide as if what he proclaimed was a revelation. "Run in place with hand reaches!" he yelled.

"Run in place with hand reaches!" we yelled back in unison as we began the exercise.

The initial start was difficult, as our muscles were stiff from the uncomfortable bunks and the cold morning air. I lifted my knees as high as I could with each step, thrusting my hands skyward and then bringing them back down. We continued the exercise for a few minutes.

"And stop! Stretch on your own for two minutes."

This was perhaps the most humane part of the day. Despite the bitter cold, exercise allowed us the chance to stretch, to move, and to warm our bodies before setting off to a day of servitude. The rules of the Collective stated that these exercises were meant to keep us healthy, the way one walked a dog, or a farmer let a cow out to pasture. I found the exercises themselves liberating, as they allowed some freedom of movement compared to the dull, ordered marches that took up the remainder of our daily duties.

Halfway through the stretches, Mead heaved and vomited again before collapsing to his knees on the snowy ground.

"What do you think you're doing, maggot?" a Black Cat yelled as he ran up to Mead.

Dry-heaving, with bile, saliva, and blood drooling from his lips, Mead was unable to answer fast enough. The Black Cat drew his baton from his belt, raised his arm up high and thrust downward, clocking Mead in the ribs. His body clearly weakened, Mead fell forward, his chest thumping the ground as a grunt escaped his lips. The rest of us continued our stretching as if nothing was happening. The weak fell, the strong survived to serve another day, which was the life of freedom in the tenement.

After the exercises were complete, the Black Cats called for us to reform ranks. By now, the sun had risen high enough above the horizon to completely cast out the grayness of the dawn, bringing a yellow glow to our dismal tenement.

Once the ranks were complete, the time came for morning recitation of the Server's Creed.

"Service is freedom!" the Black Cats yelled.

"Service is freedom," our voices responded.

"Service is our one true right!"

"Service is our one true right."

"We are free from self-interest!"

"We are free from self-interest."

"We are free to serve!"

"We are free to serve."

And on went the doctrinal recitation. We appreciated the Black Cats' constant concern for our well-being, their taking the time to instill in us the reason why we serve, why we are so vital to the survival of Our State. In a show of respect, a show of solidarity, we would respond as one voice—a collective voice. Some smiled as they realized their true purpose, as we realized the extent of our freedom. In the Collective, all men were free. The Served, or the Progs, they were free from discomfort, from worry, from work, from personal responsibility, free from accountability, free to lead a perfectly blissful existence. The Servers were free to give of themselves, free from self-interest and selfishness, free from the thoughts that complicated our lives prior to the evolution of Our State. We were free to serve others and see their rights fulfilled. Our emotions, wants, desires, and passions all but stripped away, we served those who need serving without any thought for ourselves. That was what the Provider had dictated as best, as fair, as right, as the common good.

The chanting lasted as long the Black Cats felt the collective spirit of the Servers needed reinforcing, ensuring that this part of the day, against the rigid schedule of the Server's life, was always unique. While our daily activities were a mundane play of choreographed scenes, the chanting of the Server's

Creed was always different, always tailored to our needs, tailored to quench our unrelenting thirst for the words of the Provider and ensure we were ready to meet the needs of Our State. Some days, a single repetition was all it took for us Servers to remember our freedom throughout the day. Other days, the chanting would last for nearly an hour until the Black Cats were satisfied. Today I needed more; I realized my mind had wandered as of late. Our mental discipline was the one place where the Black Cats allowed flexibility, for a Server that believed his freedom came from his service would serve well, I realized.

That morning, the recitations only lasted some fifteen minutes before we were ordered back into ranks to file into the sustenance hall. The sustenance hall was located on the far side of the exercise field, and from the front, it was virtually indistinguishable from our bunkhouses. Only once entering the hall did one realize just how large the building was—big enough to accommodate every Server our tenement could hold in a single sitting. We filed in each morning like ants to a nest.

Our meal that morning was the same as it always was: a grimy, grayish-white gruel, a hunk of stale bread, a few small strips of cured meat, and a cup of some type of liquid. I found myself packed tightly on a bench next to Arnold, who frowned at his plate before tentatively scooping some gruel onto his bread and taking a bite. His technique was practiced, as one who had been faced with the dilemma of eating stale, crusty, hardened bread for most of his life. The gruel soaked into the bread and softened it, making it bearable to eat, though doing little to improve the taste. Only the salt from the cured meat made the meal mildly palatable, though the greasy, salty nature of the meat substance coated the oral cavity, leaving a foul reminder for the rest of the day. Each of us was hunched over our trays, scooping and shoveling our food into our mouths. I held my cup up to my mouth and whispered to Arnold.

"Hey, Arnold, name's Hux," I said.

Out of the corner of my eye, I could see Arnold's head rise slightly and his chewing stop. After a brief pause, he raised his cup to hide his mouth. "Hux, huh? Welcome to the bowels of the earth."

"It's not so bad so far," I whispered. "The recitations were very inspirational."

"Whatever," Arnold said before chugging the rest of his drink. He stood up, grabbed his tray, and headed for the tray return.

Well, that didn't go as well as I'd hoped.

I gobbled down the rest of my sustenance in rapid fashion. We were only given four minutes for breakfast; leaving an impatient Black Cat waiting was the last way you would want to end a meal. Just as I moved to stand, the Black Cat at the head of the hall yelled, "End meal, end meal!" Everyone jumped to their feet and started an orderly march to the tray return.

We exited the sustenance hall the same way we had come in, a mass of bodies flooding toward the small doorway like water down a drain. Outside, the Black Cats arranged us in ranks once again, constantly shouting for us to remain silent as they prepared us for our morning march to the trains. Surprisingly, I found myself once again at the side of HSC Arnold, though he didn't seem to have noticed me. He was absentmindedly picking at a piece of food caught in one of his front teeth. As we were jostled to and fro by the crowd, I tried to give him a weak a smile, but all I received was an annoyed nod in return. The stuck food was far more important to him than the companionship of a newcomer. I could also see Mead not far off, with the vomit still crusted around the edges of his mouth, green bile and blood-red stains on his chin and down his sleeve. He looked white as a ghost, with the rancid smell from his stomach contents still pungent, floating on the breeze and growing in the warmth of the breaking day.

As the remaining Servers filed out the of the sustenance hall, our ranks grew and grew until several hundred of us were lined up in the yard. The Black Cats seemed to multiply just as quickly, appearing out of thin air around, between, and within our ranks. Most shouted simple orders as they went, straightening lines, spouting off verses of the Creed, and punishing those who were too disorderly or sickly to immediately follow their orders. Before long, the Servers had arranged themselves in perfect lines across the yard. Rank after rank, all facing the direction of the train platform, each of us in the appropriate line for our respective car numbers, waiting for orders to march.

"Okay, Servers!" one of the Black Cats yelled. "You know what to do. First line, full march to the first train. Second line, follow after. Third, fourth, fifth… Get the pattern, geniuses!"

Like a well-oiled machine, rank one began to march toward the platform.

"Last rank, stand fast for bunkhouse clean-up!"

I waited patiently, silently, as the lines slowly began to file off. All around the field, the stamping of Servers' feet echoed through the tenement, joining a chorus of Black Cats growling orders; hisses and belches of steam from the wood and iron serpent; and the snap-snap-snapping of Our State flag in the crisp wind. I was near the front of line four, which meant I would have choice pickings of seats on the outgoing train. We'd have to sit on the train and wait for the bunkhouses to be cleaned by the detail, but we'd be out of this ever present wind. I smiled at my good fortune as I marched behind Arnold in perfect step with the rest of my line. With food in our bellies and exercises complete, the prospect of sitting in a warm train was more appealing than anything else in the world at that moment.

That was until I saw who was on the train.

As I looked around for a seat, my heart skipped a beat as I found my angel's face staring back up at me from one of the benches. Instantly my mind was transported back to that secluded spot behind the bunkhouse in my dreams. I felt the soft touch of her lips against mine, the coolness of her breath on my skin, the sweet embrace of her body folding into my own to create a single, unified self. We were of one mind, one spirit, and one purpose. For that one second, my dream became a reality, and then the second passed, her eyes turned away, and we were back on the train again, apart. Another Server bumped me from behind, and I stumbled into the train as my thoughts evaporated.

I moved slowly, eyes darting from my angel seated in the corner to the grimy floor, debating the next move in my mind. *If I sit next to her, will the Black Cats notice my interest? Will they notice the look in my eyes as I look upon her beauty? Or will they notice my attention more if it were directed decidedly away from her? Will they see how I keep my gaze fixed all too steadily in some other direction? Will my affection be revealed by avoidance?* Courage or stupidity, I made the only choice I could. I sat next to my angel, willing to accept whatever fate befell me. As Servers continued to pile into the train, we were forced closer together, and still my angel failed to acknowledge my presence. Her attention was focused down to the floor, her hands quivering as they had the day before. Looking up, I saw a wall of standing bodies blocking the two of us from view, the Black Cats unable to monitor us as they crammed more of our tattered lot onto the train. I took a wild, fleeting moment to give into the crazy desires of my heart, reached over, and clasped my hand around my angel's.

"Hello," I whispered loud enough that hopefully only she would hear. I turned my head to her and gave a reassuring smile.

The side of her mouth, twitching slightly, rose to a half smile. She looked into my eyes, then returned her gaze to the floor. We sat in silence as we waited for the detail to complete its task, her hands ceasing to shake, her eyes fixed on the floor, my eyes on her. As the wall of bodies eventually began to clear, I reluctantly released her hands. The feeling that had overcome me was completely foreign: my hands trembled, palms sweated, and giddiness clouded my mind. *Does she feel the same?* Whatever this was, it was mixed with fear. This wasn't right. This wasn't allowed. But…

The train shook briefly, let out a whistle, belched a cloud of steam as if it were a heavy sigh at the start of something awful, and lunged forward. Even as we continued to feign ignorance of each other's presence, I relished the brief feeling of my angel's skin against my own. Our arms lay lazily at our sides, impotent, and yet still brushing and pushing against each other with each bump of the train. For a time, I allowed my dreams to return, dreams of raging against the Collective, embracing the forbidden slavery of self-interest, and taking this exquisite creature in my arms. Slavery to desire had never been so… desirable.

I was snapped from my thoughts by a commotion farther down the aisle. One of the Servers was trying to fight his way through the crowd away from one of the Black Cats.

"Halt, Server!" the Black Cat yelled, but the man continued to push through the crowded aisle, his eyes wild and untamed like one suffering from a break in reality or like the rabies-infected creatures I studied during my medical indoctrination.

Reaching the door, the Server grunted while pulling it open. A rushing wind blew through the car like a thundering storm, biting at our exposed skin as it passed. The sounds of the train running along the tracks, once muffled, became unbearably loud, shrieking through the open door like an animal howling and screaming. Oblivious to the danger, the Server shot through the door and lunged for the roof railing of the next car. His foot caught a stray piece of wiring, sending his colossal body falling sideways, twisting him around to face us, and I recognized him. As if he knew what was to happen next, the look on his face eased. The tight, stretched lips gave way to the hint of a smile. His eyes became serene pools beneath a relaxed brow. A calmness overtook him as if he somehow knew true peace and freedom awaited. A loud crack resounded through the railcar as his body completed its arc downward, a splash of crimson red blood splattered against the walls and ceiling of the train car. Splatters of blood blew in, carried on the bitter wind, peppering the Servers closest to the door as the train briefly swayed from one side to the other.

None of us had moved during the entire exchange, not to hinder, not to help.

At my side, my angel shrieked and began to cry again, letting out short, subdued sobs, the sobs a child would make at night when she didn't want her surrogate to know she was awake. Meanwhile, the Black Cat who had chased the man through the car approached the still-open door, where the Server's body dangled and jumped in time with the lumbering train as it made its way along the tracks. The black-clad figure stooped, inspected the headless body, and turned back toward the other Servers in the car. I could not see his eyes, as the reflective lenses of his glasses hid all signs of what went on behind them, but I got the distinct impression that he was looking for someone to do the dirty work.

"You, you're medical!" he yelled, pointing in my direction. "Take care of this body now, before we reach the Progressive."

"Me?"

"Yes, you! Get up here now!"

Deliberately not glancing at the beautiful, sobbing woman at my side, I slowly raised myself up out of my seat and began to walk to the open doorway. On either side of the aisle, the Servers squeezed into the bench areas, allowing me to pass, some still wiping the splattered blood from their faces.

"Move like you got a purpose, Server!" yelled the Black Cat.

Hurrying, my shoes slipped on the blood that covered the floor as the howling wind rushed past my ears and whipped my hair into a wild frenzy of loose strands. I reached the open door and looked down to see the body of the dead Server still dangling by his feet; a cable was twisted around his ankle. His heavy trunk bounced and bobbed against the steel wheels with every jog of the train. The Black Cat pushed me forward.

"Get rid of it!" he said.

Where his head should have been, nothing but a bloody stump remained. The wind whipped, railroad ties went rushing by. Blood continued to pump from his now exposed vessels, spraying my hands with the sticky life force. The Black Cat stood over me as I stared down at the body, impatiently waiting for me to carry out my orders.

"I… I live to serve," I mumbled, just loud enough that he could hear me over the howling wind.

Looking down at the hulk of a body, mixed with the splatters of blood, I could make out the bile-covered stains on the jacket sleeves—*Poor Mead.* Reaching down, I yanked on the wire that held Mead's foot and then watched as his body fell away from the train. It bounced and twisted as it hit the frozen snow, a bloody rolling heap splashing a stroke of crimson along the canvas of white snow. In a moment, it disappeared from view.

I fell back into the door jamb, letting out a sigh. *Mead… That was Mead. The parasitic Progs have finally consumed that host and shall no longer be able to feed upon him.*

"Get up and get back to your seat!"

"Yes. Yes, sir," I said as I scrambled to my feet.

The Black Cat touched the side of his head and spoke into his microphone. He informed the listener of the situation and told them to mark the location.

I took my seat again as the Black Cat slammed the car door closed. "I guess freedom wasn't good enough for him," yelled the Black Cat to the Servers in the car.

The Servers continued their silent vigil, hiding any remorse or fear they may have felt at the events. I sat, looking down at my hands. They were painted red and sticky with Mead's once life-sustaining blood.

Freedom… not good enough…

Chapter 3

As we approached the dismal underside of Progressive 17, the Provider's prized cattle sat motionless within the train cars. There was nothing any of us could have or would have done to alter the events of the morning.

The cars of the train tilted from side to side as the moving wall made contact. The clamping sound of the large steel claws that gripped the wheels of the train reminded me of the grip the Progressive had on its Servers. In a few moments, we would be off to our day of service, donned in our red jumpsuits, and that was all that our minds should be fixed on. The disembark procedure was the same as when I reached the tenement. We sat in silence and waited for our car number to be called. Throughout the entire procedure, I listened with my attention focused solely on the words being spoken by the Black Cats. My eyes were still fixed on the now dried blood on my hands. During my medical indoctrination, I had been specifically trained on how to deal with the sight of blood, surgeries, horrific disfigurements, and the like. While other Servers may have cringed or vomited at the sight of the dangling, headless body on the train, I had been able to approach it with ease, serving in the capacity for which I was fully indoctrinated. And yet, with the dried and cracked residue still crusted over my palms, I could feel my stomach churn. Such a senseless death, all while the Progs fed off the flesh of the living without the slightest concern for the harshness of our reality. Why did I feel in such a way at the death of a Server when I had witnessed the deaths of many Progs, but not a moment's pause had I ever experienced? Could it have been that laziness and the mentality of entitlement diminished the value of a person if the entitlement was at the expense of another? Were those who believed that the involuntary servitude of another was their right, equal in value to those forced to provide that right at the threat of fear, force, or brutality...

Stop it! Just stop with the thoughts...

"Car number four, on your feet!" yelled one of the Black Cats on the platform.

We jumped to our feet and began to move through the doorway of the railcar. Mead's blood was still sticky on the floor, as shoe after shoe stuck and peeled off while our row moved forward. As we exited the train, I found myself standing next to my angel as we shuffled out onto the Progressive 17 platform. The wind was whipping, and patchy ice had formed in the dips of the concrete. I tried my best to stay near her, but we were quickly separated.

"Get with your proper group Servers: general to the right, mid-level center, skilled to the left. Move!"

I gave a quick glance over my shoulder as I walked to stand in line with my fellow medical providers, only to see my angel on an awkward fall downward. Instinctively, I ran to her.

"Whoa!" I yelled as I put out my arms to catch her.

From out of nowhere, a baton cut through the air and slammed into my stomach. I fell to the ground, gasping to catch my breath.

"Where the hell do you think you're going?" yelled the Black Cat at the other end of the baton.

Trying to catch my breath, I mumbled, "To... To... help her."

"Not your place. Save that care and concern for the Served. It's not a Server's right. Now get your sorry ass back in line!"

As I pushed myself to my feet, I looked over at my angel. Towering over her, a Black Cat screamed for her to get up and get in line. Fortunately, she didn't experience the business end of a baton.

As we each stood, we locked eyes, just for a second, and I had to look away. I dared not watch her anymore. The Black Cats might have noticed the longing in my eyes. Instead, my eyes fixed on the doors of the train, where the splattered blood of the dead Server was smeared; footprints of red from dark to light trailed from the train car to the various lines of Servers. Even in death, a part of him took his final walk into Progressive 17. More than likely, a general Server like my angel would be tasked to clean it up before the day was out. I hoped they wouldn't select her.

"Look alive, Servers!" shouted the Black Cat at the front of my line. "Channel opening!"

I felt a rush of warm air as a large bay door opened up before us, revealing a long, brightly lit tunnel. Tunnels ran beneath each Progressive in winding paths, connected to stairwells that led into every major building in the city. This System, I had learned, was designed to keep the Served from seeing where the Servers truly came from and what squalid conditions we endured. Any questions about our existence or living condition would belabor them, stripping them of their rights to comfort and peace of mind—if it was that they actually had functioning minds. Our living conditions were irrelevant. Our comfort was irrelevant. It was our right to serve, and their right to be served. That was the way the Provider had designed Our State, and it was a System that had stood from the days of his hypnotic rise without disruption, without so much as a question of its validity or objective morality.

The Black Cat at the front of our line led us into the tunnels, and the great bay doors slammed shut behind us. The shouting of the other Black Cats disappeared, replaced only by the steady tapping of our feet as we marched along the otherwise silent halls to our destination. Our group was small, made up entirely of medical center workers, most of us Servers of "high importance" who were granted first access to the tunnels in the morning. This was the way things had been in every Progressive I had been assigned. While the Progressives were uniformly designed, I had no way of knowing which part of the city my train had entered, making determining my location difficult. I imagine that designing various entryways was intentional—wouldn't want a Server to memorize the way out, after all.

As we continued our march through the tunnels, the air took on a sweet scent, became dryer and warmer. The lights grew brighter, and the Black Cat's voice became less demanding, less intimidating.

"Left turn," he said, stopping by a stairwell and waiting for the line to go up ahead of him.

I came up near the end, eyeing the menacing figure for half a second before turning and heading up the steps myself. He would remain below, leaving our fate in the hands of a more specialized and typically more civilized Black Cat up above.

As we climbed the stairs without a Black Cat accompanying us, my brethren remained silent, their solemn faces directed at the steps before them. This was an ideal opportunity to converse, to wonder aloud, to question, possibly to plan a world where equality was based on the start rather than the finish. *Are we now so indoctrinated that we have changed our nature as social beings, that we remain silent to this treatment?*

The Server in front of me glanced back down the steps as we continued our ascent.

"Do you not grow weary of this?" I said.

A look of utter shock paralyzed his face as the words left my lips. The Server began to shake his head side to side.

"Don't you?" I said again. "Why should we be forced to serve anyone but ourselves?"

"Shhh," he said. "We're not allowed to talk to each other!" Picking up his pace, he pushed past several Servers, all the while continuing to shake his head.

I am growing weak.

It was in moments like these that I fully understood the necessity of reciting the Server's Creed each morning. The Black Cats ensured that the Creed was always the first thing on our minds, from the moment we awoke to the moment we laid our heads down to sleep. Our lives were difficult, our burdens heavy, and yet the work we did was essential to maintaining our freedom and fulfilling the rights of the Progs. Self-interest and egoism was the disease, and service was the cure—the act of foregoing reason to the collective mind of servitude.

At last, our line reached the top of the staircase, and all seditious thoughts once again quieted; it was time to serve. From my position near the back of the line, I could hear a woman's voice giving directives to each of my fellow MSPs. When I reached the front of the line and my turn came to be assigned duties, I found the kind face of the female administrator looking up at me. She was a middle-aged woman with straight black hair and warm eyes that proclaimed some mixed foreign descent. She spoke with only the slightest hint of an

accent, calm and accommodating. The name *Louise* was printed on her tag, which hung neatly above her left breast.

"Welcome to Progressive 17 Medical Rights Facility,
MSP Huxley," she said. "Today you'll be assigned to the east
wing surgery department. You have an appointment with carotid patient KB11002B at 0900 hours. A meeting room has
already been prepared. Red jumpsuits and lab coats are to be
found in the locker room down the hall to your left. Do not
venture beyond the locker room before changing; failure to
do so will result in re-indoctrination of your duties. Oh, and
please be sure to undergo a thorough steam sanitization before dressing."

With those words, she handed me a small electronic records pad—an ERP—and pointed toward the hallway to her
left. I nodded, smiled, and set off down the hallway toward
the locker room. Once there, I found a cubbyhole with my
serial number on it. I quickly removed my dirty clothes, hung
them, and then made my way to the sanitizing shower corridor. The corridor was more akin to an elongated bubble. A
conveyor belt ran along the center with nozzles situated on
both sides at varying levels. This additional cleansing was specifically for the Medical Servers, a way of minimizing potential
contamination resulting from our poor hygiene conditions at
the tenement. It was difficult to breathe in the thick fog of
steam and sanitizing chemicals. Upon exiting, I stepped to the
side to ride the parallel drying conveyor back into the locker
room, the warm jets of air a welcome feeling. Back at my
cubby, I grabbed a pair of boxers and socks, slipped them on,
then donned my red jumpsuit. With my black shoes and white
lab coat on, I was ready to serve.

Outside of the Progressive, we were given scraps of
brown cloth that barely fit and hardly protected against the
cold, worn jackets handed down from Server to Server, shoes

with wafer-thin soles. In the sterile and welcoming environment of the Medical Rights Facility, however, we were expected to look presentable, clean—models of the Provider's service. Our jumpsuits served that purpose, making us uniformly tidy and uniformly recognizable, red dots in the sea of demanding, blue-jumpsuit-clad Progs. The sharp differences in color served as a visual depiction of the division between us—the apex of social justice, as the Provider would say.

Dressed in my jumpsuit and lab coat, I set off for my first day of servitude at Progressive 17. The halls of this Medical Rights Facility were identical to the ones I had known in my last Progressives, which were all in stark contrast to the grungy conditions of our Server tenements. In our tenements, Servers slept on beds of straw, walked on floors of dirt, and relieved themselves on toilets stained with mildew. Here, the accommodations provided the Progs were clean, white, and sterile. Not a single smudge marred the walls, nor did a single fleck of dirt tarnish the perfectly reflective linoleum floors. Each step down these hallways caused shoes to squeak and echo in all directions, through the air that was infused with a clean floral scent, an aroma that would never survive in the choking, fuming atmosphere of the Server tenements.

As I moved through the corridors, I heard the cacophony of complaining voices, some moaning that the MSPs weren't doing enough to get them home faster, to honor their rights efficiently enough, others complaining that they weren't receiving the correct treatment, as if they knew what the correct treatment was. After each complaint followed the slow, steady, and comforting voice of a Server, offering an explanation as to why a certain test had been ordered or why a given treatment was superior to one the Prog was asking for. In the end, the Prog got his or her way, but this dance was important to maintaining the rights of the Progs. They had a right to treatment, a right to be heard, and a right to be listened to. The Servers had the right only to serve; a right the truth of which Our State had taught us to believe freed us from the slavery of personal conflict, self-indulgence, and individual opinion.

When I finally reached the meeting room that had been prepared for me, I placed my ERP on the desk cradle. A message on the ERP schedule screen flashed, indicating an appointment cancellation. The scheduled Prog had exercised his right to rest and relaxation, electing to take an afternoon appointment over one that required him to come in early. This was a fairly regular occurrence, one that I took in stride. I tucked the ERP away in the desk for later reference, washed my hands, and went to find the nearest administrator who could provide me an alternate assignment.

No sooner had I taken a few steps from the meeting room when I heard, "MSP Huxley, excuse me!"

I turned to see a male administrator hurrying toward me.

"MSP Huxley, you've been directed to the sterilization quarters."

"What?" I said as he grabbed my arm. I looked down at the tag on his red jumpsuit. "Jason, is it? I don't know what you mean. I'm—"

"Just come with me—the sterilization quarters."

"No, no, there's a mistake. I'm already sterilized—No! Recheck you records!" I said, pulling my arm from his grip.

"No, no, MSP Huxley—to work there, not to be sterilized. This way, follow me."

I let out a sigh of relief as I followed his lead, staying almost even with him as we hurried to the sterilization center. I had never worked in the sterilization quarters. I could feel my heart racing, my palms sweating with hands trembling. I couldn't understand my reaction to the mention of sterilization.

"What do I do there?" I said.

"I suppose you'll sterilize the chosen children and maybe some older folks," Jason said. "Don't worry. The room is soundproofed; we can't hear the screaming out here."

"The screaming?"

"Ah, here we are. Enjoy your day, MSP Huxley," Jason said.

He pointed toward the door and turned to leave. I held my hands out; they were still trembling. I looked up at the stenciled words above the doorway: *"Selection Processing Area"*... no mention of sterilization. Letting out a deep breath, I placed my palm on the scanner and the door instantly slid open.

Upon entering, I found one of my brethren from our initial march into the Progressive milling around. The man was short, balding, with wrinkled facial features. His remaining hair was gray; his eyebrows almost white with age. He wore the standard white lab coat overtop a jumpsuit, but his appeared to be about two sizes too large on him. The sleeves hung down around his enlarged knuckles. I wondered if he had accidently taken some other Server's suit, or if he had simply lost a significant amount of weight recently.

"Aha," he said, seeing me enter. "The newcomer—Huxley, isn't it?"

"That's right—Blair Huxley," I said, adjusting my own lab coat, confident in the fit.

"Yes, yes, indeed. I thought I saw you at the tenement this morning. I'm in the bunkhouse adjacent to yours."

I looked around the small procedure room for instruments or medications, but saw none.

"No treatment today?" I said.

"Just waiting on the recipient," he answered. "I'm Paul by the way—Jeremy Paul."

As he spoke, Paul pointed to a large cabinet in the corner.

"You'll find the anesthesia machine locked up tight until the patient arrives," he said. "And the other tools as well. The administrators run a tight ship here, possibly something other than you are used to." He stopped and placed his hands on the cold, stainless table that stood between us. "Something to remember here: with young children, it's best to hide the things that may scare them until after we electro-sedate them. The older subjects aren't as bad."

"I don't understand?" I said.

"You will, you will."

"What is this section?" I said, still looking around the cold, unadorned room.

"Well, this is another jewel of Progressive 17—the only Progressive to offer such a service to the Collective," Paul said. "Have you ever experienced emotions or attraction to another human—sexual or otherwise?"

For just a moment, the image of my angel appeared in my mind. "Of course not, that's… forbidden."

"Don't fool yourself into believing that your lack of emotion is because it is forbidden. It is, in actuality, a result of the procedures we will be performing today," Paul said.

He stood and looked directly into my eyes as if trying to read something. I felt as if I'd seen him prior to this meeting, perhaps at another Progressive.

"What will we be doing?" I asked.

"No matter how you may react to the procedures, remember that the work we do here today is for the benefit of the Provider and the Served of Our State."

"I'll keep that in mind," I said, moving to the sink to wash my hands. I found that I was a bit concerned over still having some dried blood on my hands from the dirty business of seeing Mead off into the snow bank, even after my sanitizing shower and a subsequent hand-washing.

"You been to many Progressives?" Paul said.

"Several over the past few years. This is my fourth. I hear it's the last one the Provider granted the Collective."

"A crater skipper, eh?"

"You could say that."

"Hope you're a lousy doctor, then," Paul said, "because I'd hate to lose a good one so fast, not that any Server ever leaves Progressive 17. This is the proverbial end of the line."

"What is a good doctor, or even medical care in general to the Served, anyway? Nothing's ever good enough for them."

Paul chuckled a little at the exchange. "Right. Kinda hard to figure out the value of something if you've never lifted a finger to work for it."

"Good point," I said.

The door to the sterilization room opened, and in stepped a man clad not in a red or blue jumpsuit, but a jet-black uniform. His collar was almost molded to the shape of his neck, rising up two inches from his shoulders. A small loop stretched over the space between the left and right side and attached to two blood red buttons. On either side of the collar, the symbol of Our State was embroidered with silken strands, the Δ outlined by links of chain, the inner emblem of two arc segments with a setting orb surrounding the eye of the Provider. The man's uniform was just as crisp, each crease as hard edged as his jaw line. Tucked under his bent arm was a short, narrow black baton, almost like a whip. He looked at the pair of us with cold, calculating, almost lifeless eyes, and yet with intensity that could burn. The man slowly worked his way around the room, occasionally running his whip-like baton along the cold, stainless surfaces. Paul and I glanced across the room at each other as our chuckles had become muted, and in their place trepidation and an aura of fear.

"Gentlemen," he said, "my name is Killary—Consular William Jefferson Killary. I represent the Provider. I will be reviewing the selection and sterilization process today. You will go about your duties as if I were not here. Do you both understand?"

In unison, as if practiced, we said, "Yes, sir!"

Consular Killary took a seat in the corner, saying nothing more.

Paul and I continued our work in silence, the joking and joviality sucked out of the room as Consular Killary's cold eyes bore down on us.

"We've got a green light on the anesthesia and instrument cabinet," Paul said, pointing to the steel-and-glass cabinet in the corner of the room. "The kits are self-contained, so just grab one from the cabinet and open it."

I grabbed a kit as Paul had instructed. The kit was a large sterilization pouch with white polyethylene at one end and a heat seal strip at the other. Tearing it open, I removed the inner blue sheets. The instruments were pretty standard: forceps, scissors, scalpel, syringes, adhesive, stapler, a small elastic cover of some type, and vials of anesthesia.

"What's this cover for?" I said.

"Ahh, that item. Yes, we'll be utilizing it to sterilize the mental and emotional constructs of the selected recipients."

"Oh, okay." I had no idea what he was talking about, but with Killary in the room, I'd dare not admit to it.

I prepared the anesthesia for our first patient of the day, while Paul lined up the sterilization equipment and carefully reviewed the electronic files that held the medical and psychological profiles of each of our incoming patients, the testing data, and all pertinent information necessary to make the appropriate decision. The door opened a few minutes later, and a young boy, no older than four or five, stepped in. No surrogate accompanied him.

At that moment, something within me pulled me down—down from a feeling of apathy to something less, something forlorn, something gut-wrenching. This time, when the Collective decided the future of an entity, of this unknowing recipient, this little boy, I found it to be... troubling.

Paul crouched down to the same level as the boy, smiled, and gave him a pat on the head. "Take a seat, young man."

The boy looked from one of us to the other, then to Killary. He slowly climbed on top of the stainless-steel stool sitting near the door.

"Ah, you are a smart one, aren't you?" Paul said while glancing down at the electronic records pad that displayed the boy's medical history and exam findings. "Top marks in math and early reading skills, spatial reasoning borderline, but within acceptable limits. Yes, yes, a smart one, indeed!"

Paul's hands begin to visibly tremor as Consular Killary watched his every move, his every action and reaction. Killary just sat there, his baton-whip coupled in his hands as they rested in his lap, twisting and twisting the baton as if it were a pencil in a hand sharpener. I couldn't recall any time in recent memory when I had been subjected to such intense tension. It was stifling. The boy's demeanor never changed, though. Killary's presence had no impact on the boy's interactions, and his ignorance of what Killary represented was no doubt blissful. The future was bound to change this.

I continued preparing the work area as Paul stammered through the remaining data in the child's record. Based on everything my colleague said, I already knew what the boy's fate would be. He was intelligent, creative, and possessed no physical defects to speak of. He could only have one fate.

"Well, well," Paul said, patting the boy softly on the knee. "You'll have the honor and privilege of being afforded the rights of a Server. You will spend the rest of your days free from want or need, you'll be taught all the wonderful mysteries of science and technology, and you will be free to put that knowledge to use in service of the Collective, a true pawn of the Provider, you lucky lad. A shackled sheep you'll be—one of us, a Server."

The boy nodded quietly as a look of confusion crept across his face. Paul lifted him up and placed him on the procedure table, laid him down, and then placed his head in the restrainer at the end of the table. A white, wooly sheepskin head with little brown eyes and droopy ears covered the dampened electrodes on the head restrainer. I attempted to place the cranial placement straps over the boy's forehead as he began to struggle and whine.

"It's just a game, little man. Don't you want to pretend to be a little lamb?" I asked, still trying to pull the straps over his head.

"No, no! Leave me alone!" screeched the boy.

"Calm down, calm down. It'll be okay," I whispered in the most soothing voice I could muster, knowing that for him, it wouldn't be okay, that he was destined for a life of gruel, straw bunks, and servitude.

"No, no! Leave me alone!" the boy shouted again, kicking his legs and thrashing his arms.

"Lay over him and grab his arms, Paul! This kid's outta control!" I yelled.

As the boy continued his frantic struggle, Paul and I finally subdued his writhing, allowing me an opportunity to strap his head in. I slammed the green button on the Taser mechanism with the palm of one hand while holding the boy's face with the other. The boy was just about to bite my hand when the electrical pulse raced down the feed cable to the electrodes on the cranial strap. The boy's back arched briefly, and his arms and legs became rigid as I was thrown back against the wall from the shock that had raced up my arm. The look of anguish on his face and the snarling, gaping mouth eased and relaxed as he turned into a lifeless lump on the table. For me, the shock was as much a memory jolt as it was an event in real time. I stood against the wall, panting; images of hands holding me down flooded in to my mind, and in a moment were gone. A bead of sweat ran down my forehead as I looked up at Paul. We were both out of breath and emotionally drained as we experienced our post-adrenaline crash, although Paul hadn't experienced much current through his oversized, double layer of clothing. It was then I knew what Jason's comment about hearing the screaming was all about.

I could see Killary out of the corner of my eye; he sat there, his knees bouncing up and down as he pushed the balls of his shoes into the floor over and over like an excited boy waiting for a cookie. His face had come alive—a crooked smile, a wicked smirk found a home there. *Bastard, the bastard enjoyed that. He just sat there and enjoyed that.*

Paul exhaled a large cleansing breath, gave me a nervous smile, and went about his work. He began to strip the boy of his pants.

"Extend the headrest," Paul said, "then make an incision at the base of the skull, around C1 and the foramen ovale. Place the sterile elastic cap you asked about earlier on the bulb probe and insert it into the incision. The control panel is at the head of the bed. Just press the *'Sanitize'* button, wait a few minutes, then remove and seal the incision. I'll take care of snipping the ol' vas deferens down here."

"Got it. And what's the bulb do?" I said.

"That eradicates the mental and emotional aspects of desire. A specific pulsed frequency effectively destroys the area of the brain responsible for all that messy stuff."

"Fair enough. Seems an appropriate reward for possessing abilities."

"Thanks to the Provider," Paul said.

When our work was done, Paul tapped a button near the door.

"You see, this boy was the recipient of the Provider's goodwill. He will now be free from the toils and potential agony of emotional folly. His attachment will be to Our State—although not emotional, an attachment nonetheless," Paul said.

With present company, I chose not to reply.

A moment later, a nurse arrived to take the boy to a recovery room before his transfer to the central processing facility, where his formal education as a Server would be initiated. My mind drifted back to my own time as a medical indoctrinee, being drilled fourteen hours a day on all the inner workings of the human body, on the differences that divide Servers and Served. Half our training was philosophical in nature, teaching us to understand why the Served had rights to medicine and the Servers did not. In order for us to be truly free, we had to serve only others, never ourselves—a basic, if at times, painful principle, but nonetheless, we were free from innate self-indulgence.

Looking up, I noticed Consular Killary staring at me from the corner of the room. His facial features had now returned to pure stone, unreadable and unchanging. I forgot myself for the briefest of moments and engaged Consular Killary.

"It seemed you enjoyed that, Consular," I said. "By the way, thanks for the help.'

Killary shot to his feet, his stone-cold body now a fiery, fierce lava flow. "You forget yourself, Server!"

As quickly as he rose to his feet, his arm raised, grasping his narrow baton, and down it came, flying through the air like a missile to slam into my shoulder.

Instant pain shot down my arm and my back as I let out a scream that made the boy's yells sound like a whisper. I fell backward into the wall and slid down onto the floor.

"Yes, yes, Consular, I forgot myself and my place. I forgot myself. My apologies, Consular, my apologies." My other arm instinctively shot up over my head to protect against another blow in case another came.

"Get up, Server—on your feet!" His voice had calmed again, now just cold and icy, as before, almost monotone. "I must say, you both handled that well. You needed no help, and besides, what difference does it make now?"

"Yes, Consular, how right you are," I said. "Yes, what difference does it make now? My apologies again, Consular."

My shoulder was on fire and my arm throbbed. I put the pain away, as I had to focus. I had a job to do. My insolence had deprived the Consular and my other patients of time—time they could not regain. *I must focus on serving others and not be so self-serving. There's no freedom in that.* Paul gave a reminder of the next patient awaiting our services as he gently tapped me on my uninjured shoulder.

Our sterilization work carried on for a number of hours after this, and fortunately we did not have any repeat incidents like the one that had welcomed our day with such glory. Each child entered, has his or her record read, and their fate determined in a swift and decisive manner. Most of the work had already been done for us. Those with physical and mental strengths became Servers. Those with deficiencies, those with marginal aptitude or less, those who were more adept at having their hands out in acceptance as opposed to those who would raise their hands in self-serving effort… these would join the ranks of the Served—they became Progs. Children who straddled the line would be given more detailed examinations by the lead MSP, but today, none of that was necessary. All our cases were appropriately red or blue. Paul was not lying when he boasted of this Progressive's efficiency. There was no gray, no purple—you were either a Server or Served.

We had just sent another child off to join the Servers when our final patient arrived. She was older than the others, somewhere around six or seven, and her record was surprisingly sparse, her induction date most recent. Despite the ongoing dread of Killary's presence, Paul immediately jumped into his playful, well-practiced repertoire, but the child never said a word. Paul glanced briefly from the child to me, then to Consular Killary in the corner, who had yet to say another word. I could see worry in Paul's eyes.

"What is your name?" Paul said as he got down on his knees to make himself level with the child's eyes. "Surely you've got one of those, eh?"

The girl turned her head away. Consular Killary's voice came from the corner; he spoke in a language I did not recognize. The girl perked her head up at the words and stared at the cold, hard face of the State representative in the corner.

"Foreign," Consular Killary said, "probably an undocumented. They get mixed into the batch every now and then. Amazing how they make it up this far."

"Aha," Paul said. "Thought I had lost my touch."

He smiled briefly at his joke, then turned to me.

"That'll be it for today, Huxley," Killary said. "This girl will join the Served."

"We haven't checked her records or tested her yet, sir," I said.

"No need. She doesn't speak our language, and she's undocumented. She'll be a Served."

"Yes, sir—of course, sir. We'll look forward to serving her the rest of our lives."

"And the lives of your brethren," Killary said.

Paul hit the button by the door, and in short time, the nurse arrived to escort the girl to her life of spoils. The thought of serving someone that would not even make an effort to understand the language just did not sit right with me. As Killary had so eloquently put it, what difference did it make now anyway? Paul and I began to clean up our instruments and the area from the day's work.

"With the exception of your insubordinate sarcasm, MSP Huxley, you and MSP Paul served the Collective well," Consular Killary said. "You'd do well to spend a few more shifts in here, aiding the Provider with selection and sterilization. I'll see your name is added to the rotation."

"Many thanks, Consular," I said, bowing.

He stared intently at us for a moment, then, without saying another word, turned and exited the selection and sterilization room.

We both let out huge sighs.

"Quite a chap, isn't he?" Paul said. "I swear if I saw that man smile, I'd have a heart attack."

"He did smile, and lucky for you, you missed it. His joy at the struggles of the young boy, our first recipient, was nothing shy of disgusting."

I stood and stared at the empty corner where Killary had sat. *What difference does it make? Disgusting.*

"I've heard tales," Paul said. "Heard one of his now dead female relatives sat and watched via long-distance monitoring—a family being brutally murdered, all the while screaming and pleading for help. Apparently the father was a diplomat of some type. Grazzi, I think his name was—Blair or Benjamin—and his family. It's told that she just sat, watched, and smiled as the killing took place—sat right alongside the Provider. A chip off the old block, I suppose."

"I'm Blair, and it's an uncommon name. Must have been Benjamin," I said.

"Right, right, must have been Benjamin."

We both stood for a moment, shaking our heads at the lunacy of the world around us.

"I've heard that Killary may be in line to take the place of the Provider once he decides to end his reign," Paul said. "I don't think I can take any more of this change. I don't think any of us can."

"Hmm... change. Who knew that such a term could take on such a negative connotation?"

After a brief moment of silence: "Well, you should probably be off," Paul said. "I can clean up here."

"No, please let me. I need a moment to myself."

"Understood. First time's always tough," Paul said, gazing at me. "There's plenty I remember about my first experience in this room, but those tales are for a different time. Anything I can do?"

"No, no, it's all on me. It's a lot to come to terms with," I said. "You seemed concerned about how I would respond, yet this process is supposed to eradicate emotion."

Paul grinned at me and winked. "Nothing lasts forever, does it?"

Chapter 4

The halls of the Medical Rights Facility, which earlier were largely empty, now appeared to be flooded with waves of blue jumpsuits, each covering the body of a creature demanding fulfillment of their right to treatment. I had entered the busiest part of the service day, when the Served had all found themselves out of bed and willing to receive treatment. Every now and then, I saw someone in a red jumpsuit scurry by, but they paid me little heed, as they were undoubtedly focused on serving. Some of the blue jumpsuits move quickly, eager to leave and return to a life of comfort, while others moved slowly, finding the sheer effort of walking about the facility taxing. I never thought I would visually see ignorance, as it was not generally an aspect of one's being that took form, but there it was, written on the faces of the Progs, etched in their shallow smiles—that clueless emptiness shrouded behind veils of bliss, the expressions of mindless happiness where what one received was at the expense of another, and no shame was apparent with the act of taking.

As I moved down the hall, I passed a Black Cat at every corner, each standing like a statue, watching the Servers through their silver-framed, mirrored glasses, not an inch of skin to be seen. I sometimes wondered if there actually was a human beneath their starched, rigid black facade. Their indifference at the ill treatment they imparted upon the Servers would suggest otherwise, but then again, aside from the physical correction they provided, their attitudes toward us paralleled those of the Progs.

My mind drifted back to the many recipients MSP Paul and I sterilized this morning, to what they thought of the Black Cats now and how they might see them when they would reach my age. To them now, the Black Cats were silent bodyguards, perhaps a little frightening, but a sign of safety and security, a sign that the System was looking out for them, for us. At least that was how I remembered them, but now not so much. Now they served as sentinels guarding the System, constantly greasing the wheels of the machine with nothing but their presence, each as much a symbol of conformity as the rest of us. The children of Our State had no parents, no relatives. They were raised by surrogates, stripped from their concubine at birth, given all they had rights to by Our State, provided by our hands and our labor in the name of the Provider. "It takes an entire Progressive to raise a Served." That was a saying I had previously heard—sounded like something Killary would have said in all of his cold indifference and power lust.

Another thought occurred to me as I passed yet another Black Cat: we had not assigned a single recipient to become a Black Cat. What were the odds, with the number of recipients we treated this morning? My mind wandered as I continue on to my destination, unaware of the twists and turns I'd made on my hurried journey. *Where do the Black Cats come from?*

Without conscious awareness of my short journey, I arrived at my assigned general exam room. Patient KB11002B was likely already inside. I took a deep breath and placed the palm of my hand on the wall scanner. With a whoosh, the door slid open, retracting itself into the wall. I stepped in, already mentally prepared to be berated for my tardiness by a loud-mouthed Prog on the other side. I was surprised when it was not a Prog "proper" in a blue jumpsuit waiting on the other side, but another State representative like Consular Killary—only this time, the uniform was more basic, much less adorned, without the trappings of a high-ranking official.

"About damn time you showed up, Server!" the man said.

As he spoke, some spittle flew from his mouth, landing on my lab coat. I paid it no mind. Instead, I headed toward the small ERP perched on a roll-around stand.

"I've been waiting five minutes here! Five minutes! Do you have any idea of the implications of that? Five minutes! I'll have you reported for this."

"My sincerest apologies, Mister...?"

"Benson—Kenneth Benson. You'd serve yourself well to remember that name next time you and your ilk ask for some extra blankets for your tenement. When they don't arrive, it'll be because THIS housing rights sub-director remembered those who kept him waiting!"

"My apologies again, Mr. Benson," I said. "I am here to serve. I have failed in delivering that service in a timely manner. I am fully responsible and ready to bear the brunt of any punishment that is deemed appropriate." I looked at the Prog and lowered my head, almost bowing, and then continued. "You see, we were providing Consular Killary with a demonstration in the sterilization room, and we had a particularly troublesome recipient. Consular Killary was able to accurately identify her as an undocumented and saved our schedule from more delay."

"Hmm... Consular Killary, you say?" Mr. Benson said, rubbing his chin while pacing.

"That's right, Mr. Benson—Consular Killary."

"An undocumented, huh? Well, I'll be... How the hell do they even get rights? What kind of bullshit is that? They're not even from Our State, so now I have to wait on a damn illegal!" He eyed me. "Yeah... illegal! That's what I call them. What do you think of that, Hackney?"

"It's Huxley, sir, and I think nothing of it, sir. It's not my place to think on such things. If the Provider, in his ultimate wisdom, has bestowed on them the rights that other Served are entitled to, then it is my duty and the heart of my existence to provide those rights. It is through the exercise of that service that I derive my freedom, Mr. Benson."

Benson paused, then the look of disgust on his face gave way to conformity. "Right. It is rightly so as you have noted, Server Huxley—rightly so. That is the proper and right answer. Well... no harm done," Benson said. "If you rely on the expertise of men like Consular Killary and me, you're sure to be a success here. Now... about my operation?"

"Right," I said, thankful that my name-dropping produced the required results. Such a technique would never work on a full Served. They couldn't care less about anyone but themselves—they were entitled. I moved into a detailed explanation of what Mr. Benson's surgery would require, being sure to stroke his ego each time he asked a question, even if I had already stated the answer. Within an hour, we had all the details worked out. I sensed that Mr. Benson was holding back during our discussions, that he actually was quite versed in medical procedures for some reason, as his knowledge seemingly uncanny for someone in such a position as his.

"Now, back to the new blankets I had mentioned earlier... You must be in a low-numbered bunkhouse—one, two?" Benson said.

"Two. It's bunkhouse two, but..." I had wanted to ask how he knew about the layout of the bunkhouses.

"But what, Server?"

"The Progs—my apologies, sir... I mean, the Served... Such luxuries as new items are to be bestowed upon them, not us. Please don't go to any trouble on my account."

"Nonsense, it's no trouble at all," he said. "The Provider knows just how cold these nights have been lately. Besides, I've gotta keep the hands of my surgeon well cared for. It's in my own best interest, isn't it?"

"We are overly blessed with the fruits of our freedom as it is. The Provider is far too generous to us already."

After I confirmed his pre-operative appointment, I once again assured Benson that his endeavors were unnecessary, knowing all along that not a shred of extra fabric would make its way to any bunkhouse. A housing rights sub-director such as Benson would never have the authority to shake the System, because to give any group or individual more than they already were allotted was likened to heresy. This was a dance every Server played with lower-tier State personnel, the same as the put-on joviality of Jeremy Paul before the scrutinizing eye of Consular Killary. We had to appear happy in our position, always happy, or else we risked upsetting the balance that kept our society standing. It was our right to serve, even if the service were an act for an undeserving audience.

Just as Benson was leaving, I was approached by one of the floor's administrative secretaries.

"Ah, MSP Huxley," the woman said. "There's a Served waiting in the next room—wants to see a Medical Service Provider ASAP. I didn't have an opportunity to obtain any info. He just ran up to the desk frantic, rambling on and on about needing to be seen. He wouldn't answer any questions and would not allow me to scan him in. I put him in the next room and assured him that he would be seen momentarily. I don't know how he made it past emergency services if his condition was so grave."

I hesitated before answering. In my experience, walk-ins were almost always trouble: usually it was a Prog convinced they were so entitled that they didn't even need an appointment.

"I guess I'm your man," I said.

The woman gave me a reassuring pat on the arm and a warm smile that said a silent *Thank you*.

As she walked away, I took a few steps to the neighboring door, took a deep breath, and placed my palm on the scanner adjacent to the door. The door slid open, allowing me to enter. I fully expected to find some hypochondriac complaining about the smallest stomach trouble or a raving psych case—walk-ins were usually one or the other.

But I saw before me a pathetic-looking, little wretch of a being. A short, skinny, sunken-faced man with downcast eyes sat perched atop the chair across from the consult desk. The man looked up at me, like a skeleton in a blue jumpsuit, and his thin, tight lips managed to form a halfhearted smile. His eyes darted to the Black Cat standing in the corner, then down to the floor. He appeared weak and tired, like the look of a worn-down animal with little will to go on, a sheep shaved of his coat, standing naked and fearful. The Black Cat, meanwhile, offered no recognition of either of us, remaining still as a statue in his place. Somehow, I always found the Black Cats' silent observation in the Progressives more disturbing than their violence in the tenements. At least in our barbaric tenement world, we knew what to expect.

"I… I appreciate your see—seeing me without an appointment. I'm fully… fully aware of how that can play—play havoc with your tight schedule," the Prog said, occasionally glancing at the Black Cat.

His face looked almost kind, his voice soft, though I heard notes of depression in it that I had not expected. I was unsure of how to handle this unusual patient. I pulled the portable ERP toward me and initialized the screen.

"Sir," I said, "I'm going to need you to place your forehead against the back of the ERP so I can access you medical history. Apparently you were not inclined to scan in at the desk."

"Yes, yes, of course," the man said as he rose from the chair, placing his head against the back of the pad.

I touched the *Gather* icon on the ERP and his record appeared. I noticed the man was trembling when his head was against the pad; he glanced up at me with a look between fear and embarrassment. His complexion flushed slightly red and then he returned to his seat. His record appeared on the screen.

Beyond the ERP, I could see the man's eyes dart back and forth between me and the Black Cat. He appeared so worn, so spent and used up, I oddly felt sorry for him. *A Server feeling sorry for a Prog? What's wrong with me?*

"If you could please give me a moment to familiarize myself with your medical history, then we can then discuss why you're here and how I can be of service." Something prompted me to swipe through the screens to check his induction data, something I wasn't accustomed to looking at. Age was listed as fifty-plus—unheard of for a Prog.

Looking up, I noticed the man's eyes still shifting back and forth between the Black Cat and myself. "Just a few moments more," I said. "I need a complete picture of your health status before we begin."

My eyes fell back down to his record. I found a number of diagnostic reports, none of which would indicate that I should be seeing a man in such a condition as the one that now sat before me. This Prog had not seen an MSP since his last State-mandated exam six months prior. The last report indicated a rather healthy, over-aged Served male. That, I would have said, was the most alarming aspect of his history: it was rare to see a Served survive to so great an age, not that I was in the habit of calculating the ages of those I served. With few exceptions, most Progs led rather sedentary, unhealthy lives.

"Okay, Mr.… Hemsworth, correct?" I said.

"Yes, yes, that's right."

"What seems to be the problem?"

"Well…" Hemsworth said, his eyes darting the Black Cat again. "I've had this feeling that something just isn't right."

"How do you mean?"

"Something's just not right. You need to look—you need to see for yourself!"

A touchy, demanding Prog… Seems normal to me.

"Please take a seat on the exam table," I said as I gestured toward the table. I looked at the Black Cat and said, "Please excuse us for a moment. I need to pull the curtain and examine Mr. Hemsworth."

The Black Cat said nothing, merely turned his head toward me and gave a slight nod, then returned to his previous statuesque position.

As Hemsworth moved his somewhat dilapidated body to the exam table, I slid the curtain closed, blocking the view of the Black Cat.

"Now, let's see if we can find out what the trouble is."

I pulled the ERP over and jotted a few notes on the screen with my stylus: *"Appears much older than listed age. Chief complaint: 'Something just isn't right.'"*

"Mr. Hemsworth, can you provide me with more details about this something that you feel isn't right, and we can take it from there?"

Hemsworth gestured me closer with his curled-up index finger, motioning me closer and closer. I leaned in as he had indicated.

"I see through this façade," he whispered, placing his frail hand on my forearm. "I see through this."

"Through what?" I said. "Are you having trouble with your sight—is that it?"

He raised his crooked, arthritic finger to his dry, cracked lips. "Shhhh. This is not right—this blue uniform I wear, the red uniform you wear, the Black Cats watching every move we make.... It's not right."

Pulling back a little, knowing on some level to what this man was referring, yet unsure of how to respond without drawing suspicion to myself, I said, "Have you been getting ample sleep? Lack of sleep tends to increase your cortisol levels and that could have a profound effect on raising your levels of stress. It's a vicious cycle. I could prescribe something to help you sleep and we could see how you feel in a week or two."

"No, no, that's not it. Our entire System, Our State... You need to look. You need to see!"

"Sir, I am examining you. I am looking."

"No!" he whispered. "Not at me, at the System!"

"Mr. Hemsworth, I realize you weren't seen as quickly as you should have been, and for that I apologize, but I assure you, the medical rights System works as it should by design."

"Do you want to do this? Do you really want to? Would you be serving me if you didn't have to? Don't you see what I mean?" he said, slapping his bony hand against the exam table.

"Mr. Hemsworth, I am a Server. I am here to serve you. My service is my freedom; my service is your right. *Want* is not part of the equation," I said, leaning closer to him so as not to alert the Black Cat.

"Brilliant, my dear boy," he said.

"Brilliant what? I don't understand what you're talking about Mr. Hemsworth," now finding myself looking between him, the curtain behind us and back again.

"You're a Medical Service Provider, so you gotta have some smarts, boy. You've seen the type of people you serve. Don't tell me you've never questioned or wondered why we get the rights, but smart, capable guys like you don't get anything. Want… Haven't you ever thought about the difference between 'want' and 'need' or 'have to'?"

"It is not within my rights to question the motives of the Provider. It is, as I have said, my right to serve and in doing so I am free from want or desire."

"Damn it, boy! I'm not crazy. I'm not suffering from lack of sleep. This System is wrong. It's not natural!" Hemsworth whispered, grabbing my stylus hand.

I paused and stared down at him, shocked that a Prog would ever unnecessarily touch a Server. That just did not happen.

"You need a sedative and a prompt appointment with the Mind Health Section," I said, not knowing what to make of this, wondering if maybe I, too, could use one.

"Stop THAT!" Hemsworth said well above a whisper, his eyes ghastly wide. "All of you are the same. You refuse to see the truth. We are slaves. All of us—slaves. I no longer feel bliss. I feel BLISSLESS and I know why… I'M NO LONGER IGNORANT! I've been… thinking!"

"No longer ignorant? Thinking?"

The curtain was ripped open with such force that it tore off the tracks. The Black Cat stood there for just a moment before pouncing on Hemsworth. He grabbed him by the collar of his blue jumpsuit and dragged him off the exam table. Unable to get his feet under himself in time, Hemsworth fell to the floor. His knees cracked against the shiny white linoleum with an awful thud. He cried out in pain as the Black Cat grabbed him and raised him to his feet.

"You're coming with me," the Black Cat said. "We'll see to your thinking!"

"I… I… I'm sorry," Hemsworth said. "I can't live like this. I can't! I've lost my bliss. I've seen that it's not real. Help me! Oh please help me!"

The Black Cat dragged Hemsworth to the door. Before activating it, he turned and pointed his finger at me as if it were a weapon. "Serve yourself by forgetting this ever happened," he said before turning again. He activated the door and dragged Mr. Hemsworth out into the hallway.

Stunned, I wondered what the hell kind of place I had been transferred to if this was only my first day. I darted to the doorway and leaned my head out to glance after Hemsworth and the Black Cat just as they neared the elevator.

"Don't forget me!" Hemsworth yelled over his shoulder.

He didn't struggle or scream, instead allowing himself to be pulled along. The Black Cat raised his hand to his earpiece, and nodded his head as he stood grasping Hemsworth by the collar at the doorway to the elevator. "Forward. Understood, sir," he said to the listener. He then lowered his hand from his earpiece as he pushed Hemsworth into the elevator car. I watched from the doorway as the two of them disappeared behind the closing automatic doors. The last thing I saw before the doors completely closed were the eyes of the Prog— Mr. Hemsworth… sunken, sad, and defeated.

I hurried over, weaving through the waves of blue to see which floor the Black Cat took Hemsworth to. *It must be the Mind Health Section.* I watched as each level indicator illuminated in succession above the elevator door. They were heading... down? *But... Mind Health is on the upper floor.* The level indicator stopped on level one, then flashed several times. The letters *MRR* appeared above the door; I had never encountered that acronym and was unsure of the nature of the intervention.

For what seemed like an eternity, I stood in the hallway, gazing at the elevator, occasionally looking to the left and then the right, uncertain of what to do. This man, Mr. Hemsworth, a Served, a Prog, was unlike any I'd ever met. Every wild and untamed thought I had ever had about the System came directly from his mouth. He had questions; I had begun to have questions. The thought that I could ever have anything in common with any Served struck me as terrifying, jolting my perceptions.

Without any semblance of a plan, I hit the elevator button and waited. Several moments later, I heard the faintest ding, and then the double doors opened before me to reveal an empty compartment. Stepping inside, I turned to the control panel and looked for a floor labeled *MRR.* It was three levels below the basement, but no selection button appeared next to it, only a card reader slot.

If it was medical imaging of some sort, certainly medical providers would have access, but there was no way they would put it so far down. It would have been on the first floor by the Urgent and Emergent section. *MRR... What could that stand for?* I couldn't question the Black Cat himself. I wouldn't even know which Black Cat it was, as they all looked the same in their all-encompassing black garb. The advice of the Black Cat popped into my mind: *"Serve yourself by forgetting this ever happened."*

Yeah... like that's going to happen.

I was at a loss for what to do; I pushed the *Door Open* button on the control panel and stepped back out into the hall. My day was only half done, and more Progs needed to be served. Whatever became of that confused mind in the lanky body, I might never know. The only way I could, the only way anyone could, would be if they openly questioned the System in front of a Black Cat, like Hemsworth did. But while a member of the Served may only be dragged off to mysterious ends for voicing doubts, I already knew the fate of any Server who rejected their right to serve. My hands had been stained with the blood of one such Sever earlier in the day.

I trudged back to the exam room, intent on finishing my notes about Mr. Hemsworth, whatever good that would do. I placed my palm on the wall scanner and the door slid open. I pondered the thought that I'd have to put in a work order for one of my brethren to come and fix the torn curtain, but I was more concerned about my charting.

What a mess. I sighed. *If he'd been a Server, I may have more concern, but even though he was a Prog, his words were so...*

I grabbed the ERP and pulled it over to the desk, snatched the pad off the roller stand and sat down. I noticed my stylus wasn't in the pad's stylus holder. Patting the pockets of my lab coat, I glanced over at the exam table only to see the end of the stylus protruding from the back edge of the table. It must have dropped during the commotion, I concluded. I pushed my chair back, stood up, and stepped over to the exam table. Bending down to reach for the stylus, I saw a small wadded ball of something a little farther under the table. I reached in, my fingers dancing on the white linoleum until they came to rest on the object.

Paper?... Paper! When was the last time I saw or felt actual paper? I didn't think it existed anymore. There had been rumors circulating through the tenements of printed matter still in existence, but no one had actually seen any for ages.

Pushing myself to my feet, holding the paper in my hand, I rolled the wad of paper through my fingers, enjoying the texture for a moment. I realized a smile had crept over my face, from a piece of paper—*How foolish*. As I began to unravel the crumpled wad of paper, I heard a voice behind me.

"Here to fix the curtain."

I froze for a moment, then shoved the wad of paper in to my lab coat pocket as I turned. A Server done up in his red jumpsuit stood in the doorway, holding packaged curtains and a small box that I guessed contained his tools.

"Sorry to startle you," he said. "I'm here to fix the curtain."

"My mind was elsewhere. Yes, yes, please come in," I said. "Please don't let me hold you up. That's quite remarkable; I hadn't even put a work order in yet, and here you are."

"Well, somehow someone knew. The Provider knows what's best for us," he said. "The Provider provides even when we don't know what to ask for."

"Nothing to fear here," I said. "Nothing wrong happened here."

"Not my business, but whatever you say," the man said. "None of my business. Just gotta get the curtain up. It's gotta be ready for the next Prog. Can't keep them waiting! Our service is their right. Our right is to serve, and serve we shall."

"Absolutely, my brethren, absolutely—serve we shall," I said after feigning a friendly smile. "On the same token, not to be rude, but I must finish this charting. Please excuse me."

"Not another word from me, then. I'll be as quiet as Mead, my brethren."

I had no idea how to respond or to feel at such a comment. Mead had only been dead a handful of hours, but now his passing was used as a pun? I sat back down at the desk and picked up the ERP. The usual blank security screen stared back at me. I swiped my thumb across the pad to unlock the security feature—only to find my notes section blank. My free text, my subjective impression, Hemsworth's chief complaint, "Something just isn't right"... Everything was gone. I tapped the *Back* icon, and the screen shut off, turned back on, then returned to the *Welcome* screen.

What the hell is this?

I re-launched the chart, and nothing appeared. The same blank screen stared back at me. After initiating a reboot and bringing up the keyboard, I tabbed to the search screen and entered Hemsworth's unique alphanumeric identifier that I had noted when initially entering my notes. The processing message appeared for a moment and then *File does not exist* glowed on the screen. I repeated the process and received the same message.

What is wrong with this System!... Hemsworth, where the hell are you? Is this what you meant—a computer glitch? Where are you? I wondered, typing in a search for all patients with the last name *Hemsworth*. Not a single Hemsworth at Progressive 17. A few moments before I was talking to him, and now he was simply gone—*Damn ERPs.* It was like he had never existed, vanished into thin air. I slammed my hand on the desk, disgusted.

"You okay, brethren?" said the Server replacing the curtain.

He'd been there working the whole time. I was so wrapped up in this mystery, I'd completely forgotten about him.

"Yes, sorry, doing well. I thought I saw something on the table—just my imagination. Long day, you know."

"And we're only half done."

"And half undone," I said to myself.

I sat there, dumbfounded, dizzy with confusion over what had just transpired. My first day at Progressive 17 and already an encounter that could unravel everything I'd been so strongly encouraged to believe as true, everything I held as an anthem, everything that we the living held to be true, to be factual—all that we had been indoctrinated into believing was reality.

Chapter 5

After changing out of my red jumpsuit and back into my tattered tenement clothes, I fell in line with the other Servers and marched the tunnel to the train depot, the stench of entitlement still hanging about me, souring my mood. With each step away from the Progressive toward the tenements, the air grew colder.

"Door open!" yelled the Black Cat to our left.

The tunnel door shot open, and the warm air sucked out only to be replaced with icy wind, engulfing each of us as it passed over and through our bodies. I was already chilled inside from the events of the day. A young boy writhing in the face of terror, turned into a quivering lump of gelatin in an instant so we could rob him of his manhood... then Hemsworth. *Why would Hemsworth describe himself as "blissless"?*

I continued to ponder this. What could have happened to him in the span of six months that a once healthy male was now a frail and sickly frame? Was it something as simple as a psychiatric condition? Did he take a fall and hit his head? I shivered from both the unforgiving wind and from the realization that what Hemsworth said might just be true. *Could we simply be slaves—pawns in someone's perverted game of power and control?* The reality was that if it were a game, the Provider used the Progs as pawns as much as he used us.

The smoking serpent on the tracks hissed as it took on its load of Servers. I stood at attention, shivering in the double ranks with the other Servers, waiting for our car number to be called. Number four again. *That'll be my train car for my duration at Progressive 17, for the duration of my remaining service.* I remembered the look on Hemsworth's face when I first entered the exam room, the way his eyes darted back and forth between me and the Black Cat. He was terrified; he was visible shaken. He came into the Medical Rights Facility knowing what he was going to say, knowing what might happen to him if he did. Maybe he had been forced to see a doctor because of his blisslessness, or perhaps he had come of his own will, but not caring. He offered no struggle, showed no concern over his fate, and yet he was frantic in his attempts to convince me of his message, to convince someone, anyone.

I gotta get it out of my mind, just a crazy over-aged man, that's all—probably the reason their care is rationed so they don't live that long.

I turned my head to look at the Black Cat barking orders to the Servers nearby. He looked just the same as all the others, full black regalia adorned with the symbol of Our State, all designed to create an aura of anonymity and terror, or to some, security. In front of the Servers, the Cats barked orders, gave beatings to those they deemed to be deserving of them, and forced us to repeat the Server's Creed ad nauseam. In front of the Served, they were silent sentinels, always watching, always listening, always vigilant, never out of sight. The Black Cats watched us all, the Servers and the served alike— just maybe… we were all pawns.

The Black Cats, Consular Killary, and Mr. Benson… all part of some shadow world between that of the Served and the Servers, swimming in and out of each like sea snakes, tasked with keeping the Progressives running as they always had. Men like Mr. Benson, I'd dealt with his ilk before. Much like what was once called a "union employee"—not too bright, not too productive, but a bunch of them could organize and throw support behind whatever cause provided them the most for doing the least. The Consular Killarys of Our State... Now there was an animal of a different color. Who and what were they? *They intimidate, enforce, determine the value of each member of Our State, and determine the most beneficial outcome for each to best suit the Collective.* I could only surmise that men like Consular Killary were the most dangerous men of all.

"Car number four! Move, Servers!" a Black Cat shouted, breaking me from my thoughts.

Our formation began to move toward the train in single file, first rank leading the way. I was in the second rank, third Server from the end. By the time I climbed the steps and entered the car, all of the seating had been taken. I found myself standing away from the benches, near the door, clutching an overhead rail. Scanning the Servers in the car, I looked for my angel. I noticed her crammed into the right-hand row of benches along with three other Servers. She glanced up, and I caught her eye—and for some crazy reason, I found myself winking at her. Her cheeks immediately blushed as she managed a grin, then she looked down to avoid being noticed.

Oh, car number four, how you now bring bliss to the end of my day...

The train rattled as if shaking off the sleepy fogginess of a restful nap, let out a whistle, belched a cloud of soot and steam, and then lunged forward. The cold within me had evaporated with the warmth of my angel's smile. Although we were off once again, headed to the tenements for a meager meal, another recitation of rights, and then to a hard, straw-covered bed, the weight of the day had just been lifted, all but for a simple smile from the one I found myself seditiously drawn to.

A moment later, my mind returned to the same old rut— every day, every Progressive just the same. We woke, we served and slaved, we slept, and we repeated. I could not help but admire the efficiency of the System, even when those dangerous doubts ran through my mind. The Progs never starved. The Servers never revolted. We all played our parts, we all exercised the rights afforded us, and the Progressives kept on running. New Progressives were built year after year, and each of those ran just as efficiently as the previous. No variation, each a spitting image of the next. We were like insects slowly spreading out over a patch of dirt, little mounds growing up over the barren, cratered wasteland that stretched as far as the eye could see—a nest of insects far and wide.

"I feel blissless"… "I feel blissless."

I ran the words over and over in my mind again and again as I stared beyond the cramped bodies of the Servers, out beyond the train windows onto the snowy, pockmarked landscape. Why were those words so telling? What made them so strange to hear from the mouth of a Prog? As much of my life as I could recall, I had never experienced bliss, had I? Was such a state solely for the ignorant, for the Progs? The feeling afforded me by my angel, was that what perfect bliss felt like? I'd lived and worked and moved as part of the System. My right to serve meant that I would never have to worry about anything such as bliss. My existence was to be void of emotions so they would play no part in my day-to-day life. No extreme joy, no extreme sorrow, only service. *So why these… these… feelings?*

I thought back to every Served I'd ever treated; I couldn't recall a single one who had ever appeared unhappy. Except for anger once the realization that their rights might be delayed slightly, most Progs displayed the hallmark empty-minded grin of the blissfully ignorant. Certainly there were those anxious to be facing invasive medical treatment; that was practically the norm. Progs were notorious for berating MSPs, or any Server, for moving too slow or failing to provide what they perceived as proper service. That was simply a part of our bane. Had I ever known a Prog to be completely without bliss, medical treatment or not?

The train shrugged as if in recognition of my question, swayed to and fro as we were shuttled back to our cold and dank tenement.

"I'm perfectly blissful."

If I'd heard those words once, I'd heard them a million times. Whenever I finished treating a patient, whenever all the complaints and protestations were complete, those same words were repeated: *"Blissful, I'm perfectly blissful."* Every time… every time.

I glanced around at my fellow Servers, then to the Black Cat at the far end of our car. No bliss for us Servers. The looks on the faces of my brethren proclaimed an absence of that or any emotion—however, not as a consequence of ignorance, but of exhaustion. Bliss was the purview of the Progs; it was the culmination of their being. They were blissful. Every one of them, their claims like a mantra.

I was once again shaken from the world in my mind at the train screeched and jostled, throwing my body forward into my fellow car mates. Murmurs swept through the car like a subtle ripple; expressions became fearful. I bent down and peered out through one of the soot-stained windows. No platforms, no structures were in sight, just fields of white stretching out away from the train. We had simply stopped. It had been approximately thirteen minutes or so since we left the depot. It took sixteen minutes from the Progressive to the tenement, always sixteen minutes, every Progressive to its tenement, always sixteen minutes.

A Black Cat pushed his way down the aisle, shoving Servers aside as if they were reeds swayed by a stiff breeze.

"You there," the Black Cat yelled. "Open that door!"

There were a few of us crowded by the door; I couldn't tell just who the order was directed at.

"Me?" I asked.

"Yes, you! You're a Medical Server—you!"

I just blinked.

"I said, open the door, you filthy Server maggot!" The Black Cat shoved Server after Server out of the way as he continued toward me.

I began to shake as I pulled the train car door open, just in time to feel the Black Cat grab my other arm. He shoved a scanner into my hand. "Go and find the head of your brethren that chose to fail his duty this morning. Get an accurate scan and return. You've got five minutes. Take any longer and we'll collect your frozen corpse in the morning, understand?"

"Yes... Yes, sir. I... I understand," I said.

I glanced at my angel just as the Black Cat shoved me out the door and off the top step between the two cars; her face was a mask of shock as she covered her mouth to conceal the gasp of fear. The Black Cat turned and eyed her. As I fell from the platform, a tearing pain raced up my leg, and an instant later I was lying in bloody snow.

The wind howled as I took a brief moment to gain my bearings. I saw a trail of red-stained snow stretching out along the high, white embankment. In my mind, I pictured Mead's blood still pumping through his carotids after his head was torn off, leaving a trail from his body to his head. *It should be easy to find, luckily it hasn't snowed.* I reached down to my leg and began brushing aside the bloodied snow that had already begun sticking to my clothes in an effort to determine the source of my pain. My pant leg was torn, and beneath the tear, I saw a gash caked with a mix of Mead's frozen blood and my own fresh blood—my injury coming from some sharp protrusion on the train when I'd been pushed out by the Cat.

Wonderful, if anything opportunistic was in his blood, as soon as it thaws, it's going to be in mine. Shit. Well, nothing I can do about it now. At least the cold will keep any inflammation down.

The plow on the front of the train had carved a channel with high banks on either side. I lay flat, slid down the snow bank, and then managed to raise myself to my feet. Glancing over my shoulder, I could only make out the upper half of the train car over the high snow as it sat huffing and puffing, awaiting the completion of my task. As I began making my way in the direction of the tenement following Mead's blood trail, I felt my feet breaking through the hardened surface on the blanket of snow, dropping me down to my knees. The going was slow and I began to wonder if I'd be able to make it back within the five minutes. I figured if it took much longer than that, I'd probably freeze anyway.

Another pain shot up my leg as I shifted my weight. The pain was becoming less of a detriment with each passing moment as I trudged through the deep drifts. The cold was already doing its work, numbing my limbs. I shoved my hands into the pockets of my tattered coat, trying to make the best time possible and still be able to have use of my hands when needed. The scanner, looped around my wrist, pulled at my arm and banged against my hip with each lunge forward. I could now make out the end of the blood trail just up ahead. *Mead's head must be around here somewhere.*

I was quite surprised the old rusted hulk of a train was capable of putting out such a bright beam, as the retreating sun took with it the last remaining natural light. I managed a few more steps as my right foot pulled free from its shoe, leaving it buried deep in the snow. Tumbling forward, I simultaneously pulled my hands from my pockets, flailing my arms as my head smacked against something solid. I managed to pull my arms up underneath me and gingerly push off the packed snow, hoping my arms would not push through the hardened top layer. Looking down, I found myself staring into a pair of dark green eyes surrounded by a face with an expression of serenity, of calm, of peace… Mead.

I paused for a moment, studying his features, wondering what must have gone through his mind in his final moments. *He is now free.* Is this what we had to achieve to experience true freedom in this mixed up world? Was death our only escape or was there something more, something greater where a man was viewed by his ability to serve himself rather than his ability to serve others?

"Two minutes, Server! Move your ass!" the Black Cat yelled from the train.

The Black Cat's command grabbed me and thrust me back into reality.

"Coming!" I yelled back, uncoiling the scanner from around my wrist.

"Sorry for this, brethren," I whispered as I smacked the scanner into his forehead. I pulled the trigger and the scanner beeped, then a flash of green light appeared, signaling a positive register. I wrapped the scanner cord around my wrist again, bent backward, and shoved my arm down into the snow hole that had stolen my shoe. Feeling the shoe in my hand, I rolled over and over, cresting the top of the snow bank, pulling my shoe with me. I gave a quick glance at Mead's head, serenity frozen over his features. I turned my shoe over and dumped out the snow. Bending to put it on my foot, gravity got the best of me as I slid headlong down the side of the snow bank, coming to rest on one of the railroad ties. I put my shoe back on and looked off to my left. I was aside car number two. I was surprised. On the other side of the bank in the deep snow, it felt as if I had traversed a mile, but it was no more than 150, maybe 200 feet.

"You got thirty seconds, snow princess!"

"On my way!" I yelled as loud as I could, hoping I was heard over the chugging breaths of the train.

I scrambled to my feet, moving as fast as I could to car number four. The going was much quicker this side of the snow bank as the plow and the Servers had cleared a wide berth. Just as I reached the steps of car four, I tripped on a rail tie that was jutting out. Flying forward, I skidded to a stop just short of the handrail.

This is not my day.

Pushing myself up, I bumped my head on a metallic object that was protruding from the car's underbelly. Taking a quick glance, as I knew I was down to only a few seconds, I noted a holding compartment of sorts, possibly for wood, tools, or… railroad ties—I'd bet that was it. There was a hinged, grated door. Peering in, I saw the compartment was empty. It looked big enough for two or three people. I was surprised they didn't make us ride down there.

"Ten, nine, eight…"

"I'm here! I'm here!" I said, scrambling to my feet. I grabbed the handrail and pulled myself up the steps onto the platform between the cars.

"Three, two… You sure live on the edge, Server. Give me that scanner and get inside!"

The Black Cat placed his gigantic hand on my back and thrust me forward. I slammed into another Server who was hanging onto the center rail, sending him forward into another Server. The door to the car slammed shut behind me as I caught a glimpse of my angel; her lips were quivering as she managed a slight smile. She then looked down to avoid revealing anything more. The earlier glance from the Black Cat was enough to instill a renewal of fear and compliance.

Safely back on the train, my body warmed with each passing moment, and with each passing moment, the throbbing in my leg intensified.

"Consular Killary…"

The name spoken aloud startled me. I turned to see the Black Cat standing at the doorway. The scanner was sitting in the base that hung from his side. Nodding as he touched the side of his head, he said, "Yes, Consular, this is Two-Zero-One-Six. Extinguished Server confirmed." The Black Cat continued his report, nodding for a moment. "Yes, sir…. Yes, thank you, sir." Dropping his hand away from his mask, he turned toward me. "What the hell are you looking at, Server?!"

"Nothing, nothing, sir. My apologies." I quickly turned and faced the other way.

Consular Killary. Go figure.

Thoughts continued to race through my mind as the train lumbered along the tracks back toward the tenement. We were ordered to disembark in the usual fashion, single file out to form double ranks on the platform. I allowed many other Servers to pass me as car number four was called for debarking. My angel approached, and I jumped in behind her, brushing my hand against hers. I leaned in as we marched, making sure there were no Black Cats eyeing us.

We have to find a way to meet. I have to talk to you…. You bring me…

She bowed her head for a moment and intentionally slowed, reaching her hand behind her back so I could reach it. She touched my hand to hers, grasping my fingers and squeezing ever so gently. Then, as quickly as the sensation had been initiated, it was over. She allowed her hand to fall back in line with her pace and moved to close the gap between herself and the Server before her…

Bliss…

We reached the assembly area and lined up in our formations. One of the Black Cats, a particularly burly man with a voice more gruff than the others, stood before the center of our formation and shouted into the mass of Servers.

"We live to serve!" he shouted.

"We live to serve," the Servers said as a group, my own mouth hardly moving.

"Service is freedom!"

"Service is freedom." This time, my response was barely audible.

"The System is perfect!"

There was the briefest of pauses at this unexpected set of words, then the whole of the group, myself included, echoed more quietly, "The System is perfect."

"The System is perfect!" the lead Black Cat shouted again.

"The System is perfect!" the Servers yelled, aware of the safety in voluntary participation.

"That's right, Servers, the System is perfect!" the Black Cat yelled, holding up his hands to stay any more repetition. "The System is perfect. It has stood for longer than you have in your current state—undisturbed, unaltered, a complete success."

I shifted my weight slightly, glancing at those around me. They all stood in perfect form, looking straight at the Black Cat. I moved my head to do the same. There was some comfort in knowing that we were all in this together. "Misery loves company," the old saying went—a sentiment proven here every day. Maybe the Black Cat in the room with Mr. Hemsworth was right: *Maybe the best way to serve myself is to just forget those events of the day.* Maybe I could just be happy with seeing my angel each day and serving the Progs. Maybe that was all I really needed.

The Black Cat droned on as my mind continued to drift in and out, my attention wandering.

"Yes, the System is perfect. Ever since the Provider usurped control, in one grand affirmative action, the Progressives have stood as a testament to our people, a testament to our ability to survive and adapt, to the one true natural order. The Collective, Our State, is the logical extension of rights and freedoms. Your service, the freedom you enjoy through your sacrifice, provides freedom to others, to the Served, to those the Provider has chosen to receive his charity."

The Black Cat eyed us, then shouted, "Freedom is service!"

"Freedom is service," we replied in unison.

"Service is freedom!"

"Service is freedom."

"The Served have the right to comfort, the right to luxury and care. They have the right to entertainment and ease of life. Their rights could never be fulfilled if it were not for your right, your right to serve. Always let this be your last thought before you take yourselves to slumber and your first thought upon your waking return.

"Freedom through service!" the Black Cat yelled, the mist from his breath evaporating into the air above us as he pumped his fist above his head.

"Freedom through service!" the Servers shouted in response.

"We live to serve!"

"We live to serve!"

"The System is perfect!"

"The System is perfect!" The increase in enthusiasm that rippled through the crowd as it responded was palpable.

"Master at Arms, get these Servers to chow," said the Black Cat in front of our formation.

We were marched to the sustenance hall for our evening meal, which looked, as usual, identical to the morning meal. I pushed and shoved through a few Servers to muster a seat next to my angel. She seemed a little startled as I muscled my way between her and a rather stocky young Server attempting to take the space next to her. The man grunted, quite displeased as he looked around for an open place to sit. I sat, and a smile found its way to my lips.

I dipped a chunk of the stale bread into the gruel and raised it to my mouth, glancing around to make sure no Black Cats were near. I held the crust of bread in front of my mouth and whispered, "What's your name?"

My angel brushed her foot against mine, then raised her cup up to her beautiful round mouth, her full lips pursed as if to sip the cool liquid.

"Julie... Jules," she whispered, then took a sip from her cup.

I took a bite from my bread and, while chewing, said, "Julie Jules... interesting name."

Dipping her bread and raising it to her mouth, she said, "No, it's Julie. My surrogate always called me 'Jules.' She said my eyes reminded her of sparkling jewels."

Raising my cup, I glanced at her for a fleeting second. "She was right. You're beautiful."

She lowered he head as blood warmed her cheeks, turning them red.

"What's your name?" she managed to say while chewing a piece of meat product.

"Blair, but you can call me 'Hux,'" I said.

The widest grin I think I'd ever worn pushed across my lips. I had to look down as I was almost giggling. I didn't know what this was, what I was feeling... I was... alive.

"Nice to finally meet you, Hux," she said as she raised herself up from the table. She turned to walk toward the tray turn-in, intentionally brushing her hand against the small of my neck. The shiver that raced down the length of my spine was nothing I'd ever felt before, like electricity without the pain.

I watched as she walked off, already counting the moments until I would see her again.

"Two minutes, Servers! Finish up." yelled a Black Cat from the doorway.

I scooped the last of my gruel with the last crumb of bread I had and took a swig from my cup. Dropping off my tray, I headed out and formed back up with the other Servers. I had lost sight of Jules, although the image of her remained emblazoned on my mind.

We marched back to our respective bunkhouses, my mind full of questions, the world devoid of answers. I stared at the row of bunks above my head, *thinking*. To either side of me, my neighbors were oblivious to my plight. Peter Mead, the deaf man who had been sick earlier in the morning, his head now gone, his body now gone, his straw bedding now laid bare. To my other side, Colin Arnold, the carpenter, lay quietly, keeping to himself.

I lay there in silence for well over an hour. Finally, unable to contain my thoughts anymore, I reached over and began tapping on Arnold's leg under his blanket. First, it was just a few taps to make sure he was awake. He returned the tap. For those of us who had been around for any length of time, we all knew and used the same code to avoid the Black Cats seeing or hearing us communicating while in the bunkhouses. It was a simple code relying on a five-space-by-five-space grid: one square for each letter of the alphabet, except c and k shared the same grid location. Each letter was two sets of taps, the first set being the row, the second set being the column. A "c," then, would be one tap, pause, three taps, while an "o" would be three taps, pause four taps, and so on. It was akin to a second language, so it went pretty quick as long as both were up on the code. I knew Arnold would be. You could just tell sometimes. Besides, this was Progressive 17 tenement—the final bastion of service and freedom... few newbies here.

I tapped out. *You ever known bliss?*

Arnold turned his head toward me, his brow furrowed with a *"What the hell kind of question is that?"* look on his face. I raised my brow and lowered my chin in a *"Well?"* gesture.

He tapped back, *We serve. Not our concern.* He had a stern look on his face; I was sensing that he did not care to engage.

Still, I tapped back, *Prog said System broke, said he was bliss-less.* Arnold just shook his head and put his hands to his ears and shook his head again. I lay there for a moment, staring at the bunks above—and then something important struck me.

The paper! The paper! I forgot the paper in my lab coat!

I tapped Arnold frantically; he tapped a rather hard tap back, almost a punch. I tapped to him, *Gave me note on paper.*

He turned to me again. *Paper. What it read?* he tapped.

I wondered if Arnold was being sarcastic.

Don't know, I tapped. *Forgot in lab coat.*

Best hope not found. No more taps. Must sleep. He rolled over, facing away from me.

What if they did find it? What if in the middle of the night the Black Cats stormed in here and dragged me out? I didn't even know what the note said. I didn't even know if it was a note. *Maybe it's nothing. Maybe he didn't even leave it. Maybe it was there before we entered the exam room*—*No! It had to be a note.* Hemsworth was trying to tell someone something and that someone turned out to be me.

I spent what seemed like an hour or so trying to remember anything else telling in my time with Hemsworth, but in the end, I fell asleep with only the face of my angel, Jules, dancing at the forefront of my mind.

Chapter 6

I awoke before the howling wake-up siren sounded; a throbbing pain stabbed at my lower leg. In the darkness of the bunkhouse, I couldn't see the condition of my wound, but I knew that infection was likely; I could feel it throughout my body. I reached down and ever so gingerly touched my finger to the wound site. I felt what was likely a scab forming; however, it was soft and sticky, indicating too much serous fluid in the area. I pulled my finger away and rubbed my index finger against my thumb; it was not the smooth, silky consistency I'd hoped for. It was pasty and gritty—pus. The wound was infected. I didn't need to see the wound to know that I was in for a long battle with some nasty aggressive organisms. The image of Mead heaving and hacking, his ghostly skin against the snowy bed, ran through my mind.

Pushing myself up, I raised my body to a sitting position, trying my best not to wake my neighbors. I grabbed my jacket that I had wadded up as a makeshift pillow. As tattered as it was, it was easy for me to pull a strip of the material from the lower hem, an ample length to tie around my leg. I reached down toward my pant leg, over the wound, and felt the edges of the material that had been torn when I dismounted the train. A small flap of cloth had been formed from the sharp object on the train that had gouged my leg. I pulled at the material, tearing a small swath of the cloth large enough to cover the wound. Cautiously, I pulled the pant leg up, doing my best to avoid rubbing the dirty pant bottom over the oozing wound, as if it would have somehow made a difference. As dirty as my pants were, the patch would have to suffice as a makeshift dressing. I placed the patch over the wound, wincing as the cloth touched the inflamed area. I wrapped the length of material torn from my jacket over the dressing and pulled it tight. The increased pressure on the wound was a welcome respite, as the pressure dulled the pain, even though I knew all the while it would do little else. After balling my jacket back up into its job as a pillow, I dropped myself back down, panting from the taxing endeavor. I could feel the sweat beading on my forehead.

I lay on my bunk, staring into the blackness for what seemed an eternity, thoughts racing through my mind of all that had happened since my arrival less than thirty-six hours ago and what might greet me with the welcome rising of the sun. The shrill piercing of the wake-up call broke the stillness and silence of the bunkhouse as the other Servers were pulled from their individual dreams, their only escape from the Collective. The clanging of the chains moved as the shutters on our bunkhouse were raised, deadening the thoughts that had occupied my mind. I quickly pulled off my clothes and jumped to the hard wooden floor. A sharp pain raced up my leg and slapped my brain as I hit the floorboards, forcing me to bite my lip to stop from screaming. Bending over, feigning a stretch, I put some additional pressure on the wound to help deaden the pain while slowly inhaling and exhaling. Closing my eyes for a moment, I took a few more deep breaths and stood erect. Hoping that no one would notice the makeshift bandage on my leg, I regained my composure and stood as if nothing had happened. I looked toward Arnold to see if he had been paying attention, but it seemed as if he was avoiding my gaze. I wondered if our gestured communication the night before had shaken him more than I had realized, if perhaps having the night to mull over my statements had altered his opinion of my assertions. Unfortunately, I had no means of verifying what his thoughts were, and at this point, I dared not venture a question. We all stood in line facing the personal hygiene area, awaiting the command from the Black Cat peering in at us through the window. Conversation would be impossible; I would have to wait until tonight. Better he had some additional time to ponder the information anyway. Once I showed him the note, then he'd believe me, then he'd start to awaken and see things as I was beginning to see them.

I did my best not to limp as the Black Cat standing outside yelled the order for us to move. As we moved closer to the hygiene area, I noticed the Black Cat was looking away, talking with another Black Cat. I seized the opportunity to jump the line and head toward the shower area with the group starting their routine there. No one ever took notice; most Servers had been broken, tamed to the point of simply going through the motions as they had done for so many days of servitude. I finally had the opportunity to look at the wound on my naked leg up close. I turned on the water, waiting for it to reach its lukewarm state. The water over my leg helped ease the throbbing. As the bandage became saturated, I untied the knot in the strip of material from my jacket and pulled back the patch of cloth. Sure enough, I found a gnarly, jagged wound approximately six centimeters long—swollen, red, and much warmer than the surrounding area. I could now see the serous fluid that I had felt just a few hours ago. Cloudy, opaque with a few streaks of blood, sero-sanguinous. I allowed the water to continue to run over the wound, then I squeezed out an ample amount of the pumice gel that we were provided as soap. I could barely stand the pain as I rubbed the gel over and into the wound. My teeth were clenched so tight, I thought they might snap off. I could feel sweat form on my head despite the water from the shower, as the pain was stabbing at my leg, only to charge and stab at my brain. I stood again, leaning on the wall, as I was feeling faint, panting, and trying to regain my composure. I felt dizzy. My complexion was not doubt similar to the one worn by Mead's frozen head that I'd scanned the previous day.

"Change!" the Black Cat outside yelled, ordering us to the next station. I squeezed one last handful of the pumice gel before moving to the sinks. Before applying shave lotion and performing oral care, I ran the patch of cloth under the water and scrubbed it with the pumice as best I could. I left the water running over the cloth as I hurriedly completed my razorless shave and a quick run of the brush over my teeth. I wrung the water and remaining pumice out of the cloth as the Black Cat yelled the command to move. Onto the toilet I went, and sitting was such a welcome relief. With the greatest care I could muster, I placed the damp bandage over my wound and tied it with the length of cloth from my coat. I knew it was a poor choice to place a damp cloth over the wound, but I had no alternative at this point. I thought that maybe I could evade the watchful eyes at the medical center and slip a clean dressing into my pocket, maybe some antibiotics, too. If I was going to commit a crime, I figured that I ought to go all out. I had to handle this injury through illegal means or it may be the end of me. My natural defenses, I already realized, would not be sufficient.

I did my best not to slow down the rest of my group, getting dressed into my filthy rags as quickly as the pain in my leg would allow. Almost certainly these clothes had not been cleaned in days, even weeks. *More dirt in a dirty wound… Wonderful.*

The rest of the morning routine passed uneventfully. We engaged in our morning exercises, and with each movement, the pain in my leg worsened. I managed to make it through everything with jaw clenched and teeth gritted, avoiding the ire of the Black Cats. Once the morning recitation of rights and the Server's Creed began, I was able to rest, droning on through the monotonous phrases we all had memorized, rambling like a broken record and letting the cold numb the pain in my leg. It was the first time during my existence in this desolate land of ice and snow that I had been thankful for the cold. The dampened cloth began to frost in the bitter morning cold, acting as an ice pack against the throbbing red gash even as the sun smiled over us.

The morning washing of our collective brain was complete, and sustenance time soon passed in a blur. I didn't even recall who I sat with, as the pain in my leg and the thoughts in my head had me in a foggy daze. I found myself marching toward the train again, the crunching of the frosted snow beneath the thin soles of my shoes, listening to the archaic train moaning as it sat awaiting the filling of its belly with our tattered, cold frames. I began scanning the columns of bodies for a glimpse of my angel, my Jules, the only image that seemed to remain clear in my mind. I didn't see her until we had boarded the train. I felt a flutter of warmth rise in my chest at the sight of her, the forbidden familiarity, the ability to place a name to her breathtaking face filling me with euphoric wonder. In that all too brief instant, when our eyes met and smiles appeared on our faces, I felt as if nothing else mattered in the world. The pain in my leg disappeared; the watchful eyes of the Black Cats were blind to me. I soaked in her beauty like an arid sponge submerged in a pail of water and allowed my mind to fill with every blissful thought my clouded state could muster.

In a flash, the moment passed. The steel sidewinder hissed and lunged forward, carting its load of livestock toward their respective day of servitude. The shouting of a Black Cat yanked me from my stupor.

"I don't want to see you looking at me again, Server!" the Black Cat yelled.

It took me a few moments to realize that he wasn't shouting at me. A few seats away, a Server was crouching in fear, muttering apologies as quickly as his lips would allow.

"I... I... I am sorry," the Server said, over and over. "I live to serve. I live to serve."

The Black Cat shouted a few obscenities and smacked the Server once on the skull with his baton, then trudged back down the aisle. A simple warning, with a simple message: "We are always watching."

I tried to catch Jules's eyes again, but she had returned to staring, teary eyed, at the floor, never a word of objection, a poor little frightened rabbit.

About halfway through our passage, I began monitoring the Black Cats with intent. After so many personal encounters with them the day before, I found myself amazed that they had returned to ignoring me. Could it be that they didn't even remember who I was? The Server they sent into the cold, the Server they mocked and belittled, nearly left behind to become an ice cube? Or perhaps they simply felt that I had learned my lesson. After all, it was not I who had received the beating this morning; it was another poor soul who likely had simply thrown them a passive glance. I was invisible once again, just another Server in a ledger of human collateral.

It was at that moment that another thought occurred to me: the Black Cats must not have found the note from Hemsworth in my lab coat. If they had, I would definitely have been confronted. I would have been dragged out of my bed in the middle of the night, bound, gagged, tortured, and left bloodied and alone in the cold, dark night as an example to my fellow Servers. Maybe I would have been bathed of my treasonous actions and thoughts like those of the runner. Yes, I certainly would have been dead or dying, and that thought comforted me. I could still find the note when I arrived at the Medical Rights Facility. I could still discover more about Hemsworth, his thoughts, his troubles, and more importantly, why he was so blissless.

———

A short while later, I was climbing the steps to the Medical Rights Facility from the underground tunnel system with my fellow MSPs, even as my leg continued to throb with pain. If I had been treating a Served, I would have recommended he or she stay off the leg as much as possible, even with antibiotic treatment. I hadn't the luxury of either. Each step up those long flights stretched and aggravated the wound. I was fortunate when I reached the top without, as far as I could tell, opening the wound entirely. A few of the other Servers gave me a look when I lumbered up behind them, seeing me favoring one side, but they quickly turned away, disinterested, focused on their own personal misery. We were trained from the day of our selection as recipients not to inquire about the medical status of those to whom the right of medical care was withheld. Doing otherwise was a pointless endeavor and would only lead to violent outcomes.

"Welcome to your second day, MSP Huxley," the Administrative Server said as I exited the staircase. She was holding a small ERP out to me. "You'll be reviewing your carotid patient first thing. Consider it a reprieve from your busy day yesterday."

I nodded, doing my best to give a warm smile. I looked at her nametag and whispered, "Thank you, Doreen." If it were not for the pain, I would have engaged in a little conversation. Discussions concerning our particular duties as they applied to the Served were the only time Servers were allowed to verbally interact. Normally, it was a welcome opportunity for conversation. Like us Medical Servers, the Administrative Servers were trained in bedside manner. Their indoctrination taught them how to interact with Progs and Servers alike, plus lessons on when to smile, to laugh, or even to become stern. In this case, she must have noticed my rapid procession of sterilized recipients the day before and concocted a story about me being given a "rest"—a common tactic I had encountered many times before. Still, I played along, thanking her once again before heading down to the locker room. My real attention was focused on what I might find once I was there.

While the rest of the Medical Servers chatted idly, discussing their patient loads and special cases, I stood silently before my wall cubby, feeling dizzy from both the wound on my leg and the anticipation of finding the piece of paper from Hemsworth. Never in my life had I encountered a Served who spoke like he did. The System was presented as being so perfect, the indoctrination of Our State so complete. What revelations could possibly be scribbled on that note? It was just chance that I was the one who had seen Hemsworth. It had been my first day, or had he watched me, waited until he knew that I would be available? Was there something else out there? Was there more than this, a place where people were responsible for themselves, not slaves to others, not a means for another to use in achieving their ends?

Perhaps the answers were written on that piece of paper. Perhaps all I had to do was unfold it and a new world would be revealed to me. I stripped out of my worn rags after kicking off my stiff, thin shoes and pulling off my socks. The bandage on my leg had begun to thaw from the heat generated on the train ride from all of the bodies crammed into our car. I could see some bloody fluid trickling down from the wound.

I untied the makeshift bandage, crumpled it in my hand, and headed toward the sanitization conveyor. Waiting until the other MSPs had entered, I filed in behind them. I turned my hand outward and allowed the bandage to unfurl. The jets of steam washed over me as I lifted my injured leg toward them. The pain was excruciating, yet I had no choice but to endure it. On my other side, I reached the bandage out toward the nozzles, allowing the steam to wash away as much of the sludge as possible. Reaching the end of the conveyor, I followed my brethren into the drying chamber. I could feel the warmth of the chemical-laden steam dissipate as the fluid dripped from the dressing in my hand. The drying conveyor did little for my fever, but the additional jets of sanitized air across my moist wound were a much-needed benefit.

Reaching into my wall cubby, I found myself breathing heavy with anticipation. Shifting my eyes back and forth, I made sure none of my fellow Medical Servers were watching. I realized that I was the only one looking around. Fortunately, a Server didn't serve a fellow Server, so we all developed a sort of tunnel vision, only concerned about our own lane, with no care or concern for our fellow Servers. That's what we had been reduced to. I must have been developing some paranoia with all that had happened. It took every ounce of self-control I had not to snatch my lab coat down and start rifling through the pockets, but what was more important: my health or the contents of the note?

I pulled my hands back from the lab coat, as experience had taught me to be careful of any watchful eyes—the electronic kind. This was one of the only areas in the Medical Rights Facility where personnel monitoring was permitted. Black Cats could see and hear everything, even when we couldn't see them. Surveying my situation, I realized that even though I had guided the bandage toward the nozzles in the drying conveyor, it was still wet. I could not replace a wet bandage over the wound, as it would soak through my jumpsuit and leave a definite stain visible to anyone. I decided to go without. I slipped on clean work socks and stepped into my red jumpsuit. The jumpsuit was a dense, heavy fabric with un-cropped strands protruding in toward the skin side of the material, smooth and shiny on the outside. The suit felt like sandpaper rubbing against my wound as I pulled the pant leg up over it. My teeth locked shut again as I completed donning the suit. I knew I was in for a day of pain with every move-ment of my lower body. However, the warmth and cleanliness of the suit was well received.

If only I could get my hands on some antibiotics, or a clean dressing and some topical antibiotic at the least... I'd have a chance at fighting this thing.

I shook my head. Those were thoughts of self-interest, of self-preservation; I had already gone far astray in just con-sidering it. I had no business thinking of myself when there were Progs who demanded those medicines. And yet... the note was right there, in that coat pocket, waiting to unlock a new world. Perhaps a Server could have the rights of medical treatment in Hemsworth's vision of the world if he himself had the means to secure it. Perhaps we didn't have to live in squalor. Perhaps we could even know bliss; perhaps all could.

For the thousandth time, I saw Jules's face in my mind, and smiled. For her, I could change the world; for her, I was willing to try. Reaching out, I lifted my lab coat from the coat hook, pushed my arms through each sleeve, and casually placed my hands in the pockets. I shoved my hands front to back in the pockets, back and forth, in and out... nothing... nothing... They were empty. A wave of panic ran through me, my eyes darting back and forth between my fellow MSPs and my cubby, wondering who had seen my motion, who might have known about the note, how the Black Cats could have found it.

No. They couldn't have found it. I would have been beaten, even killed. It wouldn't even matter what was in the note. The Cleaning Servers must have simply washed the coat in the night and thrown out the note. That must be it. Maybe it dissolved in the wash. You fool! Of course that was it...

A shiver ran through my body, bringing me out of my thoughts. The infection was bad, and I didn't have time to ponder the fate of the world at just that moment. The note was lost, but I still had work to do. I still had to serve.

Moments later, I found myself once again awash in the sea of red and blue that streamed through the medical center, a cog in the machine of Progressive 17. I made my way as best I could to a tiny office I had been assigned to review my carotid patient's records. I trudged my way along the hallway wall, hoping to avoid bumping into people. The Progs were not much for sharing anything, even something as simple as space in a hallway. I was jostled back and forth as I pushed my way to my office, stabbing pain beating on my brain with each encounter with the bodies of the Served. The busyness would likely calm down within the next half an hour or so, as mornings were usually slow, since the Progs slept in, but this morning, it was mobbed with many demanding service. I wondered how people with chronic illnesses and recurring injuries coped with such a life. I knew of many Servers who suffered with similar ailments, but I had always prided myself on managing to stay healthy despite our poor living conditions and treatment. An MSP could be expected to do no less. My one mistake, the hesitation when exiting the train door, had possibly caused me a lifetime of pain and disfigurement, and that lifetime could now be cut considerably short.

A wave of relief rushed over me as I finally reached the office and had a moment to myself. I let out a huge sigh of relief as I allowed myself to drop into the chair. While I did not have the time or resources to examine my wound further, I could at least use the few minutes to sit and direct my mind to present matters. Without wasting a moment, I typed in the particulars of the Prog I would be performing the carotid surgery on. The screen of the ERP came to life with all the pertinent details of his medical history. Scanning through the tabs, I was surprised to find that despite his buildup of vessel plaque, he was in fairly decent health. Despite a 90 percent occlusion in the left carotid artery, his remaining imagery and tests were at acceptable levels. Remarkably, he was not particularly overweight, like many Served were. Obesity was no doubt commensurate with the lack of exercise and sedentary lifestyle, when every whim—*Or should I say "right"?*—was provided for. I was quite often surprised that many of the Progs were even capable of generating enough energy to bring themselves to the Medical Rights Facility and to fuel their rants when their "rights" were not realized in a timely manner. Although not every Served was clinically obese, their inactive lives resulted in far too many a Prog expanding sideways rather than upward.

I spent the next hour reviewing the record of the Served that I was to meet with, just long enough that no administrator came looking to assign me additional cases. MSPs were tracked meticulously throughout the day, ensuring that Progs received treatment in the most expedient manner. I exited the office just in time to seek out one of those administrators myself, and he quickly directed me to where my meeting with the carotid patient would be. I smiled, nodded, and followed his directions to the appropriate exam room.

As I turned a corner at the end of the hallway, a face appeared before me that I did not expect to see. Mr. Hemsworth's features flashed before my eyes, and time seemed to grind to a standstill. His eyes were less sunken than before, but I could still see their distinctive shape. It looked as if he had the start of a Mohawk hairdo, except it was only the front half of his head that had been shaved. His overall appearance was neater, his jumpsuit less baggy, but his basic frame remained unchanged. The man passed slowly on my right, failing to acknowledge my presence, walking along like any other Prog, without a care in the world, a slight smile formed by his thin frail lips that only yesterday were twisted in fear, pain, anxiety, or who knows what. I stopped only briefly after seeing that face, stunned, in complete shock. First, the note was missing from my lab coat; now I saw Hemsworth in the flesh and he completely ignored me. A million questions went racing through my mind. I turned quickly and saw the back of his head moving farther and farther away in the opposite direction.

"Mr. Hemsworth!" I shouted, shocked at how loud my voice was.

I was pushing my way along the wall of the hallway. Fortunately, the number of Served had decreased in the hour that had elapsed since my shift had begun, back to the usual early morning low census. Despite the less crowded hall, I managed to bump into several Progs in my attempt to catch up to Mr. Hemsworth. I ignored their protestations, ignored the pain in my leg, and simply kept pushing to catch up. I called Hemsworth's name over and over, a little quieter than my initial attention-grabbing bellow, yet still he walked on ahead of me, unhearing or uncaring.

He must be terrified. They must have rattled him. I wonder if he told them anything about the note. No, he mustn't have, or they would have come for me.

When at last I caught up to him, I stopped and turned in front of him to stop his forward progress. This time, I was able to see his entire face, rather than just a flash. The hair had been shaved around each temporal area, and the remaining hair slicked back in the center. Looking at both temporal regions, I appreciated fresh, well-approximated incisions. The glint of the hall lights reflected off the bead of medical adhesive the surgeon must have used to close the incisions.

"Mr. Hemsworth, Mr. Hemsworth," I said in a hushed voice, panting as the short chase and my painful leg had me out of breath. "The note—I lost the note, or they took it. I didn't have the opportunity to read it."

He did not answer; he just looked at me as if he were being inconvenienced.

"Mr. Hemsworth?" I said again, looking the man directly in the eyes.

The eyes that stared back at me had lost some quality from the previous day. His affect had changed; it had been muted. His eyes looked like the eyes of many other Served.

"I'm sorry to have initiated my discourse in such a manner," I said. "How are you, Mr. Hemsworth? I was worried when they took you away after our appointment yesterday."

"First off, young man, let me assure you that I am perfectly blissful. You do, however, have me mistaken for someone else. My name is Hathorne—Andrew Hathorne. Now, if you'll please excuse me, I have business to attend to."

"It's me," I said, grabbing his forearm. "MSP Huxley. We met yesterday. You gave me a note. Don't you remember?"

"I have no recollection of seeing a Medical Server yesterday, and I know nothing about any note," Hemsworth said, raising his voice and becoming agitated. "Now take your hand off of me or I shall have you reported!"

"But…" I said, releasing his arm, falling back against the wall. "You said you were blissless. You gave me a note… a note I lost… a note I never read."

"Poppycock, young man, poppycock. I am perfectly blissful," he said in a tone devoid of happiness. "And a note?… A note? How peculiar. Nobody writes anymore, young man. Now be on your way and leave me alone."

With that, he continued ambling down the hallway.

"Mr. Hemsworth, what happened to you?" I said as I stood against the wall in shock.

He truly doesn't remember me.

It was only then that I noticed the way other Progs had paused to witness the scene before them. I muttered an apology and continued to watch as he walked off down the hallway.

I stood for a moment and regained my composure. I figured I still had a few minutes before meeting with my surgical patient. *Maybe the office I just utilized is still available.* During my interaction with Hemsworth—or Hathorne, as he now called himself—I had completely forgotten about the pain in my leg. Now, with the adrenaline rush decreasing, the pain began to send reminders. I made my way to the office and knocked. No answer. Placing my hand on the wall scanner, the door instantly slid open. *Great, it's available, but I have to be quick.* I jumped behind the desk and pulled the ERP toward me. Typing in *Hathorne, Andrew,* I waited for the system to bring up the record. In no time at all, the screen came to life, displaying the medical record of Andrew Hathorne. There wasn't much to it: no lab work, no imaging, no physicals, just demographic info. Like a slap in the face, I stared at the screen in utter disbelief; the induction date was yesterday, the time listed as two hours after our meeting, after Hemsworth had been escorted to the elevator. It was as if he'd actually been born yesterday—that he became blissful yesterday. My head was spinning. I had no idea what to make of this. *How can this be?* I minimized the record and typed in *Hemsworth.* The same as yesterday after our appointment: *NO RECORD FOUND* blinked in large red capital letters across the screen. I punched the *Close* icon and pushed myself back from the desk.

Leaning forward, I grabbed my head in my hands, pushing inward on the sides of my skull. I tried and tried to crush the confusion, tried to crush the thoughts racing through my mind. *What is going on around here? This is insane, or... or am I going insane?* I released my hands and stood up. *Focus! Focus! Get through the day. Move, move.*

Groggy, dazed, and utterly confused, I pushed the chair in, mustering the wherewithal to make sure the ERP was completely off, as I couldn't risk leaving those records up. Popping my head through the doorway, I looked up and down the hallway to see if everything was normal, making sure no Black Cats were running in my direction. All was as usual, red and blue jumpsuits milling about, Progs being served, Servers serving. My paranoia was getting the best of me. I made my way to my appointment with the surgical patient, all the while my confusion and pain took turns picking and kicking at my brain.

Neurological surgery was the only way someone could have changed this man's self-identity, but I had never heard of a surgery so exacting before. *The precision that would be required is not possible with human faculties.* To leave a man completely coherent, able to function as a human being and yet completely unaware of whom they were... that was something I had never learned during my medical indoctrination. I wondered if it was something taught to the neurological specialists, but even they would have whispered something about it in a stairwell or changing room somewhere. *No... No, it must be my infection. Maybe I'm becoming delirious? Did I actually meet with this person? Was there even a note? Stop it! Stop it! Remember how easy things were before you began to question everything! No... No! Just shut up,* I told myself. *Focus! Move on and focus!*

Since discovering what bliss could feel like through Jules, my angel, I knew I had so much more to live for. That small bit of self-interest, of rebellion against the system made my survival essential. I would not risk exposure over something as small as being late for another appointment.

I entered the exam room just in time. The patient was standing by the small window. I nodded at the Black Cat standing as a sentry in the corner as I passed by; he ignored my nod.

"It's a remarkable site, isn't it, Huxley?" the patient said as he gazed out the window across the expanse of Progressive 17. "This wonderful world in which we are blessed to live, exquisite starry nights followed by warm golden days, every whim a right, glorious bliss."

"Yes, Mr. Benson, you certainly live in a wonderful world—wonderful, indeed," I said, remembering the patient's name and putting on my most winning smile. "It is good to see you, Mr. Benson. Today we'll be doing a simple pre-screening for your upcoming carotid surgery. Would you like me to explain anything about the process before we begin?"

The patient, Kenneth Benson, turned to me and smiled back at the question. He was every bit the man his medical file made him out to be. Lean, yet muscled, and looking healthy enough to run a marathon. He carried himself with confidence and bravado, always smiling, and always looking up as if he were the most important person in the world. While this wasn't an uncommon trait in a Prog, he wore the attitude with an almost charismatic quality.

He turned his head to once again gaze out the window. "I believe it's all pretty standard," he said, replying to my inquiry. "I imagine you'll start off with a combination of succinylcholine and etomadate to initially put me under... use a straight blade to insert a 7.5 ET tube down to, oh, I'd say twenty-one to twenty-three centimeters based on my height. You may change over to a fentanyl push, maybe use a little propafol, or some other combo of sedative and paralytic. You'll drape and prep the site with iodaphorm or a providone-iodine scrub..."

As Benson continued to rattle off the details of his impending surgery, I began to realize that he couldn't have learned all this from a simple medical briefing. The details he described were things only a trained MSP would know, or should know. He was fluent in every nuance of the procedure, ending his monologue with a simple, "Isn't that right, Server?"

"Yes, yes, precisely," I said, still marveling at the man's intelligence. "You have quite a knowledge base. How is it that a man of your health and intelligence came to be a Served? With your skills, you would make an excellent MSP."

I realized the mistake in my words almost immediately and froze; it was as if I tried to make myself disappear. Benson's face turned from gazing out the window, and he fixed his eyes on me, the smile evaporating from his face. If I didn't know better, I would have sworn I heard a chuckle from the Black Cat standing watch in the corner. Shooting the Black Cat a quick glance, Benson once again trained his eyes on me.

"It is my right to privacy, Server," Benson said. "You'd do well to remember it in the future. Your only responsibility is to see that my rights are preserved and served. Do not question my place or yours. Understand?"

"Of course, sir, of course," I said, bowing my head low. "I was simply impressed. No offense meant. None intended, sir. My most sincere apologies."

Benson eyed me for a few more moments, and then the smile returned to his face.

"Of course," he said while moving toward the exam table. "Now, on to your physical examination, I take it? I'd like to get this over with as quickly as possible."

"Yes, sir," I said, bowing in deference again.

I then moved into a head-to-toe assessment, checking for any signs of medical issues that previous tests might have missed. This was standard practice. The exam took no longer than a half an hour. I felt convinced that a procedure clearance was appropriate—when I noticed a faint discoloration on the sides of Benson's head, around the temporal region. Although he had a full head of hair, the discoloration was visible on close inspection just below the hairline. I checked the other side of his head only to find an identical discoloration. Where my hands had moved rapidly through the examination before, I slowed to look at this area more intently.

"Is something wrong?" Benson asked, noticing my preoccupation.

"These discolorations beneath your hairline, how long have they been there? There's also a faint scar line along the cervical region of your spine."

"How should I know? You're the damned medical provider!"

I grimaced at this, but Benson did not see, as my face was still closely examining his skin. After his earlier dissertation on his upcoming procedure, I would have expected a more reasoned response. If he was hiding something, then it would obviously fall under his "right to privacy," therefore I put on another smile and completed my examination.

"Probably nothing, but I'll leave a note in your record," I said.

"Fair enough. Anything else?" Benson said as he raised himself from the exam table.

"No, I think that's all," I said. "Your surgery is in two days. Be sure to get plenty of rest and don't eat for at least twelve hours before the surgery."

"Of course, standard practice—NPO after midnight," Benson said, followed by a broad smile.

He, like Hemsworth—or should I say Hathorne—did not seem blissful, but he did not seem depressed, either. Whatever this Prog was, he was also unlike the others, but in a different way. I couldn't quite put my finger on what it was. He stepped out of the exam room as soon as I finished speaking, leaving me to clean up my instruments and finish my charting. The Black Cat followed Benson out of the exam room.

I stepped toward the window and scanned the Progressive. All of the buildings glistened in the sunlight, reflecting off their mirrored exteriors. In the distance, I could make out the rolling hills and mountains. Wonderful green pastures and the bluest of skies with wisps of fluffy clouds colored the image. The high, white picket fence that bordered the creek surrounding the Progressive created the barrier that no Prog ventured beyond. To do so, one would run into the inside of the dome, realizing that everything that lay beyond was merely an illusion. Looking down, I could see the swarms of blue jumpsuits milling about, many walking from here to there, many sitting in groups, seemingly fixated on the large screens echoing the words of Our State. *Blissful, that must be their version of blissful.*

I turned away from the window and moved to the desk, then took a seat and pulled the ERP toward me. Scanning through Benson's record, I looked for any indication that he had undergone any type of cranial surgery, any accidents or conditions that would account for the bilateral discolorations on his temporal region and the scar on the dorsal aspect of his neck. Nothing. The ERP contained no medical information that would explain my findings. Benson's almost violent outburst when questioned about it seemed even more perplexing.

I slowly twirled my chair around, spinning and spinning. With my eyes closed, I allowed my thoughts to flow freely. *How did they get there? What happened to Benson? His temporal discoloration… the scar at the base of the skull? And Hemsworth's temporal incisions? What is the connection? What is going on here? Is there a connection in all of this?*

I could feel my leg throbbing with each kick to spin my chair. Just then, like a ton of bricks falling on me, a thought smacked me in the head: *Check his induction date.*

I stopped the spinning chair so abruptly that I almost fell off. I grabbed the desk at the last moment to stop myself. Slapping the screen on the ERP, it glowed back to life. After a swipe of my hand, the ERP displayed the demographics section. *Oh no… Oh no, no, no, no…* Benson's induction date was eight years ago. *He has to be my age.* I never asked him his age. I never asked that, as all care had been standardized to all ages. *How many of these people have I treated and not noticed this? How many?*

I thought for a moment and had another idea. *Jeremy Paul! I've got to speak to him. I bet he'll know what MRR signifies.*

I grabbed my portable ERP and headed out into the hallway. Scanning up and down, I looked for a medical administrator. Seeing none around, I headed to the sterilization section, hoping I would find Paul there. Turning the corner to the west side of the Medical Rights Facility, I finally saw an administrator. I figured I'd have a better chance of garnering info if I was polite. I looked down at her name tag as I approached.

"Good day, Sharon. MSP Huxley here. I have an extremely challenging case that I'm working on for a very important Served—very important, indeed. I was hoping to obtain a secondary consult with MSP Jeremy Paul. Could you possible check your assignment pad and tell me where I can find him?"

Sharon smiled as she tapped areas of her pad with her stylus.

"But of course, MSP Huxley, here to assist. Anything I can do to help ensure the prompt and efficient delivery of rights to our patients, it is an honor and my duty," she said as she continued to tap on her pad. "Yes, yes, here he is. He's assigned to Emergent Bay, first floor west. You can simply take that elevator there down one floor and it'll be straight ahead as you exit." She pointed to the elevator behind me.

"Thank you, Sharon. Both the Served and I appreciate your assistance. Good day!" I said, smiling as I turned around.

"We live to serve," she said as I walked to the elevator.

"We sure do," I said, placing my hand on the elevator button.

A few moments later, I was standing in front of an exam area, looking at Paul, gesturing to him to hurry and finish with the Served he was seeing. Black Cats were quite visible in all areas of the Emergent Bay, making sure the Served received their rights to health care expeditiously without any conflicts developing. Paul finally finished placing a bandage on the abrasion of the Prog he was treating.

What a waste of health care.

Paul pointed to an office, and I followed his lead. We stepped into the office and a Black Cat followed us in, obviously interested in what an MSP from another floor who was not assigned to the Emergent Bay was doing here.

"I just need to consult with MSP Paul concerning a Served that I am treating," I said, looking toward the Black Cat.

The Black Cat positioned himself in the doorway and nodded, indicating this was acceptable.

I was unsure of how to discuss my concerns about Hemsworth, and more importantly the MRR, without alerting the Black Cat. I turned on my ERP and tapped the screen with my stylus until the free text section appeared.

"Jeremy," I said, "I've got a pretty difficult case I'd like your input on."

Jeremy looked at me, somewhat puzzled as there was no patient record showing on the ERP. He looked to me, then to the Black Cat, looking worried.

"Right here," I said tapping the ERP, "let me mark up these radiology prints so you know what I'm referring to." I took the stylus and tapped on the letter keys: *Had Served taken from office to MRR after saying System was wrong. What is MRR?*

Jeremy Paul read the words I had typed on the ERP, then his brows furrowed and he looked extremely anxious, scared even.

"Y-Yes... Yes," he said. "Quite interesting, quite complicated."

Looking toward the Black Cat, then back to me, he took the ERP and began to touch letters: *Memory Reclamation and Reprogramming.*

"I... er, I used to work with an MSP that had such cases," he said. "It's... It's extremely complex."

He looked to me, then to the Black Cat. The Black Cat simply stood like an ebony statue, no indication of movement or concern. This must have eased Paul's nerves, as he continued on in a more relaxed, matter-of-fact tone: "It can be a permanent condition, depending on the strength of the mind that receives the treatment, the age of the recipient, his overall health status. The more pliable, the younger the tissue is… the more open it is to manipulation."

Paul went on, substituting terms such as "tissue" instead of saying "brain," realizing that the Black Cat would not know the medical particulars of the procedure, but just to be safe.

"Those with a stronger constitution may only notice temporary effects. However, temporary could mean months up to years, even a lifetime. The patient will receive two incisions, bilateral temporal region. The contents will not necessarily be removed as in similar older procedures. The latest versions of the process involve more of a rearranging—or reconfiguring, if you will. Does that help with your case?"

I stood there, dumbfounded, awestruck. "Yes… Yes, it most certainly does. My patient is now suffering from extreme amnesia, and this certainly clears things up. Would you be willing to commit to further work on this case with me?" I asked, almost knowing what the response would be.

"I… apologize, Hux. I no longer possess the abilities to engage in the type of treatment investigations and trials I believe you're asking about. Some things just have to be left alone; sometimes we can't fix everything. We just have to realize that we are each dealt certain cards and those are what we have to play. Maybe in my younger years, but now… No, I'm resigned to the realization of what I can and cannot do. I have to get back to my caseload. Good day, MSP Huxley."

"I understand. Thank you and good day to you, MSP Jeremy Paul. We live to serve."

Paul walked out of the room, past the Black Cat, who just stood there until he had exited, at which time the Black Cat exited. I left the room, heading back to my area with a host of questions bouncing around my head.

I spent the rest of the day in a daze, my head spinning. I needed to be away from there for awhile. I needed a break from this insanity. By the end of the day, the throbbing in my leg had simply become a part of my routine. I didn't even remember to look for a dressing or attempt to scam some antibiotics. *Tomorrow, it will have to be tomorrow.*

———

On the train ride back to the tenement, I managed to find a seat next to Jules. For the first few minutes, we said nothing, and I could tell she was still shaken up from the beating that we had witnessed on the train ride out. Her hands fidgeted and her eyes stayed focused on the floor. Once the tired train had pushed itself forward, leaving the Progressive behind, we found ourselves walled off by a sea of Server bodies, granted a few stolen minutes of privacy. I intended to use them.

"How are you?" I whispered, placing my hand in hers.

"Scared," she said.

"Aren't we all?" I said, understanding the seriousness of the crime we were committing with our desires. Glancing at her face, I found her beautiful eyes looking back at me; those eyes swallowed all of my doubts as I bathed in her serene pools of blue.

"Each day, I find myself terrified," she said. "I know the Black Cats are only there for our protection and to make sure we are serving as best we can, but now I get so scared."

"It's okay now. I'm with you. I'll always be with you." I squeezed her hand and tried my best to comfort her.

"You were limping when you got on the train," she said. "Did something happen?"

"No, no… Well," I said, before correcting myself: "Yes. The injury is minor," I lied, "but so many strange things have happened to me these past few days—strange meetings with Served and Our State representatives… the new Progressive… you."

"Me?"

"You best of all." I smiled, giving her hand a squeeze.

I leaned in a little closer to her so that no one else could possible hear what I was saying. "Jules, I have something especially serious, a proposition for you."

"Yes… Go on."

"When I was made to leave the train to find and scan Mead's head, I noticed a compartment under the train, a compartment big enough for two people. We could use it to escape, to run off, leave this all behind, leave the fear, leave the serving, leave the tenement, leave the Progressive, leave all of it—just you and me."

Jules's eyes grew wide at my words, and she pulled her hand away from mine.

"Ohhh no," she said. "I don't know about that. Where would we go? How would we live? No… it's too dangerous."

"Our lives are dangerous already," I said, motioning toward the Black Cat that had just made a pass through our car, monitoring, waiting for a Server to get out of line.

"I don't know—Oh, I don't know. That's… That's a terrifying idea," she said. "I've never thought of escape… never."

I gazed out of the window, through the soot and grime condensed over the pane from the chugging, gasping behemoth, out across the barren wasteland scarred with craters, out over the charred frames that once were great trees, out over the snow-covered tundra toward the mountains. "We've all thought of escape," I said. "Dreamed of it—at least I have. Dreamed of leaving... of being with you, closer to you."

"We could die."

"Death is a part of our lives. Good or bad, we all shall die, but let it be of our own choosing, our own doing. Let us serve ourselves, our own interests, and not be forced to serve the interests of others. Let us be us. Just think about it, just think about it... That's all I ask for now."

Her eyes welled up as if she was going to cry. Her full lips quivered ever so slightly. "Okay... I'll think on it," she whispered.

Chapter 7

That night, as I lay quietly in my bunk, the pain in my leg continued to throb in slow, steady pulses. With each beat of my heart, the pain intensified slightly, only to calm during diastole, reminding me of how one seemingly inconsequential mistake could mean life or death in my miserable trappings as a Server. How a simple twist of fate could change a person's life, change the course of his or her entire existence. If I had fallen a hair in either direction, the outcome would have been entirely different. I probably would not have been here entertaining these thoughts, would not have been scheming how I was going to save myself when all interventions necessary were laid before me, yet beyond my reach as a Server. Each day, I held within my hands the serum that could end the misery I was now experiencing: a small vial of antibiotics. Physically, the mere span of an epidermis, dermis, and the thin layer of glass molded into the vial, and yet, it may as well have been a mile away. *It's not my right to such provisions.* I looked back over the last few days and thought that if not for bad luck, I would be devoid of luck altogether.

But then the vision of Jules entered my mind and that vision of her brightened and warmed the darkest recesses of my foggy mind. I pondered our luck in meeting each other, and I thought that perhaps my luck would all balance out in the end. She gave me a reason to believe there could still be something good, something moral, something worthy in this world of parasites and unfortunate hosts, and that reason brought on more strange thoughts than I could ever hope to contain. And so it was that I found myself relying once again on the carpenter at my side as a sounding board of sorts, hoping to somehow communicate my deepest thoughts through our simple series of taps and hand gestures. The amount of time it would take seemed mind boggling.

It took several minutes before I was able to get Arnold's attention. So long, in fact, that I began to fear that he had already fallen asleep. Only the loud snoring of another Server a few bunks away ensured me that this couldn't possibly be the case. No one could have fallen asleep so fast with that racket. Finally, as I was tempted to actually sneak a whisper, the carpenter finally stirred and rolled onto his back, tapping me in an annoyed fashion to indicate his displeasure that I had interrupted his attempts at sleep.

Need to talk, I tapped out on his leg.

My eyes had adjusted to the dim light, as it had been some time since the Black Cats had lowered the metal shutters on the bunkhouse windows and snapped the lock closed on the door. I could make out the outline of Arnold's face as he turned toward me. I could sense he was puzzled at my communication. I realized then that my hand had been shaking throughout the entire message. Whether it was out of emotion or out of trembling from my infection, I couldn't tell.

Steadily, I tapped out again, *Need to talk.*

Go, he tapped back.

Strange happenings.

The note? Arnold asked.

Gone. Laundered.

Not Black Cats.

I paused briefly before tapping my response: *I'm here.*

Arnold's body shook, as if he were suppressing a chuckle. He tapped back, *Noted.*

Much to tell.

Is it safe?

For several moments, I lay in silence, wondering what his question was meant to convey. As our language took so long to communicate, we tried to refrain from unnecessary words. I knew he couldn't be asking if our communicating could be dangerous. The Servers had long since believed that the Black Cats cared little for this nightly communication, if they knew of it at all. Perhaps he was once again chastising me for thinking outside the system, but he had been willing to listen before. Of course, before it was pure conjecture, possibly the ranting of a Server suffering from the selfishness of individual thought, a mental illness as it was considered. Now I was offering him concrete information. Maybe he simply didn't want to have information that may get him in trouble.

Well? he asked.

I thought for a few moments more before replying, *Is it ever?*

Another pause followed before Arnold tapped, *Go on.*

For the next hour, I tapped furiously on Arnold's leg, often having to pause as I tapped too rapidly or without enough breaks for him to determine the letters. I went through all the day's events, from the missing note, to the encounter with the amnesiac Hemsworth, and finally to the strangely knowledgeable Mr. Benson. Those events, combined with my encounters from the previous day, were all laid bare before my bunkmate's feet. The only details I left out were those concerning Jules. I wanted to say that I left those details out for her own protection, but the truth was, I simply wanted to keep my angel all to myself. She was mine, and mine alone.

I tapped on Arnold's leg for so long that at some points he grabbed my hand and gave it a terrible squeeze, followed by tapping out, *Calm, slow down.* In all that time, I didn't once look at Arnold's face, keeping my eyes fixed on the darkness that stole away at the day. I struggled at times, trying to keep my hand steady as fatigue and illness continued to threaten the stability of my tapped-out letters. When at last my story was done, I looked over at Arnold's face in the faint light that found its way through the gaps around the steel shutters and saw what I sensed to be a deep frown staring back at me.

What? I tapped, thinking that I had left out some detail again in my haste.

"Shhhh," Arnold whispered. "Listen…"

I heard that clamor of metal on metal from the door. I guessed it was the bolt being drawn back. A low moan, almost a growl, began to rise in intensity. The door flew open, and the entire room lit up as floodlights blasted the darkness into submission. A large dog sprang in and rushed down the aisle, growling, its mouth dripping white froth. Following the dog, a handful of Black Cats stormed in.

"Contraband inspection!" the lead Black Cat yelled. "Everyone outta your bunks now!"

We all scampered to the ends of our bunks, jumping to the floor below, ankles hitting elbows, Servers knocked to their knees, yelps of pain echoing through the wooden structure.

"Get in line, get in line!" the lead Black Cat shouted.

Another Black Cat grabbed the dog by its nape and dragged it to the first Server, released it, and said, "Find."

The dog then scampered from one Server to the next, sniffing at the clothing, up and down each body, behind and around each person, on and on to the last.

I wondered if this was because of me or if these inspections were customary in this tenement—they were certainly new for me. I could feel Arnold glaring at me, his eyes piercing my head as the dog made its way down the line. After it reached the last Server, it ran into the hygiene area and, in a moment, darted out, back to the waiting Black Cats.

"Lucky. You're all clean," the lead Cat said. "Let's go! Wrap 'em back up."

The Black Cats left the bunkhouse, taking the beast with them. Climbing back into our bunk spaces, darkness charged back into the room and took back the night.

You dangerous, Arnold tapped on my leg. *No more. Beware who you trust.*

Catching my breath and trying to calm my nerves, I thought about what he had just tapped. I should have been furious with him for suggesting such a thing, but the truth was that I understood his position, given the events of my short time here. Everything that had happened to me felt as if it was a fantasy—or the ravings of a person overcome by fever and illness. I would have had trouble believing it myself. If I had been presented with such a tale, I would have thought the author a traitor—a dangerous, independent thinker who threatened to disrupt the entire system and cut off the giving hands of the Provider.

Arnold sighed quietly at my side. *Anyone else know?* he tapped.

My mind immediately went to Jules. She knew far less than he, but what she and I shared was an entirely different, and potentially more dangerous, experience. My actions concerning Hemsworth could be construed as the honest concern of a doctor for a patient, and my thoughts could easily be the very natural psychological reaction to someone else throwing a wrench into the system. My actions and thoughts concerning Jules, however, were entirely deliberate. I wanted her—selfishly, passionately, and dangerously. As yet, however, I could honestly answer that she knew little of what I had just told Arnold.

No, I tapped out.

Certain? he tapped.

I paused for a moment, once again filling my mind with images of my Jules. *Yes.*

Arnold stayed still for several more moments, before tapping out, *Leg bad?*

I reached my hand down to my wound, feeling the dampness and warmth through my makeshift bandage.

Bad, I answered, before adding, *Need abx.*

What abx?

Antibiotics.

Not your right.

Must try, else die.

Then die. Not your right.

Must try.

Arnold removed his hand from my leg and rolled over, facing away from me. I tapped out a single word to him. *Trust.*

Arnold raised his hand; I could make out his thumb extended upward. I was sure my secret was safe with him. In truth, he probably didn't need to tell at all. If I tried to steal the medicine, I'd likely be caught and that would be the end of the matter. Arnold had warned me. His hands were clean.

Our long conversation done, I finally rolled over myself to get in a few hours of sleep before the blaring tenement alarms and the banging of the Black Cats on the shutters would welcome us to another day of servitude. Our snoring companion a few bunks away had finally quieted down, which hopefully meant I could sleep in peace. It wasn't long before I forgot the mysteries, joys, and pains of the day and drifted off into a semi-peaceful sleep.

———

I awoke the following morning, groggy and tired from the pain and the relatively few hours of sleep after my marathon communication efforts and the surprise inspection. Following our morning showers, exercise, and meal, I found myself in a small group of Servers being led away from the train to a small shed on the other side of the tracks. All around the tenement, I could see the snow falling in a steady shower of large, fluffy flakes. They were not, however, large enough to blanket the injustice steeped upon the inhabitants of this tenement. Two Servers with shovels had cleared the pathway to the other side of the tracks and were working on clearing the concrete walkway in front of the depot. It was looking like we'd be part of snow detail today. I'd experienced this at my previous tenements. As our group stood in line by the doorway of the shed, I wondered to myself why it always snowed, why it was always so cold. I couldn't recall ever knowing anything else. I had seen the inside of the Progressive—not a flake of snow, not a drop of rain, always sunny. How could it be so different for us? Why such miserable weather?

"Remember, Servers," the Black Cat shouted, "you live to serve! You serve in whatever fashion the Provider deems best for Our State."

"Service is freedom," we all replied.

"Look alive, then! Labor assignments incoming."

At the far end of the line, two Black Cats began scanning foreheads and sending Servers off in various directions, some grabbing shovels, some pickaxes, some racing toward wheelbarrows and carts, others grabbing saws. I was not paying particularly close attention to what they were saying; instead, I concentrated on my leg and remaining upright. The shaking was becoming worse, much worse than it had been the day before. Ooze exuded freely from the wound during my shower. I'd paid little attention to my hair and face in an effort to get enough clean water into the wound as possible. I knew the effort was futile, but it was all I had to work with. I needed the medicines from the Medical Rights Facility, or else I would soon be unable to work. In this world, no work meant no service, and no service meant you had nothing to offer and therefore had no right to your life.

With a start, I felt a rough hand come around the back of my neck, forcing my head down into a scanner.

"MSP Huxley!" the Black Cat shouted. "Not too good for a little physical labor, are you? It won't harm those special hands of yours, will it? You're on snow clearance. Get to it!"

"Service is freedom!" I yelled in the strongest voice I could marshal as the Black Cat shoved me forward.

From my side, another Black Cat thrust a rusty shovel with a splintering handle at me. I grabbed the shovel and trudged on toward the rest of the crew assigned to snow duty.

I allowed a minor curse to escape my lips once I had enough distance on my black-clad taskmasters. The only advantage to working a day in the tenement was that the Black Cats often chose to monitor from the guard towers with only a handful scattered about the Servers, which allowed the Servers to whisper quietly to one another while they worked.

An icy wind nipped at my skin through my tattered clothes as I clutched the shovel with my bare hands. I joined my fellow Servers at the tracks. I didn't recognize any of those I was assigned to work with, all of us being from different bunkhouses and specialties. The tracks stretched out on past the high fences of the tenement, through the wide, concertina-clad main gate, for many miles, out into the distance toward Progressive 17. What worlds awaited the adventurous out beyond my sight, out beyond the Progressive? What was freedom? Was this it: to be allowed to serve shoveling drifts of snow so we could be more expeditiously transported to our daily duty as a Server. *Is this it? Is this what it means to be free?* I placed the shovel handle up against my stomach and pushed forward, thrusting my shovel into the snow. With little effort, I lifted a shovel full of fluffy snow and threw it off to the side of the tracks. I focused my eyes ahead, focused on the distance, focused on freedom. I saw each Server heaving snow off to the left and right of the tracks. For those on the left, light winds carried much of the snow back onto the tracks as we methodically continued our attempts at clearance.

A loud shot rang out from the tenement behind us, echoing along the barren, snow-covered fields. I looked around and saw Servers diving into the snow; instinctively, I did the same. Lying there in the snow, my shovel thrown to my side, I cocked my head up to see what the commotion was. Off to the far left, I could see two Servers being beaten by a sizeable Black Cat. A message soon came over the loud-speakers surrounding the tenement: "All Servers up—resume duties."

Pushing myself up, I noticed others scrambling to their feet, their shovels already poised to begin their labors again, and we were soon back at it.

The work was hard, but I found myself working quickly despite the pain in my leg. My thoughts, the one thing Our State couldn't control, spurred me on. Within ten minutes of starting, most of my body was numb from the cold, a welcome respite from the heat and throbbing racing up from my wound.

"Slow down, boy," said a voice from beside me.

I turned to see a well-aged Server with a scar running down his cheek; he had a bit of a slur and a strange drawl.

"You making the rest of us look bad."

It was then that I noticed that my track of snow had indeed been cleared several feet farther than the rest, despite the blowing wind.

"Sorry," I whispered. "I'm used to being berated for not working fast enough; I didn't want the whip, baton, or a beating."

I thought about how strange it was to encounter such an old person. It was rare to see a Server that old, and one would never see a Prog even close to what I would guess his age to be, although I guessed Hemsworth was the closest I'd seen.

"Public service, eh?" the man asked, heaving a smallish pile of snow beside me. "I used to work that racket. Progs always pushing to work fast, fast, faster so they coulds get back to their precious entertainment. Well, you ain't find any of that here. As longs as we get the job done and look sad while we does it, Black Cats will be satisfied."

I raised an eyebrow at his strange dialect and his words. This was the first time I'd ever heard someone favorably compare the Black Cats to the Served. The Served were obnoxious, yes, but they didn't beat us.

"Didn't use to be that ways for me. Black Cats always beat me, bruise me. No, no, they don't like ol' Whitey, no matter how much they given. They don't like Whitey for some reason."

"Whitey?" I said.

"Rightly so, Whitey's me name."

"Huxley, I'm Huxley, a pleasure," I said. "What was all that commotion just now?"

"Ahh, yes, couple of our boys musta gotten snow blinded a bit, went walking off too far. The old Cats had to corral 'em back in with a shot or two from their shooters. No worries, the Cats like to play sometime."

"You work tenement detail a lot?" I said, slowing my pace to match the rest of my group.

"Every day for last ten years," Whitey whispered back before pausing as a Black Cat marched by, turning his masked face toward us for a brief moment before carrying on.

Half the other Servers began grunting more enthusiastically as they worked, a gesture of appeasement for our taskmasters. Moments later, the Cat had moved farther down the track, leaving us free to talk once more.

"Our rights to serve," Whitey said to me. "Don't mean we's don't pace ourselves. That's how you keeps from burning out. Just don't be in such a damn rush all the time; snow ain't goin' nowhere."

"Duly noted," I said, now completely matching my pace and guttural exclamations with the rest—heaving and hoeing in time, feigning difficulty, putting on a good show. The work was still hard, but at the decreased pace, I found my injured leg did not put me in any special danger. I took advantage of my situation out in the clean fresh snow to occasionally rub my wound with a handful. Although it would do nothing for the gaining systemic infection, at least it would allow me to wash away the crusting pus.

This Whitey, though, was one of the most intriguing people I could ever recall meeting; I wondered what secrets that old mind of his held.

"If you don't mind my asking," I said, "do you know your induction date?"

"What, boy, you is a dummy? I was born. I wasn't inducted."

"Born?" I said, not entirely familiar with the term.

"Born, yeah, born. I had a momma and daddy; they got together and made me. I came from my momma womb... born!" Whitey said and shook his head. "I thought you was one of them smart ones, boy. I could take this shovel and dig me a hole right here and I bets you couldn't tell it from you backside."

I felt foolish. I had absolutely no idea what he had just said, or what it meant. Whitey was shoveling, shaking his head from side to side, all the while laughing and mumbling to himself.

"Let me give ya a quick-like history lesson, somethin' you'd never hear from ya mind-control people," Whitey said. "Ya see, we used to come from families: a mommy and daddy would have kids, then they's would raise 'em, give 'em all the good stuff, teach right from wrong, make 'em grow up straight and narra so they makes something of themselves, teach 'em how to pull their pants up, all the ways up. Provider took all that, hacked it up. He chopped and chopped at the family code morals and upbringing until it collapsed, then he rebuilt it into this, so now he everyone's daddy." He looked around, pointing his shovel at the other Servers, the Black Cats, and back toward the tenement.

"But... But, how...? Why?"

"Laziness, boy. He went on preachin' about the man behind you and yous has to help him. Hell, it ain't nothin' about him being behind me; it's about me bein' in front of him. He wants to get in front of me, then he better move his lazy ass and catch up. Ain't nuttin stopping him, 'cept himself," Whitey said, clearly becoming upset. "Damn all them handouts to them lazy people. Now look at thems, not a one of 'em wanna do nuttin. It ain't like they can't, they just won't. I say, just take us away—that's right, take us away, take away them made-up rights, then they has no choice but to do for themselves!" Whitey was so wound up, snow was flying everywhere from his shovel.

"I... I don't know what to say. I had thoughts... thoughts something was just not right."

"I ain't lookin' for you to say nuttin. You just think 'bout what I said. We don't wear no shackles; that's cause they don't want us to know we slaves, but I know. Any man has an ounce of ability and is made to use it for others or face a beatin' or prosecution, that ain't a free man. You know thems people in the Progressive, then Progs, they slaves too, no shackles there, neither. Soft slavery, yep, that's what it is… soft slavery."

"I don't understand. Soft slavery?"

"You seen dem dogs in the yard?"

"Yes."

"You see when theys bring in a new ones. They runs the length of the chain, they tries to get away. Not the ole ones. Sees, the ole ones been mind trained. They knows how far they can go. Ain't go no farther cause they needs the handouts of the master for their livin'."

"And… your point?"

Whitey shook his head as his shovel kept going faster and faster. "My point, dummy, is they's basically slaves at that point. No needs for chains and shackles. They is soft slaves. Don't know it, neither. Don't cares to know, I reckon."

"I think I'm beginning to understand."

"Are ya now? 'Tis 'bout time. Ain't nuttin more pathetic and furiatin' than a slave who refuse to see he a slaves, outright rally against it, 'specially when his master the same cut as him. Just ain't logics. No more now, boy. My blood's a steamin'. So go on… leave me alone now."

The next few hours passed quickly with my mind reeling from Whitey's assertions… Soft slavery… A group of us moved slowly down the track, Whitey off in the distance, his head still shaking but his shovel a bit slower. Eventually we reached our intended checkpoint: a place where another team of Servers had begun clearing their own strip of track. No doubt they were dropped off along the way during the morning trek to Progressive 17. After that, we were marched back to the tenement to be given another set of tasks.

I found myself standing before a derailed railroad car, one that had been parked on the far side of the tenement, the interior stacked high with cut wood. The Black Cats instructed us to unload the wood from the railcar and pile it into wheelbarrows to create smaller piles near each bunkhouse. Another group of Servers were on the outside of the high concertina-topped fencing surrounding the tenement. It looked as if they were digging in an area that was once wooded. I would occasionally see a Server reach down and pick up an old frozen branch and place it in a wheelbarrow. The Servers would bring the wood into the tenement and place it on the far end of the railroad car, giving it a chance to dry before being used for heating the bunkhouses or feeding the aging train that shuttled us to the Progressive. The work was harder than shoveling snow, and the workers here talked much less, huffing from their labor and periodically casting their eyes to the sky, hoping to get a glimpse of the sun through the near-constant overcast skies, trying to determine a rough time estimate. It was still snowing, never letting up the entire day. No doubt the tracks would need another clearing within a day or so. *Must keep them clear. Nothing can stand in the way of our serving. Can't afford to delay the rights of the Served.*

I was huffing and puffing, pushing my wheelbarrow that was heavily laden with what felt like a ton of wood between bunkhouses eleven and twelve—when I found myself face-to-face with the person who made me forget entirely about the numbing cold and the pain in my leg. It was as if the snow had instantaneously melted and the clouds had evaporated. I felt radiance on me, like the warmth in my leg had spread out across my entire being and blanketed me in a feeling of complete serenity. The weight of the wheelbarrow became a feather. It was as if a snow angel had appeared from the falling flakes.

Jules was unloading her own wheelbarrow not ten feet from where I stood. Her eyes grew wide upon seeing me, and her smile raced from one side of her face to the other as her eyes darted back and forth in all directions for any sign of a watching Black Cat, scanning all around to make sure there were no prying eyes. There were none in our immediate vicinity, the guards on the wall being on the most distant part of their patrol. It took everything I had not to run to her and just envelop her in my arms.

"I... I didn't know you were on this detail today," she said, distractedly moving another piece of wood from her barrow to the pile beside bunkhouse eleven.

"Me, neither," I said. "For you, I mean."

As I spoke, I forgot my wheelbarrow entirely and moved quickly to her side. She backed away for fear of being caught, eyes cast back to the walls that surrounded us, like a deer waiting for a predator to emerge from a rough patch of foliage.

"They can't see us," I said, pulling her deeper into the recesses between the bunkhouses. Just the touch of my fingers on her trembling arms made the fire in my chest burn all the brighter.

"Don't," she said, pulling weakly away.

"Don't what?"

"I can't."

"You can."

"No, I can't watch you get hurt. Can't get caught, knowing what they'd do you."

"You're worth it," I said, pulling her in close and feeling her warmth against my body for the first time.

Images of a dream that felt so far removed that it couldn't possibly have been from only a few nights back flitted through my mind. I remembered every breath of this moment. The feeling of her body against mine, the softness of her skin, her breath against my neck, my cheek, my lips, every second of that memory ripped from my mind and brought into this world... finally.

The kiss was slow and uncertain, a first and yet somehow natural, somehow instinctive motion. This, I felt, was nothing like I had dreamed. My mind could never have conjured the taste of her lips, the warmth of her essence, the emotions that came when our bodies joined together in this one simple action. Time slowed down to a crawl, and the two of us reveled in that one moment, living a whole lifetime together in the span of a heartbeat. I held her beauty in my hands and rested my forehead against hers; it was as if we were one. She stood, trembling, eyes closed, a smile drawn across her face. She had been taken away from all of this, this misery, this servitude, this progressivism... this slavery. She had been taken away by our emotion, our bond, our selfishness.

When we separated, my mind jumped back to how this moment had ended in my dream, the yelling of the Black Cats, the flying bullets, the declarations of love. I would have welcomed it now, in exchange for that one kiss. But thankfully, the disaster never struck. We were not punished for our brief interlude into self-indulgence, and we stepped safely back to our wheelbarrows before the patrols spotted us. I haphazardly stacked my blocks of wood next to bunkhouse twelve, swiftly pushed the empty wheelbarrow back to the derailed cart on the other side of the camp, my mind alight with dreams of more stolen moments outside the watchful eyes of the Black Cats. Reality without Jules was meaningless. My dreams were all that mattered, for there she would always live.

But unfortunately, the cruel reality of this existence, as always, reared its ugly head. The dream world would have to wait again.

Our day drew to an end as the night charged on, stabbing at the light as its rays retreated beyond the horizon. I found myself back in the place where my day had begun: in my bunk next to Arnold. Despite frequent cleaning of my wound with snow throughout the day, it continued to look and feel worse. The bunkhouse was colder than the night before, much of the wood being spared to help feed the train. This was both a blessing and curse. The air was warm enough to keep us alive and bring feeling back to our limbs, but it also meant my leg, which had been numb most of the day, flared in pain as the warmth allowed the return of feeling, of throbbing, of heat. My body dripped in sweat throughout the night, chilled from the coolness of the bunkhouse, unable to fight the infection effectively thanks to my horrible lot in life. There was no communication with Arnold that night; he kept his back to me, his cold shoulder making the bunkhouse just a bit more uncomfortable.

Once again, I found myself not only doubting, but hating the system into which I had been brought, my inception and abilities a curse. The testing I must have had early in my childhood determined that I was capable of logical thought and comprehension, therefore I must serve. If only I had suffered some anoxic event during development, or been dropped on my head at induction, then maybe I would be a Served, a Prog. Maybe I could stand there with my outstretched hand, screaming for someone to provide me with rights, with entitlements... but no. The System kept my wounds from healing. The System kept me and my brethren in dirty, drab clothing, without respect or comfort, stripped of dignity. The System kept me away from Jules, forced to kiss in secret and love at the risk of death. The System was my enemy; my service and my abilities, a curse.

Service is not freedom; service is slavery, I tapped out onto my own leg. *Service makes me a slave. Ineptitude is rewarded, ability punished.*

I could not deny the truth that had been growing in my mind since coming to Progressive 17, which had perhaps been growing my entire life. I was a slave, oppressed and put down to serve those of lesser value, lesser intelligence, those of lesser purpose. No matter if I was allowed to keep some percentage of reward for the services I provided, it would still be involuntary servitude. *No man is free who is compelled to provide for another against his will, another who should provide for himself.* The system pitted us against each other, while the representatives of Our State seemed to live in freedom. The Black Cats, the housing officials, the bureaucrats, even the Provider himself... They were the privileged. They were the true Served. They were the ones in control.

Whitey's words bounced around my head, leaving me questioning this existence. I made up my mind then and there. I would not continue to doubt my own revelations. I would embrace them, if only in my mind. I would think for myself, and one day live for me. And that would start with one tiny step. I needed an antibiotic to live, and I would get it.

Chapter 8

My dreams that night once again returned to visions of Jules and me together. This time, however, our passionate embraces were not interrupted by the all-seeing Black Cats. We stood alone in the emptiness of the Server tenements, the entire complex abandoned and quiet. The sky was a clear blue expanse above our heads; glistening golden sunlight hovered over us like a beacon. The ground beneath our feet, no longer packed-down dirt, ice, and snow, was instead covered in lush, vibrant grasses, and the smell of flowers wafted in our nostrils, mixing with the scent of our bodies as we stood in a close embrace.

As I gradually lifted Jules's chin, our eyes met, and I felt my body slowly melt into her deep aqua pools. We were naked and alone, the flesh of our uncovered bodies pressed together, our thoughts only for each other. I whispered the sweetest symphony of words into her ears, and she smiled, pressing her body closer to my own. She giggled as I let my lips fall on her neck. We were free and we were truly blissful.

That single dream contained all of my wildest thoughts, every seditious inkling of a selfish life of freedom and self-servitude, every thought of living a life where I was an end in and of myself and not a tool for another's, nor any other a tool for mine. Every fantasy I ever had about an existence outside the control of the Black Cats, the Our State goons, and the Provider. This world was ours for the taking, a flourishing paradise free from the horrors of nuclear war, nuclear winter, and the oppression of batons and machine guns. No guards stood at the gates. No eyes watching and spying. No chanting or recitations of servitude could be heard. There was only the feeling of my lover at my side, the scent of nature on the wind, and the quiet tweeting of faraway birds who had somehow returned to retake the earth for their own, bringing restoration to a world once ravaged by mankind's power greed.

If I could have lived in that dream forever, to have stayed in that quiet paradise and never awoke, I would have. But the human mind can only maintain a dream for so long before reality is able to grip its icy fingers around its proverbial wrist and wrench it back into the outside world, back to the cold, hard emptiness of Our State.

And so it was that I awoke that next morning, cold, shivering, and soaked in sweat. Instinctively, I reached my hand down to my leg and felt the bandage covering my wound. Immediately I was rewarded with a sharp pain that seemed to extend far beyond my thigh, stabbing its way up my leg and directly into my spine. The invaders had become emboldened at the lack of resistance and were waging a bitter war on my immune system. Today would be my last chance to obtain medication. After that, I would likely be too ill to work, and from there, too ill to warrant these breaths bestowed upon me by the Provider.

As the alarms sounded and we were ushered from our beds, Arnold gave me a quick once-over. I gave a subdued whimper as my feet hit the floor when jumping down from the bunk. My limp had become noticeable. Arnold just stood there, shaking his head slightly from side to side. I imagined he must have suspected that I planned to go through with the theft of medication today. His options for deterring me, however, were limited. No more tapping notes, no more sighs, no more head-shaking could stop what was already in motion.

The daily routine soon separated me and Arnold from each other. I somehow managed to make it through the morning exercises without collapsing and then consumed morning sustenance without vomiting. With all the snow build-up over the last few days, despite yesterday's efforts at clearing it, the Black Cats seemed eager to get us on our trains as quickly as possible. As I limped behind the other Servers boarding my train, I could see a detail of Servers being herded toward the tool shed—snow detail, I suspected. *Lucky lot.* I tried to spot Jules in the crowd of Servers boarding the trains, and managed a weak smile when I spotted her. True to form, she kept her face low, her usual facial expressions unchanged, although no tears were in her eyes this day. Our feelings for each other would continue to be secret, at least until I figured out some means of escaping this putrid nest and flying free of this yoke of servitude.

As the iron serpent lumbered down the tracks, I began to work my mind, work my thoughts. I had to develop a plan for how to obtain antibiotics without drawing attention to myself. I would have to find a patient displaying appropriate signs and symptoms to warrant a strong antibiotic, but at the same time a patient strong enough to survive without them and in such a state that they would not recollect the dispensing of such medications—a tall order. The ideal candidate would be an elderly patient; however, it was a rarity to see elderly patients. Mr. Hemsworth was the oldest I'd seen as far as Progs. *Come to think of it, I've never seen any sick infants or young children, either.* The pickings were going to be slim, and ultimately I would be at the whim of the administrators at the Medical Rights Facility. I had only a limited number of patients to see before the carotid surgery with Mr. Benson, and that small pool of choices would have to do. I'd have to use someone. *As much as I've been used, it's only reasonable that I should use them for a change.*

Our train pulled into Progressive 17. As we disembarked, I once again gave Jules a quick look before heading off with the other Medical Servers toward our tunnel. The Black Cats had overestimated how much the snow would slow us down on the train, which meant we moved at a more leisurely pace through the tunnels, time being on our side. I was able to keep up with my brethren through the bright, twisting corridors without drawing attention to myself. Once we reached the stairs and obtained a few minutes of privacy, I took a position at the back of our group and feigned fatigue, attempting to persuade the others to move slowly up the stairs. I felt sure they noticed my limp, but in an interesting juxtaposition, concern for another Server was treasonous behavior, whereas concern for the Served was a duty, a right, a freedom.

We continued our march up the stairwell in our usual silence. Those ahead of me had not slowed their pace. I kept my focus on the steps ahead of me, counting out each step as I passed it, trying to take my mind off the ever-growing pain.

When we reached the top of the steps, each Medical Server approached the administrator to receive their assignments. Fortunately, I was at the back of the line, which provided me a moment to compose myself and wipe the accumulated sweat from my brow. My earlier morning shower had been a welcome relief in cooling me off, but it had little lasting value. I was certain that I looked a mess with my soaked armpits and pale skin. The administrator took the opportunity for a crude attempt at humor: "Forget to dry yourself after your shower this morning, MSP Huxley?"

"Eh, yes, I suppose I did, Doreen," I said. "I suppose I did…"

She gave a half smile, handed me the ERP with my cases for the day, and directed me on to the locker room.

Inside the locker room, I stood before the full-length mirror that was hung on the far wall next to a sink. The image I saw staring back at me was a picture of systemic illness, of a person on the verge of sepsis. Dark bags hung under each of my eyes, holding hour after hour of restless sleep. My skin was pale, as the blood found its way to my core and away from the cooler reaches of my body. My entire being quivered with chills and a raging fever. If I wasn't able to get this infection under control, I wouldn't be able to stand, let alone serve. Dreams of a future with Jules, free and uninhibited, these gave me reason to push on, to find more strength than I knew I had. I splashed cold water on my face and drank as much as I could from the sink. After stripping off my damp rags, I headed toward the sanitizer conveyor, dreading the heated steam as it was the last thing my body needed. Having dried as much as possible from the air jets, I headed to my cubby, donned my jumpsuit and grabbed my lab coat. I followed my fellow MSPs out into the main lower hallway of the Medical Rights Facility. The brightness was overpowering, forcing me to squint for a few moments. Sweat gathered on my brow, again finding its way into my eyes, stinging and making the brightness that much more formidable. I wiped my brow on my sleeve, surprised at the amount of sweat I was still able to produce. I hadn't urinated in sometime, and no doubt, when I finally did, I suspected it would be rather dark.

Checking my portable ERP, I found that my first patient of the day wasn't anywhere near what I would need to justify writing up an antibiotic prescription. Young, healthy for a Prog, with nothing more than a few muscle aches. I breezed through this first appointment without much trouble. My body still quivered whenever I broke concentration, but besides that, I was able to clear this patient out in record time. My next assignment came, and another injury stared me in the face. Apparently there had been some kind of sporting event that morning, resulting in a number of such injuries. The second appointment went much the same as the first, and when I received my third, I began to lose hope. Another injured twenty-something Prog's history stared back at me from the ERP.

But then I took note of the characteristics of this particular injury: contusions, cracked ribs, and a nine-centimeter laceration to the left shin. The age of the patient was not ideal: they would likely be sharp enough to remember a prescription properly. But with options dwindling, I had to assume the risk. I had less than an hour before the appointment with the carotid patient, and then the rest of my day would be gone. I decided I would prescribe an injectable antibiotic, ceftriaxone, for the young Prog's laceration. Dirt in the wound would be the justification if I was later questioned.

As I trudged slowly down the stark white halls trying not to limp, my eyes darted back and forth between each Black Cat I passed and the floor beneath me. Black Cats stood like statues in every corridor, unmoving, unspeaking, always watching. Did they notice my limp, my nervousness? The way my eyes shifted between them as I made my way down the hall? *My sweat… Surely they must notice my sweat. It drips off me like melting snow from a bunkhouse gutter. Could they know of my plan? Are they aware that I know this system is a scam, a fraud, a ruse—that they sell slavery as security and service as freedom and morality?*

Over the PA system, a message droned on: *"Bliss is realized through security. Security is everyone's business. If you see or hear anything suspicious, immediately report it to the nearest Black Cat or Our State representative. Remember, the Provider cares. This message proudly brought to you by National Progressive Radio."*

What a laugh.

My head throbbed as much as my leg, a sure sign of dehydration. I needed more fluids, but my thirsty body would have to wait. I reached the room where my patient was waiting. I walked in to find it much the same as every other examination room I had been in—in every Medical Rights Facility in every Progressive to which I had been assigned. The room was simple, square, a small desk with a chair, an exam and procedure table, a medical cart with basic supplies, a chair for the patient, a curtain on rails by the exam table, and of course, when a patient was in the room, so too was a Black Cat. He stood in stark contrast to the brightness of the room, like a little touch of night that had found its way here to mar the brightness of the day. The only difference was the patient inside—a man with a loud, boisterous, and assuredly troublesome attitude.

Just the attitude I need.

"About time you got here, Server!" the young man shouted, holding up his leg for me to see his injury. "Three points, just from me alone. A star player, and you keep me waiting! Get to it!"

"Of course, sir," I said.

I gave a genuine smile for the first time since arriving that morning. This person could serve as the epitome for all that was wrong with this system: a demanding imp with no ability for intelligent, coherent thought—merely a thug demanding rights that in reality were anything but.

"Don't you 'sir' me, Server!" the man said. "I see how you're judging me. You better get this stitched up quick so I can get back to the field. I have my right to exercise, you know!"

"No disrespect at all," I said, working hastily to examine his leg, which he seemed quite proud of, once the bluster of pushing around the lowly Server wore off. "You're going to feel a little discomfort as I inject a numbing medication. After that, you shouldn't feel a thing. Due to where the laceration is, I'll be using staples, because stitches would allow the edges to pull apart. You'll have them in for about ten days," I said as I prepared the lidocaine.

"Cleat tore right into it," he said. "Probably would have taken another guy's leg clean off, but not mine. I've been working out."

I suppressed a chuckle at this. Outside of the first patients like Mr. Benson, most Served were fat and lazy. The fact that they even had sporting events at all had always surprised me, as had any Served who boasted about exercise. When the end result was legally required to be a tie so as to avoid one team losing, both being winners, ambition and drive had been suppressed to the point of virtual nonexistence—so much for bettering and driving oneself through competition. This man was young and able-bodied for his sort, but he was still fatter than any Server I had ever known. Still, this Prog had provided me the ideal opportunity to obtain what I needed to survive, so I couldn't risk screwing it up just to flaunt my loathing of his ignorance—*Or his "bliss," I should say.*

"Well, I think we've got you patched up," I said. "Seven staples and the wound dressed, but nothing we can do about the ribs. Those will have to heal on their own."

"I can't wait for those to heal," the man said. "I have a game to get back to. You get me something to treat it or I'm filing a complaint with the first Our State representative I see. You hear me, Server?"

"The best I can do is to prescribe something for the pain, and you'll also need an antibiotic. There was quite a bit of dirt in that wound."

"Stop standing there talking about it and do it, then!"

"Immediately."

I grabbed the portable ERP. "Please place your head on the scanner," I said as I held the ERP up to his forehead.

The patient leaned forward and the ERP beeped, registering the patient and bringing up his immunization record.

"Good. I see your tetanus is up to date and no known medical allergies. It'll be just the one injection, then.

"Yeah, right, go already!"

I nodded and slipped out of the room. Never before had a single hallway seemed as long as the one that led from that exam room to the medication station on the other side of the wing. The PA system continued its usual message of collaboration and collectivism. *If they only knew.* Despite walking at a normal pace, it felt as though each step forward was like pushing against a powerful current, a deluge of invisible water making every moment stretch out for years unending, moving but not moving. The Black Cats standing guard grew to superhuman size, their heads seemingly all turned toward me, bearing down on me from all angles, reading the guilt in my eyes and the defiance in my heart. Every look from every Server and Prog alike was like some piercing blade slicing through my mind and seeing into my naked soul.

With my final few steps I reached the medication station. Leaning forward, I placed my forehead on the provider scanner and instantly saw the pulse of the laser scanning the credentials etched beneath my skin. An electronic voice stated, *"Place ERP in receptacle."* I followed the directive and placed the ERP in the correct port. The med station scanned the electronic file on the ERP and acknowledged the requested prescription. *"Remove ERP,"* the station directed. I grabbed the ERP with my sweaty hands, all the while looking around to see if I was being watched, expecting that at any moment, the monstrous hands of a Black Cat were going to grab me, putting an end to my plans and sealing my fate. A moment later, the station beeped and two plastic containers were dropped into the dispenser tray. I quickly grabbed them and opened them to verify the contents. The first contained twenty narcotic analgesic tablets for the patient's complaints of pain, and the second contained a vial of ceftriaxone, one gram IV or IM. I brushed my finger over the *Confirm* button and slipped the containers into my lab coat pocket.

Turning to head back, I was swept swiftly into the current of Progs and Servers as I made my way back to the examination room. Each Black Cat, Server, and Prog whizzed by as I kept my eyes focused forward, my resurrection and my life resting quietly in my pocket. Reaching the examination room, I immediately found my patient ready with a fresh set of expletives demanding me to hurry. Pacing back and forth, grunting under his breath…

"Yes, sir, yes, I'm moving as fast as I can, sir," I said, handing him the ERP. "Please verify the prescription. I have twenty narcotic analgesic tablets for you. Take one every four hours as needed, and I have an antibiotic injection that I have to administer in your gluteus muscle—your backside."

"Yeah, whatever," he said, placing the ERP on his forehead. After the ERP registered, he thrust it back at me. "Give me the damn pills."

"Certainly." I reached into my lab coat and produced the bottle of pills. Handing them to him, I repeated, "One every four hours as needed, sir."

He snatched the bottle from me, twisted off the lid, and poured out three pills into his hand, then threw them into his mouth and swallowed.

"ONE every four hours, I said!"

"Who the hell do you think you're talking to? Don't raise your voice to me! If I want to take three, I'll damn well take three. Now give me the freakin' injection so I can be on my way!"

"As you wish, sir," I said, not wanting the Prog to rush off before I completed my plan. "Right over here, sir. Please drop your pants and lean against the exam table. I'll be using some numbing medication in addition to the ceftriaxone, as it can irritate the tissue."

The nasty Prog looked at me in disgust, pulled his pants down, and leaned against the table. I drew the curtain closed, blocking the Black Cat's view.

"I just have to draw up the lidocaine and place the antibiotic vial in the injection gun; it'll just be a moment."

I gathered the materials from the cart and pulled out a small vial of normal saline. Unrolling a length of silk tape, I placed the vial of ceftriaxone, a syringe, and a needle on the adhesive side of the tape. I glanced over my shoulder to make sure the patient was still leaning over the table, looking away. My hands were shaking from both fear and fever. Clearing my throat, I quickly unzipped the fly on my jumpsuit and shoved the length of tape and ceftriaxone into the zipper opening, adhering it to the inside of my leg.

"Okay, almost ready," I said, hoping my nervousness was not evident.

"Damn it, Server, hurry the hell up! I'm gonna miss the entire game!"

"Yes, yes, here it is."

I skipped the lidocaine as I had no time and I didn't care how much initial pain I caused this slag anyway. All I could hope for was that the three narcotic tablets would somehow mask the discomfort. I drew up five milliliters of sterile saline and placed it into the injection gun. I approached the patient and wiped his upper outer buttock with an alcohol prep. Shoving the gun to his flesh, I pulled the trigger. Instantly, the gun shot forth a needle into his flesh, then the plunger flew forward, injecting the saline into his fascia.

"Oww, that's stings like hell!"

"Sorry, it'll diminish quickly, sir. The lidocaine will help," I lied, smiling to myself.

"Are we done?" the patient said as he pulled up his pants.

"All set. I hope you feel better, sir. Good luck in your game."

"I don't need any damn luck, Server—and remember, I've got your name," he said as he ripped open the curtain and headed toward the door.

As he left the room, it might have been my fever-induced euphoria, or simply that I was hearing things, but once again, I could have sworn I heard the Black Cat chuckle. I cleaned up the materials from the injection and sat at the desk. Pulling the ERP toward me, I completed my visit notes and signed out. Between my legs, I could feel the vial and supplies, still secure. I pushed against the tape, worried that my perspiration could weaken the adhesive. *I should have adhered it to my underpants,* I thought, chastising myself for the poor decision.

Taking a deep breath, I raised myself from the desk and stepped back out into the corridor, finding that the midmorning rush had already begun to diminish. An administrator found me and assigned me one last patient before my surgery. I was led to another room to treat yet another male Served with sore muscles and other minor ailments. I recommended a dose of non-prescription painkillers and sent him on his way, suffering only a few insults about wasting his time. I then took the elevator to the vascular surgery suite to begin preparing for Benson's carotid surgery.

When I entered the surgery suite, I found Mr. Benson already lying on an operating table, chatting cordially with the surgical assistant. The anesthesiologist had no doubt already prepped the anesthesia machine, as he was nowhere to be seen.

"MSP Huxley, glad you could join us," Benson said as I entered, casting a smile my direction and propping himself up on an elbow. "I was chatting with MSN Andrea. Blissful day, isn't it?"

"Yes, Mr. Benson, better by the minute," I said, moving to a sink on the far side of the room to scrub up for surgery. I thought of the vial taped to my leg and my impending recovery once I gave myself the injection. "Yes, sir, the day couldn't be better—wonderful day for a procedure that will surely have you feeling tip-top, sir."

"I was just asking MSN Andrea what kind of anesthesia I'll be under during the operation. She didn't seem to have an answer for me."

"That's because anesthesia is handled by automation," I said. "Official regulation requires that the exact proportion of chemicals used be determined by computer, but I imagine it will be as you had described at our last pre-procedure visit. We operate the machine, of course, but it makes all the decisions regarding the pharmaceutical balance. It's supposed to ensure that you receive the deepest and most blissful sleep possible. I see anesthesia has already come and gone, so the machine must be all set."

"A wise policy," Benson said, lying back again while his left carotid was marked for the upcoming incisions. "The Provider truly has thought of everything when it comes to ensuring our rights, hasn't he?"

Despite wanting to cringe, I only smiled and responded, "He certainly has your rights in mind."

The surgical assistant approached me as I finished scrubbing in. I held my hands up as she held out the sterile gown. Placing one arm through the sleeve, I could feel my body becoming weaker and weaker. The thought of the antibiotic only inches from its intended target no longer gave me the rush it had the moment I taped it to my leg. I slipped my other arm into the gown as the Medical Server Nurse pulled the apron strings around the front for me. I held my hands up, doing all I could not to shake. The MSN held open the gloves as I shoved my hands into each. I tied the gown and proceeded to the OR table, taking my place next to Benson's head.

"Are we ready to begin, Doctor?" the MSN asked.

I turned my back for a moment and held my hand flat in the air, parallel to the floor. The shaking from my fever had stabilized as much as I could have hoped for. I had no choice but to wait and see if it would hold out through the entire procedure.

"MSP Huxley?" the MSN said.

"Yes, everything seems to be in order," I said. I looked down at Benson. "Initiate the sedation, Nurse. Good night, Mr. Benson."

Just as the nurse reached to depress the initiation button on the anesthesia machine, a startling, terrible, loud banging erupted from the surgical suite door.

"MSP Huxley!" a voice called. "Open the door!"

"What the devil is going on?" Benson said.

"MSP Huxley, should I initiate the sedation?"

I stood there, terrified, unable to move, frozen with fear. *They know.*

"MSP HUXLEY! The sedation—should I initiate?"

153

"What the hell is going on here, Server? Don't you dare sedate me!" Benson shouted.

"We said open the door!" the voice shouted again.

Through the small window, I could see the heads of several Black Cats gathering on the other side.

The nurse moved quickly to open the door, ignoring my impulsive call for her to stop. As the entryway burst open, I immediately found myself surrounded by a mass of commanding black figures, a sea of limbs engulfing me, grabbing different parts of my body, and shouting a thousand different questions that I couldn't understand. The surgical suite was like an echo chamber, each voice reverberating off the walls, surrounding me in sheer thunder. I could hear Mr. Benson screaming, "What the hell is this? I have rights, I have rights, I have rights!"

A moment later, I felt a sharp pain running up my body as my legs were kicked out from under me and I was thrown to the floor. The black-gloved hands now groped every part of my body for what I could only assume was the vial of ceftriaxone, the needle and syringe still taped to my inner thigh. Each time their hands landed on my wounded leg, I let out a yelp of pain, but it did nothing to deter their groping. Another few seconds passed, and the flurry of hands stopped, the Black Cats forming a tight circle around my body, one to my left holding up the items that were recently taped to my thigh. My only chance of beating this invader, this septic onslaught, was now out of reach—my entire existence out of reach.

"So," a voice said, "rights violation, then."

On the inside of the circle of Black Cats stood a man who looked like he'd stepped out of an earlier time. He was dressed not in a blue or red jumpsuit, or even the black garb of Black Cats and Our State representatives, but in a brown overcoat that covered a body clad in a brown shirt, black tie, and brown pants. His blond hair was cropped high and tight, and round lenses rested on his rather prominent nose, magnifying his intense brown eyes. He took the vial from the black-gloved hand of the nearest Black Cat and examined the label.

"Strong antibiotic, needle, and syringe," he said. "I assume it's for the leg?"

I could do nothing but lie there in pain and stare. *This is the end, this is my end.*

"No response?" the man asked me. "No worries, it was a rhetorical question. We're aware of what it's for."

A few moments passed as the man continued to stare at the vial. He closed his hand in a fist around the vial, allowing his hand to fall to his side.

"Move," was all he said next.

In the blink of an eye, I was snatched from the floor and held in a mostly standing position. From my right, a Black Cat drew back his tree trunk of a leg and then, with full force, slammed his boot into my leg. I let out a gut-wrenching scream. I could barely stay conscious, looking down at my leg as a red stain began to increase in size on the pant leg of my surgical scrubs.

"I assume that you injected something other than ceftriaxone into your patient earlier?" said the man in the overcoat, his lips flat without expression.

In reply, I simply gave him a look of seething hate. The Black Cat at my side reeled back and delivered another devastating blow to my already tortured leg. I would have fallen and passed out if it were not from my inquisitors making sure I was alert enough to suffer as much as possible, and alert enough for them to enjoy their work.

"I'll ask again," the man said. "You injected a Served with something other than what was prescribed for him to provide an opportunity for you to steal antibiotics from this Medical Rights Facility, from this Progressive, and with utter disrespect, from the Provider?"

"Y-Yes... yes," I choked out, writhing in pain.

"Your patient did not need antibiotics?"

"No."

"And you believe you have the right to them?"

I paused for a moment, thinking of all that was wrong with this System, thinking of all I had given, or all that had been taken from me and given to the undeserving.

I whispered, "Yes."

The man nodded and the Black Cats released their grips, dropping me in a weak and tattered pile. The man in the overcoat stepped on my leg. Not hard and fast like the Black Cat kicks. His simple leather shoes pressed slowly and deliberately on the bloody gash, increasing the force at a gradual pace that left me feeling every ounce of pain as it built up in my body.

"With few exceptions, we have eyes and ears everywhere, Server," he said.

To this, I only nodded.

"For the charges of theft, fraud, sedition, and conspiracy to commit treason, I am placing you under arrest," the man said. "Our State will bestow upon you the punishment commensurate with the crimes for which you have been found guilty. Do you understand, Server?"

"But... But I only took these... these steps... in order to further serve," I said.

"Service is your right; medication isn't. Do you understand this basic tenet?

"I understand... what you say. I... I don't agree with it."

"What you agree or disagree with is irrelevant. For your sake, ask and the Provider may be merciful."

Throughout this exchange, Mr. Benson never spoke, remaining open mouthed, sitting up on his surgery table, watching the entire ordeal unfold along with the MSN. Finally, when a pause in the interrogation presented itself, he took his opportunity to question the proceedings:

"What does this mean about my surgery? What about my damn rights?" he asked.

"Obviously," my interrogator said, "it's not going to happen today. It will have to be postponed."

"Postponed?" Benson yelled. "I've been preparing for this surgery for weeks. What about my rights? I have a right to medical treatment! Rights to proper treatment by a proper Medical Server at a proper time. I am ENTITLED! A right postponed is a right denied!"

"You have the right to reschedule," the interrogator said.

"Reschedule?"

"That's right."

"My rights have precedence over this arrest," Benson continued. "My original rights—the rights I came here to exercise. I demand you allow him to perform the surgery, then cart him off to reclamation. Stealing a tiny vial of medication shouldn't stop a Server from doing his duty."

The interrogator glared at Benson. "Do you know who I am? Do you have any idea whom you are talking to?

"No idea," Benson responded hesitantly.

"Believe me, you don't want to know," the man said. He turned to the Black Cats surrounding me. "Up, and out," he said, before walking out of the surgical suite without giving Benson another look.

Seconds later, I felt myself being hefted roughly off the ground and dragged from the room, the ongoing protestations of my patient continuing to ring in my ears.

Chapter 9

The time from when I was dragged out of the surgical suite until now had been a blur. I found myself in what I could only assume was the heart of the Black Cats' local headquarters. I could only guess, as before we had reached the elevator adjacent to the surgical suite, the Cats threw a hood over my head, obscuring my view and making my breathing difficult. The rest of the journey involved being heaved into a vehicle of some kind, being constantly berated and beaten, and finally being dragged and thrown into a hard steel chair, my wrists and ankles bound tightly to its legs. When they finally removed the hood, they were dragging me in the chair to a dimly lit room. The door slammed closed behind me. A quick scan told me I had been left there alone.

At first, I wondered if the beatings hadn't taken what little coherence I had left completely out of my head. The room seemed to flicker in and out of my vision, like some horrible nightmare that my mind just wouldn't let go of. After a few moments, however, I realized that this was intentional, lights cutting off and on like a strobe, playing with my senses, distorting my perception. Despite my artificially skewed view, my fever, and my recent beating, I was able to make out my general surroundings.

The first thing I noticed, before my vision cleared, was the unbearable heat. It was as if I was in a sauna, a sweatbox; it was stifling. After spending so many evenings in the cold, unprotected world of the Server tenements, this change of temperature was all the more shocking to my already frail system. Within seconds of being dragged into the muggy room, sweat began to bead on my forehead, underarms, knees, and torso. Vents on my left and right pumped the hot air into the room in a steady, unrelenting stream, making it feel like the temperature was intentionally being ramped up second after second until I would pass out from heat exhaustion. I envisioned this as my death, a progression from profuse sweating to dryness as my bodily fluids sweated away. My heart would begin to race, my breathing would become rapid, I would heave and vomit, my confusion would increase, my thirsty muscles would cramp and scream in protest, finally the throbbing headache would cease and I would slip into unconsciousness, and then... freedom. Not the prettiest way to die, but I could think of worse.

I saw before me, just out of reach, what appeared to be a large block of ice on a small table. The ice block extended out past the edges of the table, and I watched as tiny droplets of water fell from the ice block to the ground, taunting me with its coolness. I wanted so badly to reach out and touch the ice with my fingers, to feel the soothing cold on my skin, and ultimately feel relief from the stifling heat and humidity that was being forced on me. My mouth felt parched and my head swam both from heat and infection, and I knew that if I didn't somehow inch my body closer to the ice, to fall in to the puddle beneath, to savor a few drops of the cool, life-sustaining water, I would soon die.

What a terrible form of torture the Black Cats had devised for me, the minds of Our State, so tolerant they preached to be, but in reality, so sick and twisted, so full of hate and intolerance. To put me at the point of death, within arm's length of relief, but unable to come any closer, it was the work of evil minds. I would be forced to watch my lifeline melt, drip, and evaporate away into nothingness. At that mo-

ment, in that tiny cramped cell, I realized the extent of the
danger I had put myself in. My simple act of self-preservation,
of self-service, stealing one vial of ceftriaxone, had con-
demned me to a horrible death. Despite the heat, I felt a chill
run down my spine at this realization. Whatever I may have
thought about the cruelty of the System, it was nothing compared to reality of that cruelty. We were nothing but cattle,
there to provide a service, then to be slaughtered at the first
sign of weakness or inability to be of use to the Provider.

Despite knowing it was likely impossible, I tried to scoot
my chair closer to the block of ice before me. The weight of
the chair was too much, and my body too weak to make even
the slightest progress. I would likely send myself toppling to
the floor before I ever reached the block, or the cool puddle
forming below it. I struggled to move my feet to the sides of
the chair legs to generate a pivot point. Looking down, I saw
two bolts holding each of the legs to the floor. I let out a sigh,
exhaling the heated air from my lungs into the ever hotter
room. Already draped in a cloak of defeat, I slumped in my
chair and stared longingly at the ice block before noticing
something I had not seen before. At the center of the ice,
suspended like a dark cloud, was an object. It seemed roughly
the size of a fist, but I couldn't make out what it was through
the flickering of the lights, the distortion of the ice block itself, and the cloudiness of my vision.

As I squinted, trying to make out what the object might
be, the wall beyond the block came to life. The faint glow of
the vision offered some relief to the flashing lights above my
head, and on the screen appeared the face of the Provider
himself. Behind the Provider stood the Flag of Our State, the
Greek delta outlined in chains; inside, the setting orb and eye;
behind this but obscured, another flag adorned with wide alternating red and white lines meeting a field of blue, replete

with some sort of white inlays. The Provider's face looked stern and hard, and yet an undeniable smirk began to spread across his wide, full, purplish lips. His large, almost perfect white teeth were stark against the darkness of the room; his wiry black hair with graying sides was cropped tight against his skull, making his large ears more prominent. His dark skin glistened slightly, but I couldn't make out where the light was coming from. As yet, all I could see was his face on a black background.

As I continued to stare at the Provider's face, I began to wonder how such a man could have ever come to power. Was it his twisted claims of equality? Was it the free handouts at the expense of anyone but himself and his ilk? Was it the ignorance of so many supporting his empty promises of change? His smirk grew wider with each second, and with each of those seconds, I saw more and more evil in the man's eyes. They were the darkest of brown, staring a hole through my being. My indoctrination said that he had united the people into one State, that he had created the Progressives and rightfully identified Server and Served alike, stating it was equality that one should serve those less fortunate, even if they must be forced to do so. His rise to power was explosive, like a bomb with a short fuse, the aftermath a vision of change and destruction at the same time. And yet now, seeing him so close, I could not help but wonder how anyone could see that face and not immediately feel fear and distrust. How he had won the hearts of the war-torn world through promises of a better life without the need for work or self-sufficiency, I could never know. A caged animal eventually loses his ability to fend for himself, becomes dependent on his keeper, and becomes his keeper's slave—*And so, here we are, this must be Whitey's soft-slavery.*

When the Provider's smile could grow no wider, two more images appeared on either side of his visage. At first, I thought it was a live image of me. Each screen showed a Server in surgical scrubs, tied to a chair, staring up at an image of the Provider on a wall screen. Before the man was an ice block, slowly melting away as twin vents pumped hot air into the room, lights above him flickering on and off. Then the audio cut in, and I could hear the voice of the Provider berating the man for his disloyalty and treason, his disgust for the man having thoughts of an individual nature, thoughts that freedom meant choice. The words were jumbled and filled with static, but the message was clear. The man in the chair was to be punished, the Provider image on his screen boring a hole through him as mine did me.

As I continued to watch in complete dismay, I tried to note any dissimilarity between the man in the chair and myself, but I could find none. His size, build, and hairstyle all matched my own. His face was hidden, as his back was to me, but each time he turned his head, I thought I could see my own nose peeking out from his profile. Not only that, but I could just barely make out a tiny stain of blood on the man's pant leg, right where my own leg was bleeding from my infected wound and the recent, well-placed kicks from the Black Cats.

As I was still trying to make sense of this image, I noticed one last detail about what could only be my future shown before me, projected on a screen. The ice block was smaller, the pool of water beneath it much wider, closer, much closer to the figure strapped to the chair, the metallic object in the center more visible. As the shouting of the Provider increased in volume and his face raged with disdain, more and more of the water melted away, revealing an almost pineapple-shaped, metallic looking object in the center of the ice. A small loop with a pin was threaded through a spoon-like handle on the side of the object. From the pin hung a line attached to a square block, the block precariously close to falling from the melting ice. Each second the image became clearer, and the block became closer and closer to being released.

I took a moment to glance back at my own ice block. Yes, it was definitely becoming smaller, but wasn't close to being as small as the block portrayed on the screen. Meanwhile, my own Provider continued to grin down at me, eyes alight with sickly pleasure, enjoying my squirming and struggling, chuckling in twisted pleasure, knowing that I wanted to look away from my seemingly future self and yet unable to do so out of sheer curiosity and desperation. Smaller and smaller the ice block in the video became, and wider and wider the pool on the ground grew. The voice of the Provider on the screen became more insistent, but more indistinct. I could no longer make out individual words through the static, but I could feel his emotions wash over me in waves. Anger, fury, and wrath came through the video, tearing into my soul like a festering parasite. The man tied to the chair, chided by the Provider, deemed guilty by the Provider, forced to endure punishment and torture, but for what reason? Had he rebuked the Provider and stolen to save his own self?

I wanted to cry out in warning to my other self, to somehow will him out of his bonds so he could run to freedom, but no amount of wishing on my part could make this happen. I began to yell at the image, ordering the man, myself, to break free, to run, run as fast and far as he could. All the while, the Provider laughed a sickly laugh, louder and louder as my screams broke through the heat of the air and the chill of the ice. At last, the ice block on the screen melted to a point exposing the metal block. Breaking free of the ice, it fell to the floor, pulling the pin from the spoon, which gave way to a tinny pop as the spoon sprung free of the pineapple object, splashing into the puddle below. The future Provider's voice hushed. He grinned wide like the Provider in my own room was now doing. My future self struggled, pulled at his bonds, shook his head side to side, trying to escape, screaming, "I am an individual and I am free!" It was only at that moment, when it was far too late to look away, that I realized what was about to happen.

The metal object exploded, flame and fragments blasted from the once square block of ice, the concussion echoing through both rooms, and instantly both the video screens were splattered with blood. My future self annihilated before my startled eyes, as I was forced to watch while the heat of the room melted away my own death's icy keep. And so my ending was not destined to be the agony of heatstroke, but something entirely more sinister.

"No…" I eventually whispered.

The images to the side of my Provider flickered out, and his face came even closer to the camera, staring down at me with his constant, unending grin, his image filling the wall from floor to ceiling. The lights in the room stopped flickering and instead grew intensely bright, so bright that I slammed my eyes shut in response. When at last I opened them, I blinked a few times. I looked down to see chunks of flesh and globs of blood splattered around the room. Bits of muscle, sinew, and bone hung from various parts of my scrubs, stuck by the warmth of the humid air. I screamed in horror, violently shaking my chair in an attempt to shake the bits of carnage away, to put any distance between myself and the remnants of the dead man, remnants of my apparent future.

The Provider spoke: "Server Huxley," he said, grinning down at me, chuckling ominously then pausing. "Welcome to your inquisition."

A few moments of silence followed, during which I could do nothing but watch as the Provider's face gradually changed from an all-consuming grin to a sinister, piercing grimace. Despite the intense heat, I began to shiver. His brow furrowed, his wide lips became taught, and the lighting in the room dropped back down to the previous level. The lights above my head began to flicker, and I watched in horror as the exact scene I had just witnessed began to play itself out before my eyes in real time.

The ice block gradually shrank, drip by drip, slowly revealing the instrument of my death within.

"You have only a few minutes before this icy grip on your life melts away to pain and death, Server Huxley," the Provider said, his voice low and ominous. "I suggest you answer my questions truthfully."

In reply, I simply shook my head and tried all the harder to free myself from my bonds, tugging frantically at my ropes as they dug into the flesh on my wrists and ankles.

"What is your right, Server?" the Provider said, voice still low. "Is it your right to be served? Is it your right to comfort, medicine, and entertainment?"

The ice block dripped more water to the floor as I struggled, raging to break free, barely hearing the questioning of the evil Provider.

"No, you worthless mule, you expendable tool, that is not your right. Your right is to serve, to enjoy freedom from all your petty wants and desires, to work for the betterment of Our State. You are the animal on whose back our society stands. Do you understand, maggot?"

I pulled as hard as I could against the ropes, but they seemed to grow tighter and tighter the more I struggled.

"It is your duty to serve," the Provider said. "Your duty is to serve until you die. You once served in a Medical Rights Facility, helping the sick gain their strength, helping the Served enjoy the comfort of the rights I bestowed upon them. But now, you will serve Our State in your death. Serve to remind your brethren what happens to them if they defy the System. Watch as the reality of your death grows closer with each drop. Watch, slave!"

The tool of my death was now half exposed, the block attached to the pin growing ever more precarious as its captive grip of ice slowly dissipated and receded.

"What do you have to say for yourself, Server? Where does a maggot like you get the idea that he can somehow cheat the System, usurp the rights of others?"

My body was quickly losing its remaining strength as I shook my head side to side, my arms and legs becoming flaccid as the surge of adrenaline neared the end of its run, its effects all but diminished.

"Answer me, Server!" the Provider yelled, face all but touching the camera, appearing so close as if I would be showered with spittle as he raged. I could almost feel his breath on my face, foul with the rank stench of tyrannical power lust. "What kinds of obtrusive thoughts are you having? What kind of rebellion have you fostered in that tiny brain of yours? Why do you openly defy the one who provides you with rights? Speak!"

"I... I..." I managed to mutter, my eyes transfixed on the slowly disappearing block of ice.

"Only a few moments now, slave," the Provider said, his voice now calm, but commanding. "Only a few moments before death consumes you and you will be free. Is that what you seek—freedom other than the freedom to serve? Do you know what will happen then, after the flea that you are is no longer? Life will continue without you. Our State will go on. No one will miss you. You will do nothing more but serve to instill fear in your fellow Servers, a fear that will keep them from ever defying me. Your death will be your final act of service." The Provider then roared with laughter. "In life or in death, you are still nothing but a Server, a slave. There is nothing you can do. Fight or die, you still serve me!"

"No, no, no!" I said, shaking my head from side to side, my mind instantly flashing back to the moment Jules and I kissed. She would miss me, she would notice my departure. I was not alone or unnoticed, simply fit to serve and to die. *Serving her is serving myself, which is my freedom, a freedom the Provider knows nothing of, nor could ever understand.* I could love. I could live. I could do more than serve his system. I had to live. I had to live!

"What thoughts are running through your head?" the Provider yelled. "What gives you a will to live? Why do you struggle when you know that it is I who has control? My right is to rule, yours is to serve. Answer me! What are you thinking? Why take the medicine? Why defy the system? What is the source of your rebellion?"

"I want to live! I want true freedom!" I shouted, the strength to fight the ropes reduced to an occasional tug.

"You live to serve!" the Provider replied. "Do you feel as though you somehow deserve more than the rights Our State has provided you, which I have provided you? Do you feel unfit for the responsibility of serving, as if you could go any lower? Do you have thoughts of selfishness and desire, of a freedom other than that which I have so graciously bestowed upon you?"

The Provider's next words came out at almost a whisper.

"Well, that desire is about to be snuffed out. Prepare yourself. The time of your departure is at hand. You are now free to leave this world."

As the words left his mouth, the lights in the room brightened once again, the television shutting off as they did, the Provider's image vanishing from sight. Sweat seemed to emanate from every pore of my body as the vents continued to pump more and more heat into the room. The ice block was now practically streaming with water, my death completely visible, as the block attached to the pin finally fell from its icy hold. As it struck the floor, splashing the puddle of cool water, the pin came lose, popping the spoon away to initiate the detonation.

I gave one final, desperate struggle against my ropes, screaming in fear, urinating the last fluids my body seemed to contain through my surgical scrubs. Time slowed to a near standstill as the seconds ticked by. One second... I pulled hard with my right arm, feeling the ropes dig into my skin. Two seconds... I sat, eyes opened wide, staring at my future as it sat cradled in the remains of the all but melted block of ice. Three seconds... I pulled violently with my feet, feeling the chair lift off the ground, stripping the bolts from the floor, but not taking me anywhere that could provide safety from my approaching doom. My world came to a standstill, and my entire life boiled down to just me, that bloody room, and the object that sat before me, waiting to explode.

I closed my eyes; pictures of Jules flooded my mind as I waited for the explosion to consume me, to send me to a place free from this servitude, a place without her, alone again.

Jules... her face, her lips, the touch of her skin and the feeling of her body pressed to mine, my last thoughts I had expected.

Six seconds... no explosion.

Seven, eight, nine seconds... My heart continued to pound while my mind wandered, my thighs hot from the urine and steaming humidity of the room, nostrils filled with the stench of ammonia, charred flesh, and sweat.

Ten seconds, then eleven. I opened my eyes, squinting to see the object lying on the table before me, awaiting the explosion. The pin was out, spoon lying on the floor behind the table. I should have been done already.

Fifteen seconds... My head was swimming in muck, my senses fading, I was all but spent and nothing left within me. I saw the Provider's face appear on the screen once again as my eyes rolled up within my sagging head.

"Today, I have provided you with continued life—freedom... from death," he said, and then his image disappeared.

Just then, the door behind me swung open, slamming into the wall with a deafening crash. A shudder went through me as I prepared for a beating. A Black Cat stepped into the room, silent, cool, and calm. A blast of cold air followed him, slapping at my back and head, punching an ounce of life back into my toppled frame, leaving me shivering at the instant jump from heat to cold. The Cat grabbed my arm and cut my binds with a knife, then pushed me off the chair. I crashed forward onto the floor, sprawled in a whining and crying stupor for several moments. I lay there, covered in sweat and piss, wanting to do nothing more than hold Jules in my arms and have her tell me everything would be okay. But nothing would ever be okay again, ever.

The Black Cat grabbed me by my neck, hoisted me up, and pulled me toward the far wall, tying my hands to a small loop of metal that protruded from the blood-splattered tiles high above the floor. A moment later, my scrub pants were ripped down from my waist and I felt a large needle jammed through my flesh into my right buttock. I could tell the plunger was being depressed as the pressure in my gluteus increased and the muscle burned. For a moment, I wondered if they were giving me some kind of sedative or painkiller, or the Provider had lied and it was some type of lethal concoction. Several moments passed and I felt no difference. My heart continued to beat. I continued to draw air into my lungs. I could still feel the pain bouncing around within every inch of my body.

"Antibiotic," the Black Cat said, "but that won't help with what's to come."

Seconds later, a snapping sound informed me that my leg wound would not be the only reason for the injection of antibiotics. The whip cracked in the air above my head, giving me just enough warning to brace myself before the next snap of the whip landed squarely on my back. The fabric of my scrub top tore instantly. The tightly wound straps of leather at the end of the whip cut into my skin. My voice was already hoarse from screaming during my inquisition, but I let out a scream all the same. The pain was intense, unlike anything I'd yet experienced.

"How many lashes for you, Server?" the Black Cat said, bringing the whip down on my back a second time. I could already see drops of my own, real blood falling to the floor as my head drooped between my tied arms.

A moment of silence followed, and then the third lash landed on my back, tearing more flesh beneath my paper-thin garment.

"Ahhhhhhhhhhhhhhhhh!" I screamed.

"How many?"

"I... I... I don't know," I cried, tears running down my face and mixing with the blood, sweat, and urine on the floor.

"Twenty-one lashes!" the Black Cat yelled, cracking the whip over my head again. "One for every hour your patient was forced to have his rights postponed by your rebellion!"

Twenty-one hours? It couldn't have been twenty-one hours already.

The thought was quickly banished from my mind as the next lash landed on my back. On and on the lashing went, until I felt the nerves of my back were themselves exposed and raw. I hoped I would just pass out, slip into a coma, or even die to forego this punishment. Maybe they put something else in my injection to keep me alert, or maybe I was simply too emotionally charged from my interrogation. In either case, I felt each and every lash of that whip, from the first to the twenty-first strike.

When at last the whip had cracked for the final strike, the Black Cat cut the rope holding my hands above me and I collapsed into a heap on the floor. My mind felt muddled from heat, infection, pain, and emotional torment. I was unable to mentally process incoming data, unable to latch onto a single thought, to see images in my mind, realizing that part of my faculties had shut down. Not even Jules would solidify in my psyche, her face coming in and out of focus, intertwined with images of the Provider, the Black Cats, guns, needles, batons, and explosive devices. At that moment, I hated everything and everyone I had ever known, and I didn't even know why, and maybe that's what they wanted. I just knew that anyone who had felt the kind of pain I had endured could do nothing more than curse this upside-down world and wish for death.

But as the Provider had indicated, that was not my fate. My fate was to live, to serve in this same miserable manner that had become my life, the bane of my existence.

I was soon dragged out of the interrogation room to have my wounds bound in clean, white bandages. Whether it was an MSP or some other mysterious Our State representative, I couldn't tell. My eyes were half-closed throughout the entire procedure. I did not possess enough energy to keep them open. Each touch of the cloth brought an intense renewal of the pain followed by small dose of relief, also with it the knowledge that the relief was only meant to prolong my enslaved suffering. The bandages must have been impregnated with some type of gel, as they soothed the stinging flesh shortly after they made initial contact. Somehow I had always imagined the punishment for rebellion to be quick and painless, an instant end to life, Our State spending the least amount of time and resources to extinguish the unnecessary, fruitless, unworthy life. I had never imagined what lengths Our State would go to in order to keep the Servers in line. It was truly terrifying. In those moments, all I could think of was how much I wanted to get back to my cold bunkhouse, how sweet it would be to eat our worthless gruel and repeat endless diatribes on the virtues of service, without the threat of more violence save the occasional wallop from a Black Cat.

But even then, as the bandaging was complete and I was moved along another corridor, I realized that the Provider's attempts at intimidation would be unsuccessful. I had something no other Server had: I had Jules.

And Jules was worth even this pain. Jules was worth everything to me, and I would endure a thousand lashes if it meant feeling her lips caress mine once again.

As that thought fluttered in and out of my conscious thought, not fully materializing, I finally felt my strength give out, and I passed into unconsciousness.

I awoke on a train, surrounded by Black Cats. The steely snake chugged along in a familiar way, and by the view of gray skies as I peered up out the window, I knew I was being returned to the tenement. Several minutes passed before the Black Cats noticed that I was awake.

"Consider yourself lucky to be alive, Server," one of them said. "I've seen others get far worse than you received for far less of an offense."

I simply nodded in reply, and the Black Cat scoffed, shaking his head.

The train soon came to a halt, and I was tossed out through the door, down onto the snow-covered platform. There was a brief moment of silence, then the train full of Black Cats pulled its doors shut and continued down the track to the far end of the tenement. I rolled onto my side to minimize the pain emanating from my back, only to see an entire crowd of Servers looking over at me. My heart leapt into my throat when I noticed Jules among them. As was customary amongst the Servers, they succumbed to their ingrained fears and turned their heads away from me, unwilling to subject themselves to the wrath of the Black Cats if they were to offer assistance. Jules stared at me, my beaten body a bloody, swollen lump thrown onto the snowy concrete. Her hands covered her mouth as tears began to flow from her warm eyes.

I tried to give my angel a look of warning, but her eyes were already filled with tears, obscuring her view as she approached.

"Step away," I moaned. "You'll get yourself in trouble."

"Oh, my love," she sobbed. "What has happened to you? What have they done?"

"I'm okay—no time to explain. We have to escape... soon."

"Get away from him, Server!" a Black Cat yelled as he stepped out from the depot.

Jules startled and let out a little yelp.

"Go away, go away," I moaned more forcefully. "I love you, but go—"

"Move! Move, Server!" the Black Cat yelled as he began to walk toward us.

"I love you, Hux," Jules whispered as she scampered off toward the rows of Servers that were marching toward the sustenance hall.

The Black Cat continued toward me, stopping at my back and looking down over me as a towering giant upon an ant. He swung his leg back and thrust it forward, slamming his boot into the small of my back.

"Get your sorry ass moving, Server, and stop bleeding all over my platform!"

Chapter 10

That night, I slept entirely on my stomach, the pain in my back still pulsing from the lashings I received earlier in the day, a dull ache throbbing in the small of my back from the welcome-home kick on the train platform. My thoughts drifted back and forth between the events of the day and what the future might hold. I saw the Provider's face often, his evil grin looking down on my suffering with malicious and perverse joy. My mind also filled with images of explosive devices, dark prison cells, Jules's eyes staring into mine, and that tiny compartment beneath the train where we could hide. I didn't know where we would go from there or how we would survive, but at that moment, it was the only thing that I held onto.

After what seemed like hours of clouded thoughts, I drifted into an uneasy sleep, where the same collage of images continued to float through my wind. With them came a torrent of vivid sensations: the sound of steadily dripping water and the metallic taste of blood in my mouth, the voice of the Provider taunting me. I heard him boast about his control over my fate and the immutability of the System. I was but a lamb and it was he who decided the date of my slaughter. At times, my hands were still bound to the metal chair, while other times, I stood before him tall, proud and resistant. Sometimes Jules was even at my side, standing with me in defiance rather than in fear, her screaming voice of rebellion shattering his hardened image.

Ultimately, I awoke to the morning alarm, feeling physically and mentally drained and still feverish. The antibiotics they had injected me with were not enough to wipe out my infection. The laceration on my leg, the torn flesh on my upper back, and the contusion on my lower back now throbbed with pain. I wondered if perhaps I had been wrong about them wanting me alive, if maybe they just wanted the others to see me up and walking for a day or so before my infections spread and I died in my bunk. For some reason, I didn't believe that was what the Provider had intended. He clearly wanted me to live, to continue serving, to continue providing in his name. I would have to devise some way of treating my wounds and tackling this infection once and for all, of course without subjecting myself to another round of torture.

Darkness still enveloped the bunkhouse as the Black Cats had not yet raised the steel shutters. The thought struck me to discuss some of my experiences with Arnold. I rolled myself over and reached out to initiate a little communication. My hand fell on the straw that was strewn across his bunk space. Moving my hand back and forth, I felt nothing, his bunk space was empty. I lifted my head slowly and looked around the bunkhouse as the shutters began to rise and light worked its way in through the ever-widening window space, seeking his face. It was nowhere to be found. Arnold was gone. I tried to remember if I had seen him the previous evening, if he had been one of the Servers to help me into my bunk, but everything was a haze, every face in my mind a blur without features. There were so many hands, so many faces, it was impossible to remember. Maybe he had received an overnight assignment or was sent out early for some special task. I could only hope that he hadn't done something to receive the same treatment I had.

I finally raised myself out of my bunk and lowered my unsteady self to the cold floor, joining the other Servers in our morning routine. While I was not nearly as shaky as I had been in the days before, I could feel that my senses were dull and my movements slow. I removed my bandages for my shower. For once, I was thankful for the cold water, as it both stung and soothed the lashes on my back. I turned to face the showerhead, allowing the cold water to splash against my face, believing that it would help wash away some of the cloudiness that muddied my mind.

Then my head was thrust into the grimy, mildewed tiles. I felt a hard object pushing against the base of my skull.

"Hold still, Server. Let me get a look at those lash wounds," a Black Cat said as he pressed his baton into my neck. "Yeah, they're good enough." He released the pressure on my neck and turned away, yelling to one of my brethren in the shower area. "You, Server, grab those bandages and put them in this bag." The Black Cat commanded the Server from bunk space four.

"Yes, sir, right away," the Server said as he scampered to pick up my bloodied bandages. Naked and shivering from the cold water, my brethren looked toward me, offering a look of apology. I tipped my head to him as he shoved my bandages into the bag.

The Black Cat grabbed the bag and laughed. "Carry on, slaves!"

No bandages for the day. *I should have known.* Relieving me of my bandages was just another display of their power in relation to our utter cowardice and inability to defend ourselves. This fact hardly shocked me.

During the morning meal and exercises, I strained my eyes for any sign of Jules, but I couldn't spot her in the crowds of the exercise yards or the sustenance hall. Even though this had hardly been an uncommon occurrence up to this point, I still found her absence distressing. It might have been because of my experiences the previous day or it might have simply been that my fears were compounded by the absence of Arnold in the morning. Either way, I spent the rest of the morning seeking her face in the masses, jumping up at every woman's head I saw that resembled her from behind. Eventually, I was forced to give up my search, for fear of being noticed by the Black Cats. *Maybe that's it!* Hadn't she approached me on the platform yesterday? Had the Black Cat seen us talking... or did he think it was simply pity on her part? Had she, too, been taken? Had Arnold?

Jules is safe. She has to be.

I spent most of my train ride with twitching legs, bouncing nervously, my eyes darting around the train car from face to face. She should always be in the same car, but I couldn't find her. If the Black Cats had noticed my strange behavior, then they clearly either didn't care or attributed it to my torture the day before. They carried on as normal, remaining silent unless some other Server gave them a look they didn't like. Then the customary screaming and beatings that characterized Black Cats outside the Progressives got underway.

When we reached Progressive 17, I could hardly believe my eyes. Not because of some drastic change in the way everyone was acting. On the contrary, I was struck with an undeniable sense that everything should be different but wasn't. After everything I had gone through, I somehow expected the world to be different than it had been before, that nothing would ever be the same again. But no, the torture and interrogation of one lowly medical provider was little more than a blip on the radar of a much larger mechanism. The Progs continued to be served, and the Servers continued to be berated and abused, forced to provide for the undeserving, the parasitic, the Progs. My life, my existence, had scant effect on the System, and I was watching this fact play itself out before my weary eyes.

But if everyone knew what I knew, if they knew we were all slaves, the Servers and Served alike, what then? Would things continue unchanged?

That one thought continued to ping off the walls of my mind with each pulsing of pain as my fellow MSPs and I climbed the stairs to the Medical Rights Facility. The others went about their routine as normal, somber downcast eyes focused on the steps in front of them, no sparks of purpose in their actions, never once asking me about my absence the day before when they returned down these same steps without me. Part of me wondered if they even noticed I was gone, but more than likely, I assumed, they simply were too afraid to ask. Asking questions got people killed.

When we reached the top of the steps, a wave of dizziness ran through my body, so strong that I was forced to grab the railing to keep from falling. The exertion of climbing so many steps with so many injuries had taken of its toll on me; my legs became flaccid as I grasped the handrail tighter and tighter. As I stood for a few moments shaking the cobwebs from my head, leaning unsteadily against the stairwell wall, my fellow Servers continued to ignore my condition. They all went through the main door ahead of me, getting their assignments and heading down to sanitize and change into their jumpsuits and coats. I followed shortly thereafter, moving at a relative snail's pace to avoid any further dizziness. I would need my wits about me for the day ahead. My body would not tolerate another lashing if I was unable to perform the carotid surgery this morning—if it hadn't already been completed by another MSP.

The grogginess continued to follow me down the hall and into the locker room, knocking at my joints, slapping at my brain, playing havoc with my nerves as waves of nausea crashed against me from time to time. When I came to my cubby, I found its contents ruffled and haphazardly put in place. Clearly the Black Cats had come searching for something the day before, perhaps to search for more medication, perhaps to search for notes, plans, who knows what, but I knew there was nothing to find. I said a quiet thanks to whatever cleaning person had removed Hemsworth's note from my coat pocket. If that had been found, I might never have been allowed to return to the tenement, and there would not have been a reprieve from the explosion. Jules would then truly be alone, scared and alone, faced with a life of unrelenting, unappreciated servitude.

I stepped out of the locker room after my steam sanitizing and clean clothes, and was immediately met by an administrator who smiled sweetly at me as she handed me my assignment: carotid surgery, in less than an hour.

I continued to sway from my weakness, falling backward slightly.

"How long has Mr. Benson been waiting?" I said.

The administrator looked back at me with confusion in her eyes. "This will put it at twenty-one hours late," she said. "You're the only MSP familiar with his case. When that emergency took you away yesterday, we immediately rescheduled his surgery for today. I thought you'd be pleased."

"Of... Of course," I said, trying to smile despite my worries. "I'll get down to the examination room immediately."

Twenty-one hours. Twenty-one hours, twenty-one lashings.

My worries were verified almost from the moment I entered the exam room to find Mr. Benson waiting. I hardly had a chance to mutter a hello before he slammed me into the

wall. My entire back erupted in pain as it struck the hard surface, and for a few moments, I could not even make out the
words that the Prog was screaming in my face. I felt his heated words on my cheeks before my ears finally cleared and I
was able to take in what he was saying.

"… a right to be served, you filthy Server scum!" Benson
yelled, grabbing the collar of my lab coat. "I have a right to
health care, not you! If you ever think about stealing medicine
again, I'll have you beaten to bloody pulp, you hear me? Do
you hear meeee?"

"I… I…" said as my body and mind tried to make sense
of the intense pain coming from my back.

"You what?" Benson said, mocking my apparent fear.
"You're sorry? You'll never do it again? Well, you BETTER
NOT. You think I don't have the ability to make your life a
living misery? You think one word from me wouldn't see you
beaten so bad that no one would recognize you for a month?
Well, if you ever deny me my rights again, then you're going
to find out just how wrong you are, Server!"

With that, Benson gave me one last shove and released
the collar of my jumpsuit. For a few moments, there was silence between us, as he was still huffing in anger. I was thankful to not be bleeding all over the floor. I looked up at the
Prog before me; I saw the anger and confusion deep inside his
eyes. I wondered how much he actually knew about the System he'd spent his entire life coddled in.

"Are… Are you not perfectly blissful?" I said.

It was the only question I could think of at the time. The
only question I could ask that wouldn't seem out of the ordi-
nary.

"What, are you some kind of Server wiseass? Do I look
blissful?" Benson said, turning to me as if he was going to

throw me against the wall again. "Bliss is for the ignorant, for those mindless sheep out there."

He then motioned in the direction of the main hallway, beyond the window, where the unending stream of blue jumpsuits peppered with an occasional blue flowed by. A thousand little slaves all going about their lives, unaware of how little freedom they had, unaware that their parasitism was just another form of slavery, dependent on the food and service handouts of the Provider, their master. I wondered if Benson was equally aware of how much of a slave he also was. My mind flashed back to my days of indoctrination; we were studying avian flu strains. We were shown images of various birds in cages. I remember a grand, proud-looking macaw in a palatial cage, adorned with all kinds of treats and playthings. Alongside it sat a small plastic cage with a small parakeet inside—no treats and no toys. My brethren oohed and aahed over the macaw's cage, how wonderful it was, how spacious and well appointed, all the while failing to see that despite the chasm of difference between their respective abodes, ultimately both birds were caged. Both had lost their innate abilities for survival, both had come to rely on their masters for handouts, both were simply slaves to their providers' folly.

Just as I began to process the existence of another Served who understood the System as Hemsworth and I, despite his ignorance of the fact that he was also part of the system, I heard a sound I had never heard in all my life. The Black Cat standing in the corner cleared his throat, turning his head toward Benson. It was an action I always thought too soft and too subtle for one of their kind, as even those Black Cats who worked in the Progressives typically remained silent. There was no force or threat behind the action, just a simple reminder to Benson that said, "Remember where you are, remember what you are, and remember what you are not."

Benson looked at the Black Cat and gave a subtle nod. "As I said, I am *perfectly* blissful," he mumbled unconvincingly, appeasing our sentry.

I wanted to open my mouth and object, to force him to pursue the topic further. I had so many questions that I didn't have the time or opportunity to ask Hemsworth, and now here was a man that the Black Cats didn't feel the need to carry away and perform some obscene procedure on. Every person in the room, in fact, was in on the joke that was the System. I wondered why we couldn't all just take a few moments to recognize it and discuss our respective fates. Nonetheless, I fought back a wild smirk at the fact that a Served had just been put in his place by a Black Cat. *Now who's the slave? Although my wings may have been clipped, I have been beyond this cage. I still maintain the ability of thought. I possess self-sufficiency. I am an individual. I will learn to fly and I will be free.*

Seconds later, the Black Cat motioned us to carry on. Benson slipped into the all too familiar act of the blissful served, asking questions about the day's surgery in a tone that only hinted at his previous anger and dissatisfaction. We went through all the information we reviewed the day before in the exact same detail, walking through the motions of MSP and patient with precision. The only difference this time was I hadn't the fear of a team of Black Cats busting in and dragging me off to some nightmare factory.

Once the procedure had been reviewed again, we each moved from the office. Benson was led to the pre-operative room for placement of IV line, an arterial line, and initiation of a normal saline infusion. I walked to the surgical suite to prepare and scrub in. My hands were once again scrubbed down, my surgical gown placed over my outstretched arms, and the long surgical gloves were placed over my hands by the same MSN who served as my assistant the previous day. I noticed this time, however, that she refused to look me in the eye. In fact, her entire demeanor was one of caution and nervousness, far separated from the near robotic motions Benson and I had gone through beforehand. She was obviously still shaken from the events of the previous day, terrified to be working with someone who was clearly an enemy of Our State, an individual as opposed to a link in the Progressive's interwoven chain.

Doing my best to ignore her obvious fear of my criminal status, I instructed her to initiate sedation and skin prep. Benson's head had already been strapped into the intubation holding tray. The mechanical arm swung over his throat, and the ultrasound strobe mapped a three-dimensional image of his trachea down to the carina. The sedation unit instantaneously determined the exact diameter for the endotracheal tube. The second arm positioned itself over his oral cavity as the head-well tilted back, hyper-extending his neck. With his sedation initiated and the paralytic having taken effect, the unit eased a straight blade into his open oral cavity. The endotracheal tube slid to twenty-one centimeters and the balloon was inflated, sealing the space between his trachea and the outside of the ET tube. Ventilations began based on the continuous, real-time arterial blood gas readings from an arterial line previously placed in his right radial artery. The room was quiet except for the low hum of computerized monitoring equipment and the spoken instructions between me and the MSN.

"Is the concentrated antibiotic irrigation ready?" I asked in a cordial manner.

"Yes, MSP Huxley, three liters hanging to your right," she said.

She continued to act nervously, almost dropping equipment when our hands came close to touching. When she nearly allowed the sharp end of a scalpel to cut the patient, I considered requesting a new MSN. Unfortunately, doing so would further infuriate Benson and draw more unwanted attention to myself.

"I'm sorry I make you nervous," I said in a whisper.

She said nothing in return, refusing to look me in the eye.

"I did what I did because I was afraid of dying," I said. "But I don't plan to bring any more trouble to you or this Medical Rights Facility. All I want to do is complete Mr. Benson's procedure, all right?"

Fortunately, there were none of the Provider's eyes and ears in the surgical suites of the Medical Rights Facility; the Progs would view it as an invasion of the right to privacy. Finally the Prog rights had actually been of benefit to me. No Black Cats, no unnecessary personnel were allowed in the surgical suite for both privacy and safety. Although there was a small window for viewing purposes, the anesthesia machine obscured the vision of the Black Cat beyond the door, so our conversation was safe.

I reached out for the scalpel again. There was a moment's pause, during which once again, the only sound to be heard was the gentle humming of the monitoring equipment. The MSN then nodded, placed the scalpel firmly in my hand, and returned to some semblance of a professional demeanor.

I was just beginning to think that the surgery would go smooth this time when another wave of dizziness swept through my body as I leaned down to make the first incision. I shook my head, paused; again I moved in to make the incision. This time, my hand began to shake violently as it neared Benson's skin. My fever was worsening, sweat beginning to bead on my forehead already. I called for the nurse to wipe the sweat away, took a few deep breaths, and steadied my hand. It still shook, but I slowly reached toward Benson's left carotid. I could see the vessel pulse with every beat of his heart. I initiated the incision and worked distally for approximately eight centimeters. I reached over and grabbed the irrigation syringe and directed a stream at the incision I'd just completed.

"Sponge please, MSN," I said as I replaced the syringe on the sterile tray.

I took a moment to recompose myself as the MSN sponged the fresh incision. I gingerly pulled the incision open, allowing visualization of the carotid.

"Clamps," I said to the still overly nervous MSN.

Despite her fears, she slapped the clamp in my hand with almost robotic precision. I placed the first clamp distal, checking the artery for a pulse beyond the clamp. With nothing palpated, I placed the second clamp proximal to the first.

I looked up at the irrigation bag as the MSN busied herself organizing the instruments in anticipation of my next order. I reached up and shoved the irrigation syringe needle through the port on the bag and drew out the plunger to refill the syringe. *I've got to do it.* With the MSN's back to me, I pulled down the back of my sterile pants and thrust the irrigation needle into my right buttock, wincing as it pierced through my skin and muscle. I'd just have to chance it that it didn't end up in a vessel. I depressed the plunger breathing harder and harder as the antibiotic dense irrigation fluid was forced into my gluteus. I was breathing heavier and heavier with the pain, hoping I would not pass out. After injecting as much as I could tolerate, I pulled the needle out and dropped it to the floor. The MSN turned around at the sound of the syringe bouncing of the floor tiles. She let out an irritated sigh, realizing what I was going to say.

"MSN, I dropped the irrigation syringe. Please draw up another," I said, still huffing and puffing through my mask.

"Yes," she replied in a blunt tone, expressing how much she was inconvenienced.

I picked up the scalpel and began to incise the carotid, slicing easily though the tunica layers. The degree of calcification was astounding. It was surprising he had any circulation through this vessel at all. *Maybe that's why he is such a halfwit,* I thought and allowed myself a little chuckle. The MSN looked up and I could see the frown on her eyebrows. I looked down and continued.

My dizziness and bouts of tremors continued. Unfortunately, if Benson was to survive, I had to move much slower. Every few minutes, I was forced to pause, taking a moment to allow my head to clear. More than once, I forgot entirely what part of the surgery we were in, having to examine my own work as a frame of reference. Not once did I ask the MSN any question that might have given away my struggle. To do so would likely put her back into shakes, which would have only compounded my current issues secondary to my infection, beatings, and lashings. I needed to be able to rely on her for the duration of the procedure—no more delays, and no more lashings.

I managed to continue despite my issues. I removed a great deal of calcified cholesterol from Benson's carotid. After suturing his artery, I nearly unclamped the proximal clamp before the distal, but caught myself at the last second. With the distal unclamped, I verified the sutures were holding and no sign of bleeding was present, allowing me to unclamp the proximal. I gave the area a final irrigation then pulled the closure unit over.

"Approximation," I said to the MSN.

She reached over and pulled the incision together so the edges were well approximated. I snapped a staple at two places along the approximation line. As the MSN removed her hands, I aligned the closure unit over the area and depressed the ready button. The machine sealed itself over Benson's surgical area and initiated the sealing process. Once the green light illuminated, I pulled the unit back to see that the incision site had been sutured, staples removed, and a layer of cyanoacrylate medical adhesive applied over the suture line.

Perfect, I thought, despite nearly passing out a dozen times.

"Reverse sedation and extubate," I said to the MSN as I pulled off my gloves. "Thank you for your assistance."

She said nothing, simply selected the reverse sedation on the machine and began gathering up the instruments for inventory.

Benson stirred, moving his head from side to side as the sedation and paralytic were being reversed. The intubation tray hyper-extended his neck again as the endotracheal tube was withdrawn. He began to cough as suction wands scoured his mouth and throat.

"What the hell!" Benson yelled while flailing his arms, coughing and spluttering.

"Whoa, whoa, everything thing is okay, Mr. Benson," I said. "We're all done here. You're just coming out of the sedation. Relax."

"How did everything go?" Benson said, still waving his hands around at imaginary objects.

"Well, Mr. Benson, everything went well." I said, looking up at the MSN who was removing her gown, shaking her head.

"Lucky for you, Server, lucky for you," he said.

"MSN, please wheel Mr. Benson to recovery." I removed my gown, thinking, *Now he's a full wit, but just as stupid.*

As the MSN wheeled Benson away to the recovery room, I stood for a few moments alone in the surgical suite. I wondered what could have possessed me to steal antibiotics again, after everything I had gone through the day before. Any moment, the interrogator could return, have me whipped, dragged off to that torture chamber again for more psychological manipulation. I had been a fool to steal again, a desperate fool, to use my knowledge to know how to save my own life, to take that which I needed to survive and still to be a fool. And yet I also knew, beyond the shadow of a doubt, that there was no way Jules and I could escape if I wasn't healthy.

I threw my gown, gloves, and mask into the red biohazard bag and headed out into the hall. Just as I pulled the door shut behind me, however, another massive wave of dizziness came over me and I dropped to my knees. I shook my head, trying for the thousandth time to shake free of this mind cloud. This time, however, the feeling only intensified. I had labored too hard and too long while too ill, and I couldn't fight anymore. The only thing I remembered after that was the pain on the side of my face as it struck the floor, then blackness.

I awoke in the bunkhouse. My face was still sore, and judging by the darkness all around me, it was night. I had no idea how I had come to be here, though the Black Cats likely had a few other MSPs carry me to the train. Looking around, I could make out other bunkmates asleep in their bunks, a few snoring quietly. I reached my arm out to my side, found emptiness. Arnold's bunk remained empty. Surrounded by people, I was alone.

I actually got away with it, I thought, the first coherent thought to cross my mind since coming to my senses. I had managed to usurp the right of health care from Our State without being caught or captured. I had defied the system and gotten away with it. The Black Cats had every opportunity to arrest me when I'd been unconscious, and yet they returned me here. They did not know I had stolen from Benson, from the Progressive, the Progs, or the Provider. They did not know everything after all. And that meant Jules and I had a chance, which was all we needed.

I lay awake for a few hours after that, unable to sleep after being out for so long. Without Arnold there, I had no one to communicate with. Instead, I simply lay on my stomach, dreaming of what life would be like for Jules and me after we escaped our slavery. Where would we go? What would we do?

Finally, when at last even I grew tired of those thoughts, I simply lay there, tapping one word over and over again onto my leg.

Freedom… Freedom… Freedom…

Chapter 11

Over the next few days, I kept a close watch on my wounded leg. It seemed as though the antibiotics were finally doing the trick. The redness had significantly decreased, swelling diminished, and the area was no longer warm to the touch. My legs felt stronger under my body, and the shaking in my hands had all but calmed. As yet, it didn't appear that Benson or the Black Cats had discovered what I had done, and for the moment, I was simply thankful that my desperate impulse had paid off. I would go on living, and it would be because I had chosen to act—not because the Provider had knowingly allowed it. Nonetheless, it was merely surviving and serving; it was not what I would henceforth consider as living.

With my strength returning, I made a final decision about my time at Progressive 17: it would end. I would be in charge of my future, of my life. I would leave this curse behind. Every morning routine, every forced exaltation of the morality of service, every dollop of gruel, every lazy and agitated Prog, every Black Cat staring at me through reflective lenses… They had all become like shackles to me, dead weight that needed to be cast off. Freedom was the one thought that pulsed through my mind every second of every day, true freedom where I was the master of my own destiny, not the wants passed off as rights of a Collective of undeserving beings. I thought through every possible means of escape, trying not to miss any variable that might get in the way, might hinder our chances. Ultimately, though, I kept coming back to the compartment below the train. It would be the only way to safely hide and slip away. I could only be thankful that it would accommodate the both of us.

Several more days passed before Jules and I were positioned on the train in such a way that allowed us to talk, but when the opportunity presented itself, I wasted no time. My strength had now all but returned, and I was ready. Our car was packed extra tight that day, thanks to some sort of breakdown with one of the rear cars, which left an unusually tight crowd of Servers between us and the Black Cat that forced his way through the train car. As soon as the rattling of the cattle cars began, I swiftly reached my hand over to Jules only to slow and place it gently on her knee. Her eyes looked up into mine, all the fear and sadness gone, a look of tranquility, of peace and acceptance now there. There was a new strength behind her eyes. She had become aware, and that awareness had dissolved the doubts and hesitations. She had now come into her own.

"Today is the day," I whispered.

"What day?"

"We're leaving, escaping. The compartment under the train, it's big enough for two," I said. "We'll slip down there on the return trip, wait until we're halfway, and then we'll slip out of the compartment, fall on to the tracks, and allow the train to pass over us. Eight minutes... Eight minutes is halfway."

"The train... to pass over us?" she said.

"It'll be fine. There's plenty of room between the wheels and the underside of the car."

A small gap opened in the crowd before us, as one of the Servers began coughing uncontrollably and the others pushed and shoved to get out of his way. Jules and I quickly pulled away from each other, hands out by our sides. Then, as quickly as the gap had appeared, it closed again, unable to sustain itself against the pressure of such a mass of Servers.

"Where will we go? How will we live?" Jules said, taking my hand in hers.

I nodded my head toward the window, where in the distance I could see a charred tree line covered with a light layer of snow. The trees were dead, of course, but they stood tall and dense just the same. The snow was a detriment I chose not to worry Jules with. Once the Black Cats became aware of our escape, they would surely find and follow the tracks, and the image of the runner entered my mind. All I could rely on was the frequent snow falls to cover our path.

"We'll head there, and then figure out what our options are," I said. "You have to make sure you keep your jumpsuit on. Pull your clothes on over it. It'll be cold, and we'll need the layers. Eat as much as possible at midday sustenance and save scraps if you can."

Jules said nothing, but her eyes twitched slightly at my words. A single tear found its way down her cheek, but the smile… the smile said the tear was not born of despair, but from the possibility of a future. The last thing she said to me before the train pulled into the Progressive was a simple "I trust you, Hux."

The train relieved itself with its usual belch of soot and steam. Black Cats were lined up along the platform, ushering the Servers off the train. As our number was called, the Servers who were standing, jammed arm to arm, began to move forward, pushing through the doorway out into the cold morning. As the Servers began to clear, I stood and moved into the aisle, allowing Jules to follow behind me. We touched hands briefly as we were pushed forward. It struck me, stepping off that train, that for better or worse, this would be my last day as a Server in Progressive 17, my last day as a forced member of a Collective, an awakening from the nightmare of indoctrinated ignorance, of serving up false bliss. This would be my last day as a Server of anyone but those I would choose to serve. My brethren had a lifetime of servitude ahead of them—days, months, and years of the same oppression. That was their choice, however. They were so beaten down they had succumbed to fear and complacency years ago and were now nothing more than shells, empty husks that no longer recognized the concept of choice. They would never know love, or freedom. They would never know anything but the hard surface of a Black Cat's baton, the crunching of hard soil beneath their feet, the whining voices of the Progs, and the cold, dark insides of a bunkhouse, surrounded by their ever-weakening fellow Servers.

"Get your ass in line, Server!" a Black Cat yelled as I daydreamed about my final steps from a Server train car.

Startled, I looked back for Jules as I ran toward the line of MSPs awaiting the opening of the tunnel door.

With a loud CLANG, the tunnel door began to pull away from the concrete floor.

"Door opening!" yelled a Black Cat standing to the left of the tunnel. "Get ready for another day of joyous servitude; count yourselves lucky to be alive on such a glorious day!"

Our group mumbled the usual sentiments in response. As the door was raised higher, the warm rush of air pushed against us as it escaped the concrete tunnel and rushed toward freedom in the open landscape. The warmth was welcomed, but it brought an air of trepidation and worry. *Will everything go as planned today? Will something happen to prevent our escape? Will freedom have to wait until another time?* All these thoughts swam around my head as we marched down the tunnel toward the steps rising from the trenches of reality to the fantasy world above where good and evil, vice and virtue exchanged definitions.

The tunnel seemed narrower today, confining, almost suffocating. My brethren around me shuffled along, faces blank, lifeless bodies moving in unison toward their respective duties. *I can't be the only one to question this system. Surely I can't be.* It was so difficult to not just scream in defiance, to let everyone know that I knew, but that would be fruitless and would signal my end, but maybe all it would take was one to open the floodgates, just one to make a positive change. If I died trying, the story would be twisted, perverted, used as propaganda in the media machine of the Progressive.

We arrived at the steps that led up to the Medical Rights Facility. On either side of the entranceway stood a Black Cat armed with a weapon in addition to their baton. I'd never seen this before. I looked off to my side as I passed them, giving them a quick once-over. It seemed as if they did the same, checking me out, turning as I began to ascend the steps. I could feel my palms become moist and my heart begin to make its presence know in my chest. *Calm down, calm down. This has nothing to do with me, nothing to do with Jules.*

Reaching the top of the steps, our line of MSPs made their way toward the medical administrator sitting in the assignment area. And another first: on either side of her, standing like fixed sentinels to a wondrous city, were two Black Cats—again, both had additional weapons. I wiped the palms of my hands on my ragged pant legs and stepped forward as my turn came.

"Good morning, MSP Huxley, here is your first assignment," the administrator said, handing me the portable ERP.

"Thank you," I said, feigning mild excitement while looking down, doing my best to avoid looking directly at the

Black Cats. "It's a wonderful day to serve," I said followed by a halfhearted smile.

"Yes, it is," she replied. "You may proceed to the locker room, sanitize, change, and begin your day of service." She gestured with her head toward the locker rooms.

I nodded in return, keeping my gaze down, away from the sentinels. "My pleasure, indeed."

Soon, I stood motionless in front of my cubby, taking deep breath after deep breath. This would be the last time I would don this red jumpsuit, the last time I would slip into the stark white lab coat, the last time I would act a part in this twisted play. It was an overwhelming feeling. I had what could be considered clothing, what some would call food and a place to sleep, a bed of wooden slats and straw. I was also bestowed by Our State with a purpose. All of this I would give up in exchange for the freedom to choose my own existence, to provide myself the necessities of life on my own terms; that was my purpose. My life was my purpose. Servitude and the State were not.

I noticed the rush of Servers around me, busily donning their Server garb, their skin fresh and sanitized. I snapped out of my momentary daydream and slid into my jumpsuit, slipped on my socks and shoes, grabbed my lab coat and headed toward the door. I pulled on the coat as I reached the door. For some reason, my hands dove into the pockets, moved around and around, hoping to find some remnants of paper, but no, there was still nothing there.

Hemsworth, what were you trying to tell me?

I stepped through the door into the Medical Rights Facility hallway, startled to find another two Black Cats stationed on either side of the hallway. I couldn't recall seeing this many Black Cats on my way to previous assignments. I guessed there must be some type of routine change for their patrols.

With my improved health, I figured I had to be more in tune to subtleties. Surely it couldn't be anything else.

Making my way to my first assignment, I glanced down at my portable ERP. The Server I was about to see would be a routine follow-up from a noninvasive procedure from a few days ago, nothing too in-depth. I had questioned myself over and over again whether or not to gather some medical supplies for our escape: some bandages, a suture kit, topical antibiotics, and tape. With the increased presence of the Black Cats, I decided not to—better to not push it. In the corner of the exam room stood the ever-present, ever-watchful Black Cat, so no chance to gather anything anyway.

With each appointment I was handed, I found a Black Cat within a few yards of where I stood. Every administrator in the building seemed to be shadowed by one, even though the Black Cats usually maintained static positions in every corridor. Today they seemed to mix and flow with the stream of blue and red jumpsuits and white lab coats of Servers and Served, like little black specks of dirt being pushed to the surface of a rushing river. And maybe it was my oversensitive imagination, but it seemed like those black specks were always congregated around one place, denser and more watchful: they were always near me, everywhere I went.

At first, I thought I was just being paranoid, that I was nervous about our planned escape. Psychologically speaking, it made sense. This would be the third time in a month I was planning to break the law. It was reasonable to assume that I would be a bit jumpy. But then there was a definite change in security procedures; this was not a part of an overactive imagination. The Black Cats seemed to be everywhere, around every corner, tucked closely in every room. I couldn't make a move or speak a word without them being nearby. Even the

Server restrooms had a Black Cat standing outside the stalls, just watching.

Several times throughout the day, I would turn a corner and find a Black Cat standing in the center of the hallway, staring in my direction. Servers and Progs would pass them by as if they didn't exist, as if they were just some pillar holding up the ceiling that needed to be walked around but paid no mind. As I walked down the hall, the Black Cat's gaze would stay fixed on the place where I turned the corner, but even so, I couldn't help but feel that they were waiting for me, watching my every move.

Could they know? Could they have somehow overheard Jules and me on the train?

The thought was ridiculous, of course. They couldn't have eyes everywhere, no matter what the Provider may have wanted us to think. Besides, Jules and I had spoken before. We had held hands, held each other close, kissed, and all those things were forbidden. If the Black Cats were able to see my every move, then I was a dead man already. But I couldn't shake the feeling that something more was going on than tighter security. I decided to see Jeremy Paul one last time. I hopefully wouldn't be here long enough to engage in a discussion with him at the sustenance hall, so it had to be now. I had noticed something in him during our last interaction. I had an idea that he knew the system was rigged, somehow flawed—I could sense it. He had knowledge of an older time, so maybe there was something he could tell me.

I found the floor administrator and questioned where I could find MSP Paul. I was informed he was assigned to the Intensive Care Bay. Making my way to the elevator, I tapped on my portable ERP and pulled up the record of the Prog I had just seen in case I was stopped and questioned by a Black

Cat. Stepping in to the elevator, I found a behemoth of a Black Cat stationed in the near corner by the control panel.

"Excuse me, please," I said. "I need floor three. MSP consult."

The Black Cat took a step to his right, leaving just enough room for me to reach the panel and select floor three. He didn't say a word or make any gestures to acknowledge me otherwise; it was as if he were made of steel—black matte steel. I glanced at him out of the corner of my eye. I could see my reflection in his mirrored glasses, a timid man in white in comparison, but I had determination and a newfound purpose.

The elevator arrived at the third floor, and the doors opened to show another Black Cat directly across from the door. I stepped out and headed down the hall toward the Intensive Care Bay. I reached the entrance and placed my hand on the wall scanner. The screen beeped and a green light appeared, then the door slid open into the wall. I had never been in this Intensive Care Bay, but it seemed to be the same as in my previous Progressives. I saw Jeremy Paul through the clear glass doors that separated each of the ICB rooms. It looked as if he was inserting a triple lumen catheter into a Progs internal jugular, a fairly standard ICB procedure to gain access to a Prog's vascular system.

A few moments later, MSP Paul reached up and pulled his sterile gown off, stepped on the actuator to access the red biohazard bin to his left, and threw his gown and gloves in. He then turned toward the door while pulling off his mask. Seeing me standing there, he allowed himself a small smile.

"Hux, great to see you. What brings you to this neck of the woods?" he said, almost beaming. "Another consult, I'd guess."

"Jeremy, great to see you too. Yes, exactly, another consult," I said, then smiled in return. "Is there somewhere we could go?"

"Follow me. I've got a burn patient I have to check on—sterile room, so no cats allowed... if you know what I mean." He winked at the last word.

"Got it. Lead the way."

We walked down the narrow hall past the glass fronted bays to a set of special treatment areas equipped with positive pressure anterooms. Paul stepped past the Black Cat standing watch at the door, depressed the switch to open the anteroom. We stepped inside and the door slid closed behind us. The pressure equalized as we donned clean gowns, masks, and gloves. The inner door opened and we stepped in. On the bed before us lay a sedated patient wrapped in various types of dressings designed to assist in healing burns.

Paul stepped over to the patient's monitor, and looking up, he said, "So what brings you here, Hux? How can I help you?"

"Are we secure in here?" I said, somewhat concerned while looking through the glass partitions at the Black Cat.

"Absolutely. Tight as a funeral drum."

I feigned a quick smile, not quite understanding the reference. "The system... There's something gravely wrong with this System."

Paul dropped his head from the monitor, his gaze falling on the floor before him. "I thought that was the path you were on based on our last meeting. I sensed you were not here to discuss a case. Yes, there's very much wrong here, very much. Your point?"

"My point...? My point...? Wait, you know this and you do nothing? Why didn't you say something when we last spoke if you thought that I knew?"

He turned to me and stepped forward, looking me directly in the eye. "For what purpose, to add to your discomfort, to add fuel to that fire that consumes you? I have lived for some time now with the same feeling—no, not the feeling, but the knowledge that this is wrong, that an imposed equality is not equality; that equality begins at the starting line, it is not guaranteed at the finish. Freedom is unbridled choice as long as that choice recognizes the equal rights of others to choose, that when choice begins to become limited by a self-proclaimed authority, then freedom has already become abrogated. Is that what you want to hear, Hux?"

I stepped back, shocked. "You... You... know. Why are you still here? Why haven't you tried to escape?"

"Oh, I've thought about it from time to time, but not for many years. I'm getting on now; I've played my hand as best I could. I have some latitude as an MSP, much more than some—like now, our conversation. This is a blessing, one that many of our brethren do not have. I can't chance throwing away what little I have, not after this long. I've done things, Hux, things to people that I'm not proud of, but this is my lot now."

I looked down, away from his gaze. I was feeling something that I had never experienced: a deep sadness. I had not known this man that long, but it was if in leaving, I would also be losing a long lost friend.

"I see," I said. "I had hoped to convince you of such a move, an adventure of sorts, but yes, as you say, it may just be folly."

"Don't be foolish, Hux, it's not much, but it's more than many have. Don't throw it away doing something rash. I've seen you with her... at the tenement. It's an amazing feeling. I wish you wouldn't risk losing it, but if you do decide to venture off somewhere, I won't stop you or say anything. I hear southeast is the best direction to go."

"You hear... So there've been others, then?"

Paul paused for a moment, fidgeting and wringing his hands. "Has been, and most probably always will be. What has happened to them, I can't say. We as beings—humans, you know—we're not designed to serve others like this, unless we choose to, of course. We didn't evolve this way. If we did, we wouldn't have to be fooled, coerced, or forced into it."

"What... What can I say? What can I do?" Looking up into his eyes, I could sense a smile behind his mask; I could feel his warmth and sincerity brighten the room. "Thank you, Jeremy. If we don't cross paths again, it has been a sincere pleasure serving in your presence."

"Serve yourself, Hux, as you should—that'll be my thanks. If you make it back, remember, Hux, in the realm of the human condition, when the unjust acts of one are justified by pointing to the unjust acts of another, tyranny is sure to follow. Don't change no matter what change someone else promises."

I dropped my head, turned to the door, and hit the switch. The door slid open and I felt the rush of air at my back as I stepped into the anteroom, pushing me away from the sterility of the room, pushing me away from Paul. The door slid closed behind me.

"If you make it back..."

As I walked toward the elevator, I pondered Jeremy Paul's words and thought, *Head southeast... Make it back... To where... or... to when?* What was there to the southeast that was so different from what we had here? I continued walking, looking down at my portable ERP, checking to see if I had been assigned another case, not looking where I was going and then—

It was like I hit a brick wall. I looked up, rubbing my head, only to find a statuesque Black Cat standing alongside the elevator.

"Forgive me," I said, "I wasn't paying attention."

The Black Cat pointed to his right, toward the elevator door. "Not to worry," he said, "we're paying attention."

Furrowing my brow, I quickly glanced back at him as I stepped inside the elevator. Another Black Cat stood inside the door, as before. I pushed the first-floor button. The Black Cat just stood there, unflinching, unmoving, a silent omen. What was it that the previous Black Cat had meant: *"We're paying attention?"*

An uncomfortable knot was forming in the pit of my stomach. *Maybe we should call it off, attempt our escape another day. There just seem to be too many eyes on me today.* I wondered if Jules was experiencing the same heightened level of surveillance, or was it just me, just my overactive mind? I put the thoughts out of my head and carried on to my next assignment.

When my last day of service was finally winding down, I had a few moments' reprieve to organize my thoughts and, in my mind, walk through the plans for our escape. Sitting in a tiny office, I changed my focus and took a few brief moments to wrap up my day's work before I would venture back along the corridor to my final stop at the locker room.

In an unusual move, without a Prog patient present, a Black Cat stood quietly in the corner of the office, like an immovable permanent fixture. He stood in the same spot as always, not making any movements, generally ignoring my existence altogether, although I was in the office alone. I thought it best to take a moment to check my schedule for the next day, in case Jules and I couldn't find each other on the train or we had to abort for some reason. Some small part of me also hoped that this tiny act would make me seem more trustworthy in the eyes of Our State as I played the role of a docile Server, a sheep to the wolf. I pulled the portable ERP close to me and typed in my personal code. The ERP displayed a series of dots, over and over as if it were thinking, and then it pulled up a screen that showed—

I gasped out loud and pushed my chair back against the wall. The Black Cat turned his head toward me; in his mirrored glasses, I saw my reflection, a tiny head on a tiny body, one in each lens.

"I'm sorry for the outburst," I said. "I typed in the wrong patient and the information shocked me. My mistake."

The Black Cat turned his head back to its original straight-ahead position; he said nothing.

I stared at the screen in complete dismay. On the screen in large red capital letters read the words: *SERVER DOES NOT EXIST IN DATABASE.* I grabbed the ERP and held it to my forehead while depressing the scan function button. The ERP beeped, accepting the scan. Once again, the series of dots appeared on the screen as the electronic pad went through its record scan. *SERVER DOES NOT EXIST IN DATABASE* flashed on the screen for the second time. This was similar to the message I had received when entering Hemsworth's identification after he had been dragged from our appointment.

That's it, then. If I make it to the train today, Jules and I must escape. This must be the day.

With that thought, I quickly tidied my desk, grabbed the ERP from its cradle, turned it off, and walked out, clutching it under my arm, tight to my body. I was terrified. On the other side of the door, I found another black-clad sentinel, mocking me with his presence. He was looking straight ahead, unmoving. I took a quick glance as I hurried past, looking back to see if he was following me, but he wasn't. Shuffling back to the locker room, I never felt I had seen so many Black Cats crammed into a single space, but still not one made a move toward me or seemingly recognized my presence in any way. I was running a little late, as most of the other MSPs were leaving the locker room as I was entering.

Perfect. I had planned on putting my own clothes over my jumpsuit for extra warmth. I hoped Jules had remembered to do the same. Out of view of the Cats, I pulled my pants up over the suit, yanking the pant legs up. It was a tight fit, but I managed to get them over the jumpsuit. My shirt was in such tatters, I would have to risk the Black Cats seeing the jumpsuit underneath. I was relying on my jacket to cover up the holes in my sleeves. I double-checked that the ERP was off, slipped out of the locker room, and handed it to the administrator before heading down the steps to the tunnel system. I caught up with the rest of my brethren midway down the steps. The last few moments had flown by so fast, and now that I found myself in the slow-moving tide of numerous empty bodies, the change of pace was almost unbearable. I had to find Jules; we had to escape.

When our group of Servers reached the train, I found it once again packed tight. Apparently, the broken-down railcar had yet to be fixed or replaced. I was stuffed tight into my usual car with an extra two dozen sacrificial Servers, pressed in at all sides. *This will serve us well.* With the Black Cats distracted with the continued boarding procedures, I pushed my way through the train car, taking in every face for any sign of my angel. Each woman I came across caused my heart to jump, only for it to fall deeply into my stomach at the realization that she was not the one I was looking for. At last, I spotted Jules tucked in the back of the train, near the rear door. *Perfect place. She knew to sit by the door. Perfect.* We made eye contact for just a moment, and I prayed that she would see the concern in my eyes and be ready to move. I suspected she was.

At last, all the Servers were crammed into the car, and the train whistled, gasped, and hissed, then began to pull away from Progressive 17. I remained still where I was, standing fixed with a million thoughts racing through my mind, allowing the Black Cat to complete his head count before shuffling farther down the car. As soon as his back was turned, I squeezed my way through the bodies, grabbed Jules by the hand, and pulled her up next to me to stand by the door. One of our brethren, a fellow MSP, turned to look at us with a quizzical look as if to say, *"What are you doing?"* I returned his gaze, an almost pleading look painted on my face, but at the same time, determined. I raised my index finger to my pursed lips and whispered, "Shhhh." He simply nodded and turned his lifeless head.

As the Black Cat up ahead opened the front door, completing his sweep of our car, Jules and I crouched down. I opened the back door and out we shuffled onto the platform beyond. I pulled the door shut, making sure it properly latched. We remained outside for only a moment, Jules pressed tightly against the wall of the train, eyes fixed on the ties below us, moving ever faster as we picked up speed.

"Don't worry," I said. "It won't be going much faster than this."

She looked at me with trust written in her eyes.

"Down there... We have to go down there. It's been about one minute. In seven more minutes, we have to jump." I pointed to the compartment below us. "I've got you," I whispered in her ear, grasping her hand.

"Yes, you do," she replied, then smiled and kissed me.

This is why we're doing this, I reminded myself, the warmth of her lips on my cheek, staying against the oncoming cold wind.

Jules reached her other arm down, holding onto the large steel compartment door. She turned her body, pushing her legs in, wiggling her body farther into the compartment. I let go of her other hand once she was almost all the way in. I repeated the same procedure, squeezing myself into the compartment beside her. It was the closest we had been to each other since embracing between bunkhouses the day we shared our first kiss. Her breath was on my face, her arms holding me tightly, and her body bracing me against the cold.

For a few magical moments, I had forgotten the danger of our predicament, forgotten the uncertainty of our future, and simply held my angel. The sound of the tracks disappeared, the roaring and the whistling of the iron serpent replaced by the slow, steady breathing of my love at my side. Instead of the cold, hard metal walls of the compartment, I could feel only the softness of her skin and the warmth of her breath against me face. All was quiet, still… blissful.

The moment overtook us, and then the sound of a hard metal plate crashing down over the compartment door woke us from our fantasy. I kicked my feet once against the plate, but it didn't budge.

"Oh no…" I whispered.

Already I could hear the screeching of the serpent's steel wheels against the steel track as the brakes were engaged. Through the steel mesh walls of the compartment, I could see the sparks of anger as the beast was forced to stop its march toward the tenement. It sat there for a moment, huffing and puffing. Its breath rose up around us, then with a loud gasp, the iron monster resigned itself to its fate and slowly began to turn its round legs back toward Progressive 17, back toward the Black Cats, back toward Killary and the Provider.

"Hux, what's happening?" Jules cried, the fear evident in her voice.

"Kick, kick, kick!" I shouted as loud as I could.

We kicked and kicked at the iron trap, but it didn't budge.

"What have I done to you, my dear, my love?" I yelled above the din of the protesting train, pulling her tight against me. "What have I done to... us?"

Already the train was beginning to slow again. Through the metal grate, I could see the main platform of Progressive 17. I imagined I could already hear the Black Cats gathering outside on the platform, their black boots snapping in step, then coming to a halt, just waiting for us to emerge. They would pull us apart, take us away, separate us, torture us, kill us if we were lucky.

What have I done to my love, to my angel?

I tasted the uncertainty of freedom as I inhaled the steam from the serpent's throat. I imagined at that moment, as the train came to a stop, Jules forced to sit in that hard metal chair, watching a block of ice slowly melt away as the Provider sneered at her, telling her how worthless she was for trying to escape, for denying her freedom to serve. I couldn't bear to see it, couldn't bear to hear those lies spewed at the woman I loved. She was not worthless. She meant everything. She was the whole world to me.

"Jules," I finally said, as the train came to an eerily quiet halt. "I... I love you, Jules. Whatever happens, know that. Know that I love you and will never forget you. With you, I'm... I'm perfectly blissful."

Just then, I heard another loud bang as the latch was knocked off our iron keep. The rusty hinges squealed in protest as the compartment door was hoisted open. I felt piercing fingers as two strong hands reached into the compartment and grabbed at my feet like locking pliers. Desperately, I kicked my feet back out at them, feeling my right foot connect with something hard. For a few brief seconds, the hands retreated, then seemed to multiply and came all the faster. I feebly kicked against them again, but to no avail. Seconds later, they grabbed me tight by the ankles, and I was dragged out of the compartment, over a few hard, wooden railings, and onto the frozen, cold ground below, my head coming to rest on a concrete slab.

"Don't you touch her!" I yelled as I saw a group of Black Cats reach in and grab my angel's legs.

"No! No! No!" she screamed as she was dragged out and thrown onto the ground beside me.

"Shut up, you treacherous swine!" yelled one of the Black Cats.

Above me hovered a bright shining light, pointed directly into my eyes. It was too bright to be the hazy, cloud-covered sun or any of the typical lights of railroad platform. The instantaneous brightness of it, compared to the darkness of the train compartment, forced me to close my eyes and look away. When at last I opened my eyes again, the light was still there, but it was like a halo surrounding a face.

"Well, well, well, it seems we meet again, MSP Huxley," said the haloed figured with a mocking laugh—a laugh I had heard before.

I turned away from the halo to see a face I'd never thought to see again, wearing a sheepish grin—Arnold.

A split second later, out of the corner of my eye, I saw a long object, probably a baton, on a one-way, rapid descent in my direction.

Thunk!

Pain… then blackness.

Chapter 12

As my eyes fluttered open, an intense pain pounded throughout the forefront of my head, interspersed with sharp stabs at the side of my left temple. The pain came in and out in waves, making me dizzy, the space around me seemingly spinning. I became vaguely aware, as my foggy mind began to clear, that I was seated in a chair, not bound, but slumped uncomfortably forward, my chin resting on my chest. With some effort, I was able to straighten my neck. The pain became more intense, but I was determined to open my eyes and see what I had brought upon myself. I cautiously turned my head from side to side, anticipating the oncoming increase in pain. I took in my surroundings, wondering if I was in for yet another torture, or maybe this time, they would move straight to execution. I couldn't see Jules; she wasn't in the room with me. Feeling the unlawful emotion welling up, I wondered what had become of her.

The room was similar to the one I had been placed in during my first interrogation, although thankfully there was no television monitor or block of ice, no jets of super-heated air. Instead, I found myself in a metal room that, except for me and this chair, was completely bare. On either side of me stood a door. The door on the right was adorned with a small slit-style window, the other completely solid. The room was surprisingly clean, the steel walls glistening from the single light bulb hanging from the ceiling, while the floor looked as though it had been cleaned just prior to my being placed inside. Mop streaks swirled around the floor with hints of red here and there. The red streaks brought me back to the nightmare of my inquisition, the blood and body parts strewn throughout the room.

If that is what is in store for me, just make it quick.

I was just turning my head to find the same bare wall behind me when the windowed door opened and a Black Cat stepped in. I instantly sat lower in my chair at his presence, pulling my head down into my body while instinctively raising my shoulders in an ill attempt at self-preservation. From the corner of my eye, I saw him approach with something in his hand. I squinted my eyes and shrank even farther into the seat as he neared. A deluge of cold water hit my face. I gasped at the intense cold, huffing and puffing as the icy fluid slapped me.

"Whoa, whoa!" I screamed.

"Shut your mouth, maggot!" yelled the Black Cat as he dropped the bucket to the floor. "Now stand up."

I shook the cold water from my head, and with each shake, the throbbing intensified. Pushing down on the platform of the chair, I attempted to lift myself to a standing position. As I was nearly vertical, my knees gave out and I began to drop. At that moment, the Black Cat shot out his hand and grabbed my arm, steadying me and pulling me up to my feet again. We stood there for a moment as I regained my composure. The abrupt standing had almost caused me to black out as the blood drained from my head. The Black Cat's patience was uncanny, something I'd never experienced before. I grasped his arm as he held it out to me.

"Let's go," the Black Cat said in a soft, direct voice, a complete reversal of tone from his initial command.

He then led me toward the door without the window slot. He entered a code on the panel next to the door and the door instantly withdrew into the wall.

"Oh… my," I said, gasping as the Black Cat led me through the door.

"Be quiet, Server!"

The room was unlike any I'd ever seen before. A wide, cylindrical expanse climbed up and up to a small, round glass ceiling. It looked… majestic. Beyond the window, I caught a glimpse of the sun surrounded by blue unfettered skies. The walls and floors were white with the exception of two narrow lines: one red line running from the doorway from which we had entered to a small chair in the center of the circle, and an equal-length blue line running from the chair toward the only other doorway in the circle, situated on the opposite side. The room smelled of a mix of sterile spray and fresh crisp air—the air that one enjoyed when out in open spaces. It was almost lively.

The Black Cat led me along the red line toward the chair. As we approached, I could make out that something had been placed on the chair, something small, almost round and crumpled. For some reason, my heart began to beat even faster than it had already been beating. I had seen it before. As we came to within a few feet of the chair, I could see the object more clearly. My heart was racing, my respirations increasing to the point I was almost hyperventilating.

What if he sees it? What if he gets to it before me?

Without waiting for a command, I pulled free of his grip and lunged forward, grabbing the sides of the chair, then spun myself around just as the Black Cat gave the order to sit. I slammed my backside down onto the chair, covering the object and hoping that he did not see it. I had completely forgotten about the throbbing in my head.

How did it end up here?

I held the sides of the chair as tight as I could in case the Black Cat tried to lift me up. I couldn't lose it again. I could feel the sweat bead up on my forehead and start to run down the sides, racing down my cheeks. My eyes were starting to sting from the salt. I dropped my head and waited to see what the Black Cat was going to do, clenching my eyes against the salt and the apprehension. Nothing happened for what seemed like an eternity. I opened my eyes slightly and tilted my head to the side just as the Black Cat was reaching the door. He turned, staring directly at me.

"Don't move," he said before the door slid closed behind him.

For several moments, I didn't move. My hands remained clamped around the base of the chair, my knuckles white from the intense grip. As a few more minutes passed, I began to loosen my grip. The throbbing in my head had returned. I reached up and delicately ran my fingers over the area from where the pain emanated. A large goose egg the size of a small walnut adorned the left side of my head. I could just imagine what it looked like. I suspected that I had a mild concussion at the very least; it would explain the pain and grogginess.

I turned from side to side, twisting around as much as I could while still holding onto the arms of the chair, keeping the object beneath me. The room was so unique, so clean, and so perfect. I noticed a narrow slit in the wall directly across from me. I followed with my eyes to the top where a small half globe protruded from the wall, almost like a halved egg stuck on a rail, or a droplet of water precariously perched on a gutter, waiting to fall. A dull hum hung in the air, like the sound of ventilation. However, I couldn't feel any breeze, but it was comfortable.

With the blow I had taken to my head, I was having difficulty making sense of time. I couldn't tell how long I had been sitting there. Had it only been a few moments, or had it been hours? I couldn't tell.

I raised my buttocks off the seat ever so slightly and reached my hand under. The object was there, no longer round from my weight, but it was there. I extended my fingers, placing my index finger on the object, and slowly pulled it out. I grabbed it and held it as tight as I had ever held anything before. Sitting back down in the seat, I scanned the room looking for video cameras or anything else that they could be watching me with. *Eyes and ears... Eyes and ears.*

I waited longer, and still nothing had happened. No doors had been opened, no screaming Black Cats had entered, and no torture had been initiated. I reached my hand up, close to my face, and began to unclench my fingers to reveal the object. Then I heard the sound of gears engaging. Clenching my fist again, I shoved my hand between my legs, burying the object.

I looked up and saw that the raindrop, the egg, had begun to lower itself down along the track that was cut into the wall. *What form of torture is this?* The egg emanated a bright white glow, increasing in intensity the lower it descended. When it was a few feet above me, it slowed to a stop. It was difficult to make out the shape any longer, as the light was so bright. I squinted, raising my hand up to block some of the light just as the light eventually dimmed and extinguished itself. The inside of the egg took on a more subtle white glow, and I could see an embryonic shape within.

The top half of the egg pushed forward and then dropped down, following the curvature of the lower half until only the lower portion was enclosed. Within the egg sat an older gentleman, dressed in what looked to be a white robe. His beard was short and neatly trimmed, white like his robe. He didn't seem to have a single follicle of hair on his head. His eyes were covered with mirrored glasses, small circular lenses that reflected my image back toward me, much like the

Black Cats' did. I gripped the object tighter and tighter. For the next few seconds, we simply stared at each other. I had no idea what was about to happen. I couldn't read this man or even begin to imagine what was to become of me. Finally he spoke.

"Before we begin with the formal proceedings, you have something that you would like a few moments to look at. Please take your time and be done with it," the man said in a calm and genuinely cordial voice.

I was completely shocked at what the man had just said. I just sat there, unsure of what to do.

"Well, go on then, young man. You can't sit there gripping it forever."

I looked down to my lap, back up at him, then down again. My hand was buried deep between my legs, and in my hand the object that I had been longing to see again.

"Open it. See if it is everything you were hoping for. See what words of wisdom it may proclaim. You've no doubt lost many an hour of sleep wondering as to its whereabouts and its contents."

I pulled my hand from between my legs, turning my fist over, looking at my fingertips as they dug into the palm of my hand. My fingers were as white as his egg, my nails carving trenches into my skin. I slowly released my grip on the object. The note that Hemsworth had left under the table in the exam room, the note that I thought had been laundered by the cleaning Servers... Now it sat in the palm of my hand. I was almost in tears as I plucked the note from its sweaty prison and began to open it. It was larger than I had imagined. It was an old newspaper clipping, actually—so thin and delicate, so fragile. Smoothing it out on my leg, I looked down and was amazed at what I saw, what I read. I held the clipping up, closer to my eyes. A beam of light from overhead shot down to brighten the area around my chair.

"That should make it easier for you to see," said the man in the egg.

On the paper, I saw a picture of a much younger version of the Provider—same evil, dark brown eyes, same wicked grin, and the same tight, cropped hair, only not as much gray, same overly large ears. His thin, lanky body stood behind a podium with rectangular glass objects on stands positioned slightly in front and on either side of him. Behind him were a gold curtain and two banners on poles. On one side was the same banner I had seen in the interrogation video, the one behind the banner for Our State, the banner with the alternating red and white lines converging on a blue area that was adorned with white star-like objects, only this time the banner for Our State was missing. The banner on the opposite side was a dark color, maybe a dark blue, with some type of circular emblem in the middle, a bird of some sort. I could only make out two words: *States of*.

The man in the picture stood tall behind the lectern, his chin raised high, head tilted back as if he were looking down on subjects, directing them, lording over them, hands with exceptionally long fingers pointed toward those he was addressing, as if he was admonishing them or ordering them. Despite it only being a picture, his ego and arrogance were overpowering and all too obvious. On the front of his podium was the word *FORWARD*, only the *O* was not simply an *O*. Within the circle was a symbol that looked remarkably similar to the emblem of Our State, the arced lines and setting orb. Across the picture, Hemsworth had written in a carbon type media, *MUST GO BACK*.

I sat and looked at the picture; the similarities were eerie, as if the Provider had existed before, somewhere else, presumably where this picture was taken. *What does 'Must go back' mean?* I thought. Was it a time of freedom? Was it in reference to the *Forward* on the Provider's podium, back to a time before he existed, before he came to power? What did it mean? Did it refer to a place or a time?

"Don't know what to make of it, do you?" the man in the egg said, then chuckled. "No, I didn't think you would. A little knowledge is a dangerous thing, young man, as you are no doubt finding out. Go back... to what, where... to when?"

After a long pause, "Yes... I suppose so," I said, confused.

The wind had somehow been knocked out of me, as I couldn't make out what Hemsworth was trying to tell me. If only I'd had more time with him.

"You can just drop that on the floor now. You won't be in need of it any longer."

As much as I wanted to hold on to it, as much as I knew there was something better before this, before the false claims from the Provider, I relented, dropping the clipping as the man instructed, looking down at it as it fluttered to the blue stripe on the floor below.

"And now on to our business. Allow me to introduce myself. My name is Comrade Andrei Zamyatin. I am the Overseer of Bliss and Harmony for this Collective," he said. "You are an intriguing young fellow. I've been following your antics for some time now. I always have to question the validity of our indoctrination programs when a Server develops rational and logical thought outside of that which is required for their position." He paused for a moment before continuing. "You have noticed Served with scars, discolorations around their temporal lobes since your arrival here. Possibly it was an oversight on our part to bring you here, as you are possibly a little too astute. Despite our improvements in the corrective procedure, perfection still eludes us, as you have seen."

"Perfection?" I said, unsure of what he was referring to.

He simply waved his hand, disregarding my question. The Overseer exhaled and continued. "Medical Server Provider Blair Huxley," the man said, his voice direct, but soft and unrushed. "This hearing has been arranged to ensure that you understand your offenses, in order that fair and just repercussions may be placed upon you at the pleasure of Our State and the discretion bestowed on me by the Provider. Do you understand your reasons for being here?"

"My desire to be truly free."

The man dropped his chin, raised his eyebrows, and glared at me over the rims of his glasses. "You are charged as follows: sedition against Our State and the Provider, theft of medication belonging to the Served by way of their rights, attempting to escape, subversive indoctrination of a fellow Server, thoughts of an individual nature, thoughts in general that are outside of those required for your assigned duties, introspection, and finally, the most egregious offense of placing your own needs above the wants of others, ergo, selfishness. Once again, do you understand the reason you are here?"

I paused at the question. I did not understand why I was here. I did not understand why I had to be held captive to serve those who should serve themselves. I did not understand this system, and in my mind, progression meant to move toward something positive, not to regress toward a system of slavery. How anyone could refer to something so backward as a "Progressive" was completely beyond sanity.

"Where's Jules?" I said.

"Jules?"

"Jules, the woman I was with when we were unjustly assaulted and subsequently incarcerated!"

The Overseer chuckled. "Assaulted, were you? What an interesting perspective." The Overseer continued to laugh softly, then said, "You must be referring to Julie. I take it 'Jules' is your pet name for her."

"She's not a pet. She is a woman, and she is an individual!"

"I suggest you watch your tongue, young man, before I have it removed. And we'll have none of that 'individual' nonsense in this chamber unless it is something I alone initiate. Do you understand?" he said. "I suspect you have developed an emotional connection to her—what you may refer to, or perceive, as love. A foolish decision, I can assure you."

He tapped on a computer screen for a moment, then looked at something on it while rubbing his chin. "Love is a most dangerous variable," the Overseer said. "Love drives men to criminal actions, as you've seen in your own life. It also drives them to bitterness, anger, and revenge. People have been murdered for love. Wars have been fought over it. The kind of love doesn't matter. Love or passion for a partner, a child, a friend… It is this passion that disrupts the system because it leads to selfishness. Server Huxley, your search for love, knowledge, and understanding has caused you to violate our laws, attempt to harm your fellow Servers, and blatantly usurp the rights of the Served."

I lowered my head at his words, looking down at my hands, before balling those hands into fists. Yes, I did have passion. I had love. I had reveled in the thought of freedom. And no matter what this man said, I knew my way was better. I was willing to be selfish if it meant a better life for me and for Jules. And somehow, I knew that this was the better way. Despite all my indoctrination, I couldn't deny that the knowledge I had was liberating. There was simply no other way to think: ignorance might have been bliss, but knowledge was freedom.

"You understand now, why we sterilize and sanitize the minds of the children so young," the Overseer said after a time. "The older a child is before indoctrination, the less blissful they become, and the more aware they are of the possibilities before them. As they become better able to choose, their happiness decreases. To be able to offer a more blissful society, we must sterilize and educate them before they become wholly disillusioned with choices. Should they be allowed to grow attachments as you have, then our entire System would crumble. Instead, we give gifts of ignorance, sterility, service, and bliss, and take away the curse of passion and choice. We retard the process of development away from knowledge and toward ignorance, allowing them to maintain bliss and fully integrate into the Collective."

"I understand what you are saying," I said, "but I question more than just the absence of logic in your position. Humans are not capital to be used or developed to suit your visions. Now, Jules, she has nothing to do with this and does not deserve punishment. Where is she?"

"While the Server with whom you were found during your crude attempt at escape and how you came to be in her company do have bearing on this case, her current whereabouts do not. Rest assured, it will be you who delivers her punishment. Now you will answer my question: Do you understand why you are here?"

"Who are you that I should have to respond?"

"You are certainly testing my patience; however, this exchange is most fascinating to me. Once again, I am the Overseer of Bliss and Harmony for the Collective, Server Huxley.

But who I am is only of minor importance. What is important here is... who are you?"

"You know exactly who I am."

"Oh, I know ABOUT you, indoctrinated as a Medical Server, transferred between several Progressives. A fine doctor you are, generally respectable bedside manner, hundreds of successful procedures and almost no disciplinary records, these last few weeks notwithstanding. Hell, I even know your initial induction date, not that it matters. What I want to know is, who ARE you? Who is Blair Huxley?"

The two of us stared at each other for several moments. I had never been spoken to this way by any representative of Our State, whether it was a bureaucrat, Black Cat, or Prog. The man was almost friendly, in his own superior way. He spoke to me like I mattered, like my existence was important in some way. He spoke to me like a person, an individual. Because of this, I couldn't help but think that it was his identity that was far more unique and worthy of attention than my own.

"What is it that you do?" I said.

"I watch, Server Huxley," he replied. "I watch to see if there are any disruptions in the bliss and harmony that Our State provides for its people."

"You watch for people like me, you mean?"

"Well, seeing as we haven't yet been clear on just who you are, I cannot fully say. But I have been watching you quite closely for some time. I find you to be an elaborate puzzle that I must solve. I'm curious about what could have gone wrong with your indoctrination that you developed such rational and logical thoughts, thoughts that should be specifically directed toward the confines of your position. It does happen, once in a while, you know, as the note on the floor beside you can attest to. Like you, I use observation to make judgments about my subjects and to select the most appropriate corrective intervention."

"So you don't just watch the Servers, then?"

"Of course not. To do so would be like checking a train's engine for maintenance but not the track on which it runs. Both must be maintained in order for society to move onward, to proceed forward. We have had cases of a Served developing troublesome cognitive abilities after selection and sterilization, and corrective steps must be taken in those instances."

"Which are we: the train or the track?"

"You know, I hadn't thought through the metaphor that far," he said, then smiled, moving his hand as if writing a note into his computer terminal.

"I suppose it doesn't matter," I said, continuing to study his face. "But if the Servers and Served are the track and train, what does that make you?"

"I am the conductor for Progressive 17," the man said, seeming to enjoy the philosophical discussion. "And the maintenance man, when it comes right down to it. I and the other representatives of Our State choose the course on which the train will run. We direct its path according to our interests and the directives of the Provider. It is a simple process. We decide what the people should want, carefully selecting that which is in our best interests, and we then instill in them those desires through a host of audio and visual inputs, then satiate those desires in the form of rights. We allow Servers such as you the right to provide those services that satisfy their desires and make manifest their rights. By extension, we maintain our power over the System, and the people can continue living in their private little utopia. It's that simple." He smiled at the perceived simplicity of the system. "Our current conversation, this is one of my maintenance functions. This interaction is one of the many ways we keep the train running and on the tracks. It's our version of a snow-clearing detail, if you will."

"Trains, tracks, rights, utopia… Ha!" I scoffed. "I haven't been living in any utopia."

"No, not you," the man said. "That's what's so fascinating. You don't live in a utopia at all. Somehow, you've come to see the life of a Server as one of slavery rather than emancipation from all that burdened mankind before the System. And look where it has led you, all this pointless thinking and questioning." At this point, the Overseer glanced at his computer screen. "Looking at your list of offenses, it's clear that you have developed a taste for rights not designated to your station, usurping the rights of others."

"One cannot usurp a right, not that it has stopped your System from trying," I said. "Rights are a concept independent of another's input. They aren't reliant on others for realization, nor are they granted by the likes of you or the Provider. They are simply an inherent trait of humankind. What you claim to provide for one must first be withheld or taken from another, which hardly makes it a right."

"And you presume to have the same rights as one of the Served?"

"I presume nothing. I am a complete entity in and of myself. I have no more and no fewer rights than anyone else. I do not request or require another individual be enslaved or placed in a position of involuntary servitude in order that I realize anything more than I could and should realize myself. Nor can a Prog claim a right that entails that I be enslaved to them for the realization of their so-called right. I took medication, and to this, I will admit that I do not have any right to medical treatment. No one does, because it entails that the service be provided by someone else. What of the rights of that person? The person who is forced to serve, what do they receive that is on par with what they provide? There should be an equal exchange, a voluntary equal exchange at that, both parties in agreement. Self-sacrifice to a lesser value is the folly of weak-minded and illogical beings," I said with the most respect I could muster.

"To a lesser value... Hmmm... But if the value were equal, if the person were of equal value, I should say that would be entirely different I suppose. Fascinating..." the man said, making more notes in his computer.

For a few moments, the only sound to be heard was the gentle tapping of the man's fingers against his computer screen. He then continued.

"Could it be simple observation that has brought you to these conclusions, to this new philosophical world view, or could it be something deeper, something born of emotion?"

My mind flashed to Jules again, to the life I imagined we could have together, to the closeness we had experienced in such a short time. She had made me see the value in myself as I had also grown to see the value in her. She deserved something more than servitude could provide, something personal, something hers. And if my affection could make that a reality for her, then the same reality should be available to everyone.

"Based on your pause, I would assume she has consumed your thoughts again," Overseer Zamyatin said.

I said nothing.

"Very interesting. This, of course, proves why we feel our sterilization and emotional sanitizing process for Servers is so important. We can hardly have Servers running around developing emotions and fornicating all over the place. Who would take care of all of those unwanted children? Certainly not Our State, and the Servers have no time for such things. They have the Served to please."

"So… not population control, after all," I said, finally making sense of a question that had long plagued me. "Not even just to keep us docile. You don't want us to fall in love or to value life outside the Collective, or outside our role as Servers."

"You see what dangerous thoughts it brings about," he said. "You are living proof that we are right in stamping out that desire. It creates too many choices, too much conflict and bondage."

"Bondage?"

"Yes, bondage. Choices are bondage. Decision making itself is bondage. In the days before the Provider came to power, people were constantly enslaved by decisions they were forced to make. They were constantly forced to decide how to care for themselves and their families, what financial choices to make, what educational choices to make for their children and themselves, and a myriad of other decisions. That is not freedom, Server Huxley; that is the epitome of bondage. Every choice a person makes ties them into an unending list of consequences, an unending list of additional choices and variables and concerns. Their entire lives, rich or poor, were consumed by worry over these kinds of choices and the possible consequences."

The Overseer was smiling broadly now, his eyes glistening with a sickly affection for the alternative he was about to offer.

"But what we did was to offer the people true freedom. We freed them from the choices that constantly plagued their lives. Now we make all the choices for you, and you don't even know it. You don't have to know it. We convince you what to decide before you decide it by manipulating what you believe. We decide what you should think is important and what you should think it is that you need. We decide what and who you should rally against and why. You are allowed to simply live; free from decision making, free from consequences, free from thought, and that is true freedom. Un-tempered and radical thoughts like yours lead to difficult choices, consequential choices, and these choices are the chains and shackles that bind you. That is slavery, Server Huxley, make no mistake. We are the emancipators here."

I could only shake my head. "When you provide everything for someone, when you have removed personal choice, shielded them from the consequences of choice, you have somehow stolen a part of them from themselves. You have weakened them, enslaved them. And you think this makes people happy... blissful? You think the Servers aren't free from worry or harm? We're beaten and abused. The Black Cats torment us, belittle us, work us like cattle until we drop dead from exhaustion. What kind of freedom is that?"

"And yet so few of you rise up," the Overseer said. "Throughout human history, the enslaved always rose up against their masters. This is because they believed they had some influence over their fate, some choice in the matter. And that choice left them angry and unsatisfied. They wanted more and killed their oppressors to get it. But outside of anomalies such as yourself, your brethren apparently live contently. They work, enjoy their right to serve, and die without consequence. The entire Collective enjoys peace and stability thanks to them."

"You call daily beatings 'peace'?"

"Peace is a collective state of mind. It is not found within the confines of an individual's skin, an individual's mind, but in the Collective mind. A Collective at peace is by definition equal to the sum of the individual peace of its members," the Overseer said. He paused and typed additional notes into his computer. "Do not think that you could rally the masses to give up their lifestyle, the rights they have become accustomed to, and the benefits Servers such as you provide. Sheep never turn on the wolf. A flock of sheep could number in the hundreds and a single wolf could reduce them to puppets, to prey, despite their superiority in numbers, and that, Server Huxley, is exactly what the Served, or Progs as you Servers refer to them, are: they are sheep, we are the wolves. They, unlike actual domestic sheep, have voluntarily sold themselves; they chose to forgo individual freedom for collective freedom and obedience, all in exchange for a few handouts coupled with the promise of security and an unknown to them: revised equality."

"Equality? What equality?"

"We are all equal in that we enjoy freedom; however, different levels of freedom have different restrictions. There are attributes of the Collective that require us to forgo certain liberties for certain levels, but I assure you that it is all worth it, you have my word."

I felt myself becoming agitated, more defiant. "And the scarred land, the destruction of the earth, was that also a result of your Collective peace, security, and freedom?" I was having trouble containing myself. This man's openness to hearing what I had to say left me rambling on. "I've seen this land; it's torn apart. I've been to several Collectives. You fool the Progs into believing they live in a world of sun and blue skies, but the reality is a barren, cold wasteland. The landscape is dotted with craters, scarred trees, the sky is overcast, and we spend days in the dark only to have to endure unending days of light. Is this what your peace has brought?"

The Overseer roared with laughter. His head tilted back as he let loose the howling outburst. After a few moments, his laughter died down. "Well, it's good to see that part of your indoctrination was successful. There has been no second revolution, at least not as of yet. Our northern latitude lends itself to periods of seemingly never-ending darkness and periods of seemingly never-ending light. You see, Server Huxley, the Provider is still engaged in an ongoing campaign to rid those who would rally against the Collective of their means to wage any type of revolt. We provide security in exchange for a mere relaxation of the term 'freedom,' a new definition repeated time and time again; it's all in the sales pitch, if you will."

"What you are selling as security is servitude. Even the Progs are in servitude. They are simply too ignorant to understand it."

"Mankind is born ignorant, blissfully ignorant. We simply assist individuals in maintaining that level of mental maturity. It is the core of our indoctrination, the common core. Ignorance, MSP Huxley, is the utopia of the masses."

"But if people knew they were being manipulated, they would never settle for the lot you've given them. The Servers and Served could rise up together against you."

"That is your belief? That the Served and Servers will make peace and rise up against the Provider and all he has given?" the Overseer asked, raising an eyebrow. For the first time in several minutes, he stopped writing on his computer. "If that is the case, you've failed to understand the Collective. You've failed to understand the symbiotic relationship of the sheep and the wolf, failed to see the truth."

"What truth?" I said, expecting more of the same, more justification for the existence of such a sordid System.

"Physically, mankind may stand upright, but the minds of most are still crawling about in the mud, groping around on all fours or swinging from tree branches." He leaned his mirrored lenses directly toward my eyes as he continued. "An interesting point you are undoubtedly unaware of as it pertains to the accumulation of power and influence: rats. Yes, rats, Server Huxley, will stop breeding when they realize the area in which they reside can no longer sustain any more, but not so with many humans. It used to be that these humans would continue to breed like animals, bringing child after child into the world despite lacking the means to feed and care for them. What do you think such a human would do after that, Server Huxley? Well, I'll enlighten you, as I'm sure you're not aware: they would breed again, simply to gain more from the system. There would be cries of foul treatment, cries that they needed others to assist them, cries that it was not the baby's fault, all the while ignoring whose fault it was, cries that they were entitled to assistance even if that assistance came at the expense of others unknown to the subhuman animal—'entitled,' they claimed they were, Server Huxley. I see the look on your face. Yes, who are the real animals? Yes, indeed, who are the real animals?"

I slit my eyes at him. "Why? Why was nothing done to stop this behavior? It's barbaric, inhumane. It's... disgusting. It's bartering in human life, fornicating for financial reward. Our surrogates don't even do that!" I couldn't control myself at the thought that such behavior was condoned, let alone encouraged by the continual processing of payments to those who would engage in this.

"You're quite inquisitive, Server Huxley. Guilt is a powerful tool, as powerful if not more powerful than fear. If we simply ignore the cause, ignore the savage and uncivil behavior that leads to such outcomes, if we simply direct people's attention to the child, we achieve a very usable degree of guilt. You see, the whores that engage in this will support us in return for that which we take from one and provide to them. The guilt-ridden will support us to avoid the backlash of others. Their guilt makes them easy to manipulate, easier to mold, and they freely submit rather than face the repercussions. On that we capitalize. We have successfully destroyed the family unit and replaced it with the Collective; it takes an entire Progressive, you know." The Overseer continued to look down at me, a slight smile adorning his lips. "We have progressed from those days. Now we don't allow such behavior, but still provide for the masses in exchange for their support. Granted, we must utilize a few Servers such as you to provide and bring to fruition the rights we've promised—an acceptable price."

I threw my hands up. "And yet you refer to your leader as 'the Provider'!" I yelled. "Provider... Provider? Nothing is provided that is not first taken from someone else. Our sweat, our toil, our abilities... All that we produce is usurped and distributed to the inept, gluttonous, and lazy. The Provider is a charlatan, a thief, a fence in goods stolen from the rightful owners. You enslave the Served as much as you enslave the Servers; it is simply a different form of manipulation."

"You are convinced this is some form of slavery. Well, in some fashion, maybe it is. History is replete with acts of slavery. Involuntary servitude or slavery has been around for centuries. It is the wheel upon which history turns. At times, the masters become slaves; at others, the slaves become masters. It's all relative. Ponder for a moment the numerous decisions required to care for yourself, to raise a child, a family. You are a slave to the process, whichever process you choose to think of. You are devoid of a moment's rest from the process, never allowed a moment of calm. We free you from that. We make your decisions for you. We tell you what to like, what to dislike... We provide the rights to be served for some; for others, the right to serve. That's true freedom. Thought and choice are but links that form a chain that shackles you to the process. A chain of bondage—that's the real slavery, Server

Huxley. Are you beginning to understand the common core of Our State, of our Progressive, of the Provider? Have I iterated and reiterated this enough? The truth of the Collective is power."

"I am beginning to understand much more clearly that if everyone knew what was going on, if they had any idea, things would be different. I was at a point where I wondered if all of the pieces were falling apart or whether they were falling into place. They have fallen into place. I see the bigger picture. Taken individually, each of your assertions could seem sensible, logical, but I have had time to step back and see the pieces fitted together into this Collective. In its entirety, it is evil, sinister. It lacks logic and it lacks respect for individual human beings."

The Overseer steepled his fingertips together in front of his face. "Knowledge creates choice; choice leads to chaos. Chaos begets pain, strife, conflict, and the insidious act of thought. We offer the people something far better: ignorance. The body is but an easel, ignorance the blank slate of the mind, an empty canvas upon which we freely paint, in brush strokes of various hues, the images of bliss. Rest assured, Server Huxley, we are not tyrants or villains, we are not despots or dictators; we are visionaries, we are emancipators, and we are artists. A person cannot want what they do not know exists. We keep the Served blissful by keeping them ignorant. It is as though the Served are a donkey following a carrot on a stick. We keep a simple pleasure before them. They will always go the direction we wish for them to go, for we are the carrot."

"As to ideas, such as those that afflict you, ideas can be like a cancer, a cell with no contact inhibition, and their spread can be insidious. We cannot have Served running around with ideas in their heads; they wouldn't know what to do with them. It is best to condition them to believe that they are entitled to something, even at the expense of another. In this sense, issues of morality fall by the wayside and greed takes over, and then just watch that spread. Did you know that the term 'greedy' was once ascribed to those who desired something they didn't earn or deserve, those who wanted to take the rightful property of others? Well, we changed that. Greed is now ascribed to those who will not give what is rightfully theirs to someone else, whether that someone else deserves it or not, those who will not serve others with the abilities they possess. We simply changed the definition and repeated it time after time; eventually it was accepted as truth."

I shook my head. "That is disgusting. Morality has definitely fallen by the wayside. Is morality now to be based on how highly you value strangers and equally how little you value yourself? Are we to be sacrificial animals to any whim, any cause, so long as it is not our own? For, what sacrifice do these Prog parasites make, save effort and personal responsibility, that they should be so rewarded? Is theft now to be determined by end result rather than the act itself? Does charity equate to guns, clubs, intimidation, indoctrination, and propaganda?"

The Overseer stared at me without speaking. He turned to his computer and once again began typing; a troubled look overtook his features. So I continued.

"And security... You keep speaking of security. Why are there gun towers surrounding our tenement, all the tenements that I have been assigned to?"

"Precisely for that reason, Server Huxley: for your protection and your security."

"The guns are pointed inward!" I shouted.

"Calm yourself. As you know, there are times when Servers lose their faculties; you experienced this the other day when one of your brethren jumped from the train, unfortunately ending his term of service—Mead, I believe his name was. It is because of situations such as this that we must also protect you from yourselves."

"I must ask," I said, "who is it that protects us from you?"

The Overseer laughed. "Rest assured, you hardly need protection from us. We are the people who have your best interests at the forefront of all that we do. You can trust us, I assure you."

"I don't see it that way. Your own interests and maintaining power are all you're concerned about."

"The world cannot be without leadership, and leadership requires power. We create the situations that make the accumulation of power possible."

I shrugged. "'Situations that make power possible'… What exactly does that mean?"

"Power does not exist in a vacuum. One must create and derive power from the differences between two or more factions. If one wants power, simply pick a minority based on any appreciable aspect of difference, such as color, gender, sexual orientation, income, anything that differentiates people, then divide the people along these superficial, self-contrived lines. Once separated, provide or rally for rights to subscribe to one or the other group by virtue of their perceived difference, then use derogatory terms to label those who oppose their newly subscribed rights, and foster that division. The result is power, much like the discussion we had pertaining to guilt—quite similar principles." The Overseer smiled. "And as far as support, support is not free. If we must abrogate the freedoms and property of some to purchase the support of many, then we shall."

I dropped my head again. My mind was spinning. How could people have allowed such a system to evolve? At what point did humans degrade themselves, cast off personal responsibility and self-respect, and sink to such a level where their ends were derived from the means of others? When did individual charity become dictated by a derisive and divisive system wielding the threat of punishment as a weapon of compliance? The contusion on my forehead was throbbing again, or maybe it was the overwhelming flood of drivel from the Overseer. I was spent. The Overseer cleared his throat, and I looked up at him.

"Our State owes you a debt of gratitude, MSP Huxley. For centuries, nature had the greatest control over the lifespan of an individual, but now we do. It is your work and the work of your fellow MSPs that allow us to thin the herd, or flock, so to speak. Your testing, your diagnoses... All these data provide a picture, a trajectory of an individual's health status. When the information you enter into every electronic records pad is analyzed, decisions are made. We must justify the dissemination of medical resources. Yes, MSP Huxley, your work not only directly affects those whom you see on a daily basis, but indirectly leads to decisions outside of your control about how much to expend on a given individual. You play a part in determining the longevity of your patients. There are only so many resources, and one must use them wisely. If we determine that a shorter life for some will provide a better life for others, then so be it. You do not merely assist in sustaining life; you indirectly dictate death. Our State thanks you for that service; it was taken into account when your correction was determined."

He continued. "As I have said throughout our discussion, you are an intriguing specimen, Blair Huxley, but all good things must come to an end. So now our time has come to a close. Our State is not as vicious as you have come to believe, Mr. Huxley. Your life will be spared."

I furrowed my brow. "Mister? Why do you refer to me as 'Mister'?"

The Overseer waved his hand over the screen before him. The door through which I had entered opened, and a Black Cat stepped in. He was not the same as the previous Black Cat. He was much bigger, a giant of a man. He walked toward me, and the shadow created from the light behind him stretched over me as he neared. For a moment, darkness enveloped me as the hulk reached and grabbed me from the chair, his frame blocking the light behind him. Standing me up, he turned and looked to the Overseer for direction.

The Overseer waved his hand over the screen in front of him again as he said, "Forward."

The door through which I had entered slid closed, and the door at the end of the blue painted line slid open. The Black Cat began to lead me to the open door.

"Forward... Forward? What the hell does that mean? Where is he taking me?" I yelled. "What is going to happen to me? Where is Jules? What is going on?... Where is Jules?"

The Overseer stood. He was much shorter than I had imagined. He put his hands on the console before him and leaned forward. "It is time for you to become a link in the chain, Mr. Huxley. We offer you hope and change, and with this change, I hope you find bliss." Once again, he nodded to my towering guard. "Forward."

The Black Cat pulled me through the entryway, and the door slid shut behind us.

Chapter 13

*O*h, my head... my poor head... Please make it stop...

I opened my eyes, blinking from the sudden brightness in the room. Above me, I saw a clean white ceiling, whiter than anything I could ever recall seeing—sterile. *Recall...* I thought to myself. *Why is my mind so foggy? So... So... empty...*

A fan with expansive white blades whooshed around above me, and a cool, fresh-scented breeze washed over me. I stretched my arms out from my sides and felt a smooth fabric beneath my hands, and beneath that a soft surface. *How wonderful.* Pushing the sheet and blanket off, I found myself dressed in stark-white pajamas, a silky smooth material caressing my skin. *I've never worn pajamas before, I don't believe.* They felt warm and comforting. I reached behind my head and discovered a pillow, fluffy like a cloud. *Where am I?*

Managing to push myself up, I swung my feet off the bed and onto the floor, my head pounding and punching with every movement. For a moment, I leaned forward and held my throbbing head in my hands. My hands felt extremely clean against my face, and a pleasant scent enveloped my nostrils. Breathing in the aroma calmed me, relaxed the cacophony playing in my skull. Lifting my head and opening my eyes fully, I saw before me a wall, three-quarters high from the floor. What lay beyond was obscured. Everything was white, just like the ceiling, even the floors. My feet bumped up against a pair of slippers as I attempted to stand. I sat back down, leaned over, and picked up one of the slippers. *Slippers?*

I pulled the slipper over my foot, feeling the supple inner material. *Perfect fit.* I grabbed the other slipper, pulled it on, and once again attempted to stand. Although I felt a little shaky, I managed to stand without too much trouble. The extra effort sent my head throbbing again.

On the left side of the bed, the outer wall became a sheet of glass. I slowly shuffled my way to the window wall and looked out over all that was before me. Buildings stood like giants, their skins shining and sparkling in the brilliant sunlight. Trams shuffling people on rails that seemingly floated above the streets crisscrossed the common areas. I could see groups of people below, some sitting in front of giant screens, others walking in single file like lines of blue lemmings. Dots of red, blue, and black swept along the white walkways like paint splattered on a canvas.

As I moved along the glass, the wall parted, pulling back on itself, opening onto a glass-floored balcony surrounded by glass outer rails. Hesitantly, I stepped from the room, out onto the glass balcony. Looking below, I counted numerous balconies below me; I was on the nineteenth. Above me, the sky was a beautiful sight, the bluest of blues dusted with wisps of fluffy clouds, a glorious image. I turned up my face to allow the sun to warm me, but it didn't. There was no warmth from the rays, only the glow. I could feel a slight breeze at my side, and with it was the warmth I had expected to feel from the sun. Off in the distance, I could see the mountains, and before them sat vast fields of grass and flowers... *Perfect.* Large screens appeared to float above the grassy fields, all displaying the face of a person speaking to the crowds. Along the top of each screen, a large scrolling banner: *Media Servants—Nationalized Broadcast Conditioning,* it read.

How peculiar... Broadcast conditioning...

As I turned from the balcony to view the rest of my domicile, I heard what sounded like a loud whistle; I turned, but couldn't make out the location from where it had come. After a brief pause, it sounded once again, then no more. Moving along the inside of the window, I passed the three-quarter wall, entering into what I believed was the living space. A white seating platform was situated in the center of the room next to a long, narrow white table. On the wall in front of the platform, a huge screen that spanned the entire wall was displaying the same face as on the screens I saw from the balcony. The face was that of an elderly woman. Her features were drawn tight; thin lips surrounded yellowed, crooked teeth. Her hair was an auburn color, very thin and brittle looking, eyes brown and sunken into dark bags, a very unbecoming sight. The sound was off. I decided that with the ache in my head, it was probably best to relish the silence. To the left of the screen was a closed door. On the back side of the three-quarter wall, a large white animal hide with a black number *17* was hanging.

I walked to the door and stood looking at it for a moment, wondering whether or not I should open it. *No… Maybe I don't want to know.* A small square panel was situated next to the door with the outline of a hand etched in the center. A few buttons were next to the hand, one etched with the word *VISUAL.* I reached my hand out, noticing my tremor as my shaking finger came to rest on the button. I took a deep breath and pressed the button. In an instant, the door vanished to show an empty, stark-white hallway, and across the hall, another doorway, with the number *83* etched into the wall above it. Lowering my hand from the button, I took a deep breath and stepped forward. My foot hit a hard object, and the motion continued to propel me forward as my forehead hit against the same solid surface. The blow shot through me like a bolt of lightning. I stepped back and reached my hand out, only to hit against a hard surface. *VISUAL... see through.* Reaching toward the button again, I pushed and the doorway instantly appeared before me. *Incredible...* Feeling a little more comfortable and knowing what was on the other side of the door, I placed my hand in the etched outline on the panel. As I looked down at my hand, I noticed a delta etched on the top side, the apex pointing toward me. The door shot open in a flash, disappearing into the wall. Repeating the process, I closed the door.

Off to my left was a cubicle of sorts with a long counter, the back wall adorned with various small doors and control panels. Beneath the counter were numerous additional doors. I pulled open a few of the doors to see if anything was behind them. Sets of plates and drinking vessels sat neatly along the shelves, a small tray of eating utensils next to them. I scanned the entire room before me, looking over the counter into the living area and along the wall of glass to the sleep quarters. *Where to relieve myself?*

Gazing out the windows as I made my way to the sleeping quarters, I noticed the same groups of people sitting in front of the large screens, the rows of lemmings still scurrying about, each on their way to somewhere. *What a life... just sitting around while others wait on you...*

I entered the sleeping area again and noticed there was a doorway on the other side of where I had raised myself off the bed. Also, there was a wall of narrow, full-length doors. I walked to the row of doors, grasped the small handles, closed my eyes, then took a deep breath and pulled them open. Hanging from a rod that spanned the length of the recessed space were several blue jumpsuits. Below the jumpsuits were three pairs of black boots. A small chest with drawers flanked the right end of the recess. I reached over and pulled out each of the drawers. In the drawers were blue T-shirts, blue boxer shorts, and pairs of black socks. I assumed, like the slippers, they were all my size. Everything seemed so new to me. *Why can't I remember any of this… and yet everything seems to be mine?*

As I backed away from the recessed area, I noticed movement out of the corner of my eye. Startled, I turned toward the movement. It was the wall: the far wall had come to life with the face of the person talking, just like in the living area, just like outside. I slowly exhaled and felt my heart begin to slow, beginning to relax from the initial shock. I slumped back onto the bed and sat staring at the wall, looking at the lips of the hideous woman on the screen, how they moved, how they contorted. It was perplexing that such an unattractive face would be broadcast to so many places. The sound was still off, and I chose to leave it off as I sat there, fixated. After a few moments, my bladder was nudging me to relieve myself. I pushed myself up off the bed and shuffled to the other door in the sleeping quarters. Upon nearing, the door automatically slid itself into the wall. I peered in to find that the same stark-white motif had been carried into the hygiene room. On the right hand wall, white towels were draped over two white rails, the letter *H* embroidered on their corners. Beyond them sat a toilet. On the far wall, directly across from the door was an enclosed shower stall. As I walked toward the toilet, the left-hand wall came alive with the face of the unattractive woman, her lips constantly moving, constantly mesmerizing with each word. I stopped.

"Oh, no," I said out loud, leaning against the sink counter below the screen.

The screen instantly went blank and became a wall again. *Hmmmm…*

"Yes… Yes…" I said.

The screen did not return. Only the wall stared back at me.

"On."

No sooner than the words left my mouth, the woman returned with her oral dance.

"Off."

The screen went blank, and again the wall returned. *Easy.*

I continued to the toilet, and upon stepping in front of it, the lid automatically recessed itself into the wall. I pulled my pajama pants down and relieved myself. I noticed that my urine was extremely dark. I wondered how long it had been since I'd had a drink. I couldn't remember. Pulling up my pants, I shuffled over to the sink, noticing that the toilet flushed automatically. I placed my hands under the tap, and the water, a perfect temperature, began to flow. Soap was dispensed onto my hands automatically from a small tube behind the water stream. At virtually the same time the water flowed, the wall that was the screen became a mirror. I glanced up as I rubbed the soap over my hands.

My head was wrapped in white bandages, and dark circles enveloped my eyes. I stood straight up in disbelief and reached up to pull at the clips that fastened the bandages. My pace increased as I unwrapped and unwrapped the lengths of material. As the final meters fell, I stood there, staring at my reflection. A small square of compress was attached on each side of my forehead. I reached up and pulled away the dressings, allowing them to fall to the counter.

"Oh no! No, no, no, no!" I sobbed, looking at my reflection in the mirror. "This can't be me! Who is that?!" I yelled.

I dropped back against the wall behind me, the edge of the towel rack digging into my back.

"Owww! Noooooooo!"

I dropped to the floor, sobbing.

Who is that in the mirror? Who is it? What has happened to me?

Several minutes passed as I sat crying. *Okay, get yourself to-gether, get a grip, just get up and take a look. I'm sure you'll start to remember, but first you've got to get up.*

I reached up and grabbed the towel rod, pulling myself up off the floor. The water had long since stopped and the mirror had changed back into a blank white wall. I stepped back over to the sink, placing my hands under the tap. The water flowed and the wall became a mirror. Cupping my hands under the tap, I allowed my hands to fill with water. I threw the water onto my face and rubbed, wiping my eyes and clearing my vision. Looking up, I saw a person I didn't recognize. The face staring back at me had a large contusion on his forehead, raised and angry looking. *My hair… What happened to my hair?* Turning my head from side to side, I could see my hair has been shaved off the sides of my head. I raised my hand to my temples, where the dressings had been, and felt a ridge of tough, shiny material covering what looked to be incisions. *What happened? Was I in an accident? Did I do something wrong? What happened?*

"Off," I said and the mirror became a blank white wall again. I stood hunched over the sink, forcing myself to try to remember, but nothing came to my mind. Looking down at the pile of bandages, I noticed something scribed on one of the compresses, in black letters: *Nothing Lasts Forever* was written. I repeated the words over and over in my mind. I had no idea what to make of it.

Startling me out of my thoughts, a high-pitched chime sounded, unlike the whistle I had heard earlier. I turned and grabbed one of the embroidered hand towels and wiped my face and hands. The chime sounded a second time, then a third. I grabbed the compress and threw it into the toilet, then walked out of the facilities room while tying the silk belt of my robe around my waist. I wasn't sure why I disposed of the compress, but I felt I had to. Looking down along the wall, I could see that a soft blue light had illuminated the perimeter of the door to this domicile, and it pulsated with each chime.

Someone is here. What am I supposed to do? Who could it be?

The chime sounded again and again, the chimes closer and closer together. I crept through the sleeping quarters, out into the living area, seeing the soft blue lights surrounding the front door, glowing on and off. I edged my way closer to the door. Reaching out to activate the transparent viewing mode, I saw my hands were visibly shaking. I was terrified. I pressed the button on the door panel. On the other side stood a man looking joyful and energetic with a nametag stamped on the front of his shirt reading *Mr. K. Benson*. He reached out toward the door and chimes sounded again, the soft blue flickering on and off.

Why won't he just go away?

Despite my fear, I took a deep breath and placed my hand on the panel. The door swooshed open as it slid itself into the wall. I took a step back and stared at the man.

"Greetings," he said. "My name is Mr. Kenneth Benson. I'm with the Housing Authority."

Mr. Benson stepped into my domicile before I had a chance to respond. He continued to smile broadly as he entered.

"Can I help you?" I said, giving the man a once-over.

"You don't remember me?"

"Remember you? I don't know who you are or why you think you can just walk in here."

Mr. Benson laughed in response. "No, I suppose you wouldn't remember me," he said. "As far as my presence here, we had heard that you were having some problems with your memory. Not surprising given the size of that goose egg." As he spoke, he motioned to the lump on my forehead. "You fell down a flight of steps and took a nasty bump to your head."

"A bump," I said and pointed to the side of my head. "I have this because of a bump on my head: shaved hair and scars? I can't remember anything. How long is that supposed to last?" I asked, thinking of the words scribed on my dressing.

"I'm no MSP, you know—Medical Service Provider—but..." Mr. Benson said and shrugged. "I do believe there was an issue with inter-cranial bleeding and some pressure build-up. I heard something about an operation to relieve the pressure; at least I think that's what it was. I don't have any idea how long the memory thing will last."

"A fall, huh?" I scanned my mind for even a thread of recollection, but came up with nothing. I stared at Benson as he looked around my living quarters. I noticed a fresh scar on the side of his neck as he walked past me.

"I see you, too, have a fresh scar. Did you fall down?"

Benson chuckled. "No, no falls. It was an operation done by skillful hands, a wonderful MSP. I doubt you'll get to meet him, though."

I said nothing.

"If you don't mind, I didn't come to talk about medical issues, Mr. H," Benson said. "I came to discuss your rights as a Served. Due to your fall, you've no doubt forgotten all of the wonderful things the Provider has bestowed upon you—rights and services. I'm here to remind you of them"

"Of-Of course," I said. "If you say so, I've got many questions." My mind was a blank slate, like an empty canvas.

"All in time, all in time. For now, just realize that you will have full rights to entertainment, comfort, the use of this domicile, and, as you can see, any medical attention you may need. You have also been allowed a week to convalesce before you will be required to participate in mandatory Collective Integration Sessions. At that time, you will need to join one of the Our State support groups here in the Progressive to continue the spread of bliss. Do you understand so far? Do you recall any of this?"

"I think I understand what you're saying, but I've no recollection of anything."

His words made sense in my mind, but somehow they continued to feel off in some way, as if Benson ought to be saying them to someone else. During my silence, he walked farther into my domicile and stood near the window, looking out over the Progressive.

"Exquisite, isn't it?" he said. "It's staggering how much the Provider has given us. We should be thankful for every minute of the life we lead here. Don't you think so, Mr. H?"

"I suppose," I said, somewhat distracted by an insignia I noticed on his sleeve. It featured a delta like the one on my hand, made up of chains, lines, and shapes. "What does that mean?" I said, pointing at the insignia.

"Ah, yes. Inquisitive, aren't you, Mr. H? Good to hear your mind is at least functioning," Benson said, tugging at his sleeve to flatten out the shape. "The delta here signifies change, with the legs of the delta being made of chains that represent each person in Our State. Each of those links form an unbreakable, collective bond, just like us. The stripes below the setting orb signify the black and white differences between the Servers and the Served. The orb signifies the end of egoism, with the sun setting on the mantra of self-interest, while simultaneously the sun rising on the Collective, on Our State. Finally, the eye within the orb is the symbol of the Provider, forever watching over us. An ingenious design, don't you think?"

I furrowed my brow in response, and then added a nod of appeasement after I'd had a moment to process his words. I turned and pointed at the animal hide on the wall.

"What about this one, this skin of some creature?" I said.

"That is a sheep's hide. The sheep is the symbol of Our State, the docile lamb easily led, easily herded. We use the hides of the sheep as reminder that the Provider is the shepherd who leads us all; we are his herd, his flock. We do not question, we do not attempt to think of anything other than which the Provider wishes us to think, we are provided all that we desire, all that we are taught is best to desire, and we are his sheep. Because of him, the Served can remain blissful and safe within the walls of our Progressive. Because of him, we enjoy all the luxuries we have and live a life free of worry, pain, and doubt."

Benson then smiled. "I'll take my leave now," he said as he placed a small tablet on the table. "This is your PIP, or personal information pad. Just swipe your thumb across it and it will initialize. All of your appointments and Our State requirements will be listed, along with any communications." He glanced up at me while continuing. "For now, I suggest you change out of you robe and pajamas. Your domicile Server will be here shortly. Of your many rights, one is to instruct them on any tasks you wish for them to complete. Please try to remember that Servers will often try to play games with unseasoned, pliable Served, trying to guilt them into special treatment, especially the female Servers. They know they will be working with you for an extended time, and will try to set you up early. Do not fall for it. With your memory issues, you're basically a newbie."

"Of course," I said. "I'll be on my guard."

"Good," Benson said. "I'm off, then. I'll be back tomorrow morning to see how you are progressing. Forward, Mr. H."

"Say what?"

"Forward, Mr. H. 'Forward' is generally said as a farewell. It means we always progress, we always move on from where we are—forward."

"Forward, huh? I'll try and remember that," I said, still feeling somewhat unsettled, something scratching at the corner of my mind.

Benson stepped toward the door, placed his palm on the scanner, and the door slid open. He stepped through the doorway, turned and gave me a peculiar grin as the door slid closed. Once he had gone, I moved to the kitchen table, sat down, and tried to remember anything in my life that had occurred before this morning, but I came up entirely blank. Whatever fall I must have suffered, it had to have been serious.

I trudged my way to the sleeping area, the irritation of the word "Forward" still scratching at my mind. Opening the narrow door, I reached up and grabbed the first blue jumpsuit. I opened the drawers and pulled out blue underwear, a blue T-shirt, and a pair of the black socks and black boots. I laid them out on the bed and looked at them against the white of the bedding. They were screaming at me, but I could not grasp the meaning of what I saw. After disrobing and removing my pajamas, I noticed a scabbed area on my leg and felt the pull of numerous scabs on my back as I pulled off the pajama top. I couldn't make sense of why I had so many bandages in so many places from a simple fall. I went through the awkward ceremony of donning my new clothes as my empty mind turned and turned, looking for something to grasp.

Although the clothes fit as if they were made especially for me, they didn't seem to fit in other ways. They felt odd, as if I didn't belong in them or they didn't belong on this body.

Making my way back to the kitchen table, I sat and gazed out through the wall of glass, wondering where my memory had gone. Before me, on the table, was my PIP. I picked it up and swiped my thumb across the screen as Benson had instructed. The screen came to life with a bright-colored image of the delta insignia, the same that I had seen on Benson's uniform, the same that was etched on my hand. Across the top of the screen, a tab labeled *Incoming Message* flashed. As I moved my finger to touch the tab, I was startled by the chiming of the door again. The soft blue hue emanated from around the door, glowing on and off, urging me to respond. I stood, clutching the PIP and approached the door. Having become more accustomed to my surroundings, I activated the transparent viewing mode before opening it. On the other side, I saw a beautiful woman, with deep, dark blue eyes and a downcast expression. She was dressed in a red jumpsuit that was in stark contrast to her aqua-blue pools I found myself swimming in. For a brief moment, I felt inclined to reach out and touch her, but then realized I didn't even know her, and of course, the door was between us. Staring, I could see that she was incredibly fidgety, as nervous as an animal that had just been beaten by its master. She, too, wore a name tag; it read: *Julie.*

Julie… I said the name in my mind, trying to connect it with some lost bit of memory, but there was nothing. My mind remained empty, except for the incessant scratching at the corner, the intrusion of the term "Forward."

For a moment, I considered not opening the door, not allowing this stranger to enter into my domicile, into my world. If the Servers were as manipulative as Benson had said,

I might have been better off without her. But the door kept chiming, the blue lights flashing, and the Server continued to stand there as if compelled to do so.

"Yes, yes, just a moment," I said through the door. "I'll be there in a moment."

The woman jumped at my voice; her hand almost shot to her mouth as if someone she knew was calling to her. She held her hand there, quivering before her lips. Perhaps my voice was harsher than I had intended. Or, as Benson suggested, she might have been priming to manipulate me already. Maybe she knew that I'd be watching.

Finally, I opened the door, looking down at her feet so as not to be taken in by her teary-eyed beauty.

"Can I help you?" I said.

She immediately began to sob, both hands now up in front of her mouth, clutching each other. "Hux…"

She pulled a hand away from her face as a single tear fell upon the tip of her finger. I looked up and watched almost hypnotically as the tear traced down the length of her finger, down to her palm, following along a crease in her skin, the path of least resistance taken, as if the end had been predetermined. The back of her hand was adorned with the same insignia as on my hand, only her delta pointed away from her.

"Hux…" she whispered again, barely audible.

"You must be my Server," I said.

"I thought I'd never see you again," she said as her tears continued.

She lurched forward, her arms outstretched as if she were going to grab me. Turning aside, I pushed her away, not sure whether to feel anger or pity as Benson's words ran through my mind.

"Just who the hell do you think you are?" I said. "I've been told about these games. I may have just had an awful fall, but I am no fool. Don't play me for one, Server. You're lucky I'm not contacting someone at this moment to have you reported!"

"No, no, Hux! It's me—Jules," she said. "We don't have to be sad any longer. We're together again."

I stood, shaking my head, not knowing what to make of this Server before me. The PIP in my hand continued to flash and vibrate. I glanced at it, then touched the flashing icon. A message appeared…

SUBJECT: F/U MSP VISIT—JEREMY PAUL

"Just a minute, Server," I said.

I swiped my finger across the pad as the message scrolled by. As I read, the woman's sobs continued to pull at my ears. Completing the message, I looked up to see this woman in such an awful state. Turning my head side to side, I scanned up and down the hallway, noting the evenly spaced reflective domes along the ceiling, the occasional blip of red indicating the watchful eyes behind them.

I glanced back into her deep aqua pools, tears cresting the lids. Even now, she seemed almost… hopeful.

"Look here, woman," I said, scanning the hallway eyes once again, then glancing down, enveloped in the sight of her soft features. "Server…" I looked down at my PIP, scrolled the words across the screen for the second time, vaguely cognizant of the stirring within me. "My name is Hemsworth." Looking up at the teary-eyed Server, a grin reached across my lips. "Sad, you said?… No… I'm perfectly blissful."

Made in the USA
Charleston, SC
03 February 2017